I0720872

PART I OF THE EARTH DAWN SAGA

EARTH DAWN

IN THE BEGINNING

Revised Edition

PHILIP A. KLAUE

Zeta Publishing
Ocala, FL

Copyright © 2015, 2018 Philip Klaue

All rights reserved. No part of this publication may be reproduced, distributed, or transmitted in any form or by any means, including photocopying, recording, or other electronic or mechanical methods, without the prior written permission of the publisher, except in the case of brief quotations embodied in critical reviews and certain other noncommercial uses permitted by copyright law. For permission requests, write to the publisher, addressed "Attention: Permissions Coordinator," at the address below.

Zeta Publishing, Inc
3850 SE 58th Ave
Ocala, FL 34480
www.zetapublishing.com

The views expressed in this work are solely those of the author and do not necessarily reflect the views of the publisher, and the publisher hereby disclaims any responsibility for them.

Ordering Information:
Quantity sales. Special discounts are available on quantity purchases by corporations, associations, and others. For details, contact the publisher at the address above. Orders by U.S. trade bookstores and wholesalers. Please contact
Zeta Publishing: Tel: (352) 694-2553; Fax: (352) 694-1791 or visit
www.zetapublishing.com

First Published by CreateSpace Independent Publishing

Rev. Date: 10/3/2018

ISBN: 978-1-947191-93-8 (sc)

ISBN: 978-1-947191-94-5 (e)

Library of Congress Control Number: 2018957337

Printed in the United States of America
www.brusheezy.com

TABLE OF CONTENTS

◊

AUTHOR'S NOTE

I was raised as a Christian and I was taught to believe the things I was being told. That everything in the Bible is true and un-altered. Then I grew up in a world where schools taught science and history; I was told that all of these things were also true. That dinosaurs ruled the Earth for millions of years and we humans only came into the picture some ten to twenty thousand years ago. Then I was shown a futuristic word through technology, specifically the television set. I watched shows like Star Wars, Jurassic Park, Indiana Jones, Blade Runner, and The Terminator. It all got me thinking about what I've been taught to believe; contradicting theories of our past mingling with things of the future. Things like cloning, gene splicing, and Nano-tech to name a few. I began to see a bigger picture of things, combine it all with the last 200 years of our history; the wars that were waged. The level of cruelty that human kind is capable of brought me to an even deeper image of our past. The feeling that what we have done what we are doing to ourselves right now, it's all been done before, and we have the records to prove it. The proof lays in the combining of science and religion and not in the ways of those secular scientologists. This is everything! The combining of religion, science, spirituality, and the past.

As we begin to connect the dots here, we will begin to see where exactly we have come from and that the process has been arduous. We have come close to being wiped out completely several times, not just by ourselves but by an alien race that I believe still exists today and is leery of our actions and intent but resolved to not interfere anymore. Now we live in a nuclear world where the possibility of extinction is high. Not only are we stretching the means of this planet to provide but we are constantly aiming these nuclear weapons at each other and threatening to press the button. Is it in our nature to implode like this or can we find a better way? To understand our past will help us shape our future; to see what mistakes we made and make the right moves to avoid repeating them.

One day soon we humans will travel to Mars and then beyond it and I believe that when that day happens, what we find then will bring credibility to my story. I encourage everyone who reads this to do their own research into everything I write about. If you don't know what a "Rail Gun" is, or who "John Hutchinson" was, then seek it out on the internet. If you never saw a "Tesla coil" or heard of the "Kuiper belt"; internet. Research things about crystal skulls and crystal pyramids. Look up how big bugs were in the Jurassic period and read up on "Dark Matter" in Wikipedia. Expand your mind and dare to believe that our journey as a race of sentient beings through this universe is an epic one. Full of real dangers along with deep, spiritual battles and great scientific mysteries. My only hope as an Author is that I can do the story justice in the way that I tell it.

I have written a lot of grade "A" papers and passed exams on my ability to write a good story, but who reads stories anymore? People have become accustom to seeing stories play out on a big screen as a movie. So here I am writing about some crazy stuff, trying to make it all make sense and hoping it gets to be a movie one day… Please read on and enjoy the story and help me build this to movie status. I have two sequels to this and want to share these with the world.

In writing this book, I've found that music definitely helps to paint a picture of the mood involved in any given scene and so I've added (in brackets) between some of the paragraphs, suggestions of the musical artist and their songs that best suits the mood of what's going on in the book. The pictures have been generated by a paper artist program and are there-for are original. Please enjoy this book.

x

ACKNOWLEDGMENTS

I would like to acknowledge the Bible for laying out some of the ground work on this story. I do not wish to take credit or credibility away from the original tale found in the Bible. I only wish to enhance people's awareness of their place in the universe; our place. A place full of dangers and opportunities; to either thrive through peace and wisdom or perish by our own stupid deeds and ignorance.

I wish to also acknowledge Nicola Tesla, and all the other unknown inventors for being believers in something greater than themselves.

Special thanks goes out to all my family and friends for supporting me in this endeavor to write such a complicated novel. A special shout out to my brothers David, Joel, Stephen and sisters Esther and Tammy.

Earth Dawn: "In The Beginning" Part One of the Earth Dawn Saga Intro: In a Brave New World

Trees and shrubs whip past him as he dashes through the forest; his senses are at their peak as he chases after his prey. Suddenly he stops and listens for any noises... The sound of rustling branches beckons him to quickly resume his chase straight ahead and to his left; within the span of fifty paces the trees suddenly thin out as the forest floor takes a somewhat steep incline in the form of a lengthy hillside with sparse vegetation. He stops at the bottom and waits holding a long spear with a razor sharp stone carved tip, jabbed into the wood shaft and bound with twine. He scans the hillside from left to right and as he looks to his right a big, colourful Turkey darts out from a bush at the bottom of the hillside just twenty feet to his left; just when he was looking the other way...

With lightning quick reflexes he whips his body into position and hurls his spear through the air. He sees it in slow motion as the shaft gently wobbles through the air on its way to its intended target. It's a perfect cast as the tip plunges into the midsection of the big Turkey, just seconds after the throw and pins its corps sideways to the forest floor. Walking up to it he stops at the Turkey's side and kneels... "I'm truly sorry to take your life, but my life and that of my family depends on your sacrifice and for that I'm truly thankful... I bless your energy to find its way back to the <u>One</u> and be at peace." With that said he stands up, grips his spear, steps on the dead animals side to hold it down as he yanks the spear free from its flesh.

His name is Adam; he stands just over six feet tall and has pale white skin that is exposed to the elements as clothing is scarce and not really needed in the late days of summer on this planet he now calls "Earth". Adam is wearing an animal pelt around his waist to hang down and conceal his genitals though. He also has bright blue eyes and a healthy head of sandy brown hair; his body is also ripped with muscle over muscle. He's what you'd call a perfect Alfa male but he doesn't give any of that a thought; for all he knows he's the only human male on the planet. Draped around his left shoulder is a length of rope that hangs cross ways over his body so the low end hangs at his right hip; keeping it in place while he hunts. He now undoes the knot on it and stretches it out before him; taking the one end of it, he ties loops around the bird's legs. He slips the spear shaft through the loops and then tightens the rope up so that he can hoist the bird up and rest the weight of it at his back with the spear shaft braced on his shoulders.

His trek back to his home is slow and hard with the added weight of the bird but he makes the two thousand paces journey home, through the forest just before nightfall. The forest abruptly gives way to a large clearing; all that grows on it is different types of grasses and flowers. In the midst of the low growing vegetation is Adams holdings; a well fenced up property with one long rectangular home, made up of stones and sticks bound together with lots of bark woven twine and clay from the river bank which runs through the west edge of the clearing then vanishes back into the forest, the same way it comes out of the forest. Adam pauses at the forests edge to gaze upon the beauty of this serene little plot of lush land with his yard and long house in the midst of it, just as the sun sets over the forest shading it out in a silhouette and lighting up the golden colored dry tips of the grasses in the field; a wonder to behold it is to him.

It takes Adam another ten minutes to cross the length of the field to reach the fence of his yard. Sweat drips from his brow and every muscle in his body is burning from traveling so far with an eighty pound bird at his back without pausing for more than two minutes. Distance + weight + gravity makes every journey a hard one. He plops the bird down at the one and only gate on the entire fence. "Eve!" He yells between big breaths. "Eve! I'm home! Open the gate!" The gate is tied into each flanking wall of fence by four strong lengths of bark strand rope that loops through small holes at exact locations on both fence and gate, tying both tightly to each other. The knots are only undoable from inside the yard; the left side ropes are short while the right side ropes are long. Adam hears footsteps on the other side.

"I'm here Adam." Eve says from the other side. "Give me a second."

Adam watches the ropes begin to move. The short ropes she loosens first just a little and then loosens the long ropes and lets them sag down. Grabbing the edge of the gate, she lifts it and pulls it open, coincidently keeping her body concealed from his view. The top rope stretches tighter and lifts into the air; so does the bottom one but not enough to lift it off the ground. Eve peeks over the edge of the gate.

"Holy smokes that thing's huge!" Exclaims Eve upon seeing the bird. She comes around the gate so Adam can see all of her in her pregnant glow. Eve is also wearing leather hide garments; one animal hide covers her breasts and another covers her at the waist. She has long, flowing black hair and pale white skin just like Adam.

"Well hello beautiful. Any chance I could get some help with this creature?" Adam asks his pregnant wife. Eve walks over and grabs hold of the end of the spear without the tip. Adam kneels and picks up the other end and together they haul their prize to the back yard for gutting and hitting the meat with smoke of the Alder wood. Once in the back yard with the bird they both drop it and go back; Adam to re-tie the front gates ropes and Eve heads inside via the back entrance and retrieves some torches from inside the long house to brighten up the back yard for Adam to do his work. They both meet again at the stone slab; a large slab of stone long ago deposited by a glacier in that spot, which Adam based the whole property on before building. The slab serves many purposes, such as Adam's forging hut on the far left corner of the slab. Only a base of solid stone can withstand the weight and heat of a forge made up of many smaller stones yet big in their own way, compared to what a human can manually move. The open, circular fire pit sits at the far right corner. The rest remains open for what Adam is about to do (Slaughtering) and the storing of chopped wood. Eve places the two torches in notches made just for them on the surface of the stone slab. Adam uses his sharp spear blade and gets to work; Eve retreats back inside the long house not having any taste for the things her man does to make sure they eat and survive through this worlds harsh winters.

After his work is done and the bird is cleaned and hung above the smoking fire, he peeks inside the long house to see Eve folding dough for making flat breads in the kitchen; which has a crudely built, yet sturdy wooden table along with a stone made fire place with a sheet of steel going over the middle of it. Adam spent over two years collecting and melting the ores out of rocks to create that steel, and he's put it to good use as a hot plate for cooking. He's made a few other things. It also took him two years to build his forge to be able to extract the ores, so it's taken a whole four years in the making for one hot-plate. He looks farther inside and also sees his two sons playing in the play area; a flimsy, short fenced area of the houses interior, just for the kids. He looks down at himself and notices the stickiness of the drying blood all over his hands. He looks down the back of his right thigh and sees a lengthy trail of blood there too from back while he carried the bird home; he can't go in like this.

He knows that the river is his only choice so he circles the outside of the house with his spear in hand and undoes the ropes to the gate quietly. Sneaking away, Adam gently closes the gate on his way out but unable to do up the ropes, which is fine for him because he hopes to sneak back in and surprise Eve with a somehow clean and un-bloodied Adam.

At the river now, Adam walks in to the water till it's up to his groin. He pauses, steps back a pace and proceeds to wash the spear clean. Once he's satisfied with the weapon, he throws it on the sandy riverbank just feet away; it stabs in and points straight out like a pro toss. He now gets to cleaning the blood off himself, as he does he stares into the dark water. He sees it rippling like black liquid glass and it reminds him of his past; his enemy once wielded a sword and wore armor as black and shiny as the water in front of him and for that reason a flood of memories hits his mind. The clash of swords and images of sudden death pierces his vision and he has to shake his head to come back to reality. Once all the blood is washed away, Adam makes his way back to his long house still dazed from his visions. He realizes that he's been gone so long he no longer fully remembers the exact details of how he happened to leave in the first place, but it's coming back to him now.

He tried not to give it much thought, just accepted his new world and set out to make his home in it. Now, as he enters his yard and reties the gates ropes; he remembers it all.

"Adam! Where the heck were you? I was just looking for you."

"Cleaning myself off in the river my love." Adam answers his wife.

Eve detects a hollowness to his voice and knows something is amiss… "What is it Adam? Did something happen at the river just now?"

"Yes Eve; I remembered it all and it was like… Like I just lived it all over again… The battle where we lost Dar." Adam gets cut off now.

"Don't say his name Adam; please… The pain of it is also close to my heart; so much so that to hear his name now will make me cry for sure." Eve says to him on the edge of tearing up.

They quickly close the short distance between them and embrace each other in a big hug.

"Why did we make it Eve? Out of all the others who deserved it more than us; it's us two who made it out alive. Why!?"

2 Weeks Later

THE DAYS PASS BY QUICKLY for the young family. Eve gets closer to giving birth to their third child. Adam stays busy with fixing up the long houses roof before the heavy rains of fall; along with other varied duties.

The outhouse location has been over used and needs to be dug over and replaced to a different spot, and he does a lot of fishing at the river to add some variety to the family's diet. Night settles in over the land and inside the long house Adam is stirring the fire in the living rooms stone fireplace, which is a ten foot section to the west of the north wall, just beside the kids fenced off play area. Cain has been playing with his brother Abel for a while now and is getting bored with the wooden blocks. Cain is thirteen years old now while Abel is four years old, so Cain has the right to leave the play pen at any time. Cain decides at that moment to do just that. He walks over and sits on the bear skin fur that sits in front of the fire place and joins his father in staring aimlessly at the flames.

"Father?" Cain asks to get his attention.

Adam looks into his son's eyes seeing some important question about to come. Adam elects to listen.

"I saw the bent hairy people again today while you were out hunting."

"Please son, call them the Chromags; like we talked about."

"Ok… I was in the cherry tree and could see over the fence and there was five of them heading towards the river." "Ok son, what's so interesting about that? We've seen them several times before. Why bring them up now?" Asks Adam.

"Because… Why are they like that?" Cain counters with his own question.

"I don't really know Cain… Your guess is as good as mine."

"Why are there no other people like us around?" Cain now asks.

"Well now you're asking smarter questions Cain…"

"Although I really don't think you want to know the answer to that… I'm not even sure if it's the correct answer." He answers his son while still staring into the flames of the fire in the fire place. He doesn't realize the curiosity he sparked in his son just now.

"I actually do want to know the answer Dad… I'm bored here with just Abel to play with and want to know if there's others out there to play with, or you know… Get to know… Why is it just us?"

"It's a long story Cain and it's only my version of it… I can't yet make any sense out of the reason no one else is here right now. I can only tell you what your mom and I went through to make it here."

Cain lights up with excitement upon the prospect of a long bed time story; especially one that's true and about his own parents. "Please father, tell me your story… I'm not the least bit tired right now… And I can't stand playing another game of blocks with Abel right now… Please!" Cain begs his Father to divulge all he knows.

"I'm not sure Cain… Not sure where to start… Or even how you will handle the extreme acts of violence that can't be left out of the tale."

"I know about violence and I assure you Dad that I will take it like anyone else would, as a story. I wouldn't ever try to hurt anyone of our family or any other living being except out of the need to eat. And in that case, I'd make it quick like you taught me to do." Cain replies and sits down next to his Dad.

Eve is in the kitchen area of the longhouse and now picks up on their conversation. "Um Adam. I'm not sure if that's a good idea." Eve says as she pauses in her preparation of the next day's meal.

"Eve, he's not going to stop being curious… He's human like us and has a right to know where he comes from… Wouldn't you want to know if you were him?" Adam counters and Eve stays silent knowing that Adam speaks the truth. If she was Cain, she wouldn't relent until the truth was told.

"If I tell you this, you have to promise me that you won't interrupt with a thousand questions. Deal?" Adam asks his son.

"It's a deal Dad."

"First of all you have to try to imagine that there's two worlds like this one that are full of life forms and humans like us." Adam says.

"Really Father!? Two worlds full of people like us!?" Exclaims Cain.

"What did I say about questions Cain?"

"Right. I'm sorry Dad. It's just so hard for me to believe."

"Yah, and that's just the first sentence of the story… We were once a strong civilization; that means we had lots of us who made incredible things… Buildings as big as mountains and machines that did everything for us; from moving mountains to moving people… From building space ships to sweeping our floors… We had it all…" Adam pauses expecting some sort of question from Cain but his son remains silent, simply staring into the fire like he was moments ago.

"There was actually three worlds but the third one was only barely occupied by our kind; that third world is this one we are on right now… We were young, your mother and I. In our early twenties we were… I was a step brother to you mother… Our worlds were almost always in a battle over something or another and it created orphans. That means children without parents… My mother adopted Eve when I was ten and she was eight… We became best friends, and as we grew older we became more than best friends. My parents didn't find out about our love because it only flourished just after they…" Adam coughs and skips the rest of that sentence… "My father wanted me to follow in his footsteps and wanted to provide the safest living conditions and so we moved from the planet called Gorgon to the planet called Mire. Yet he had me attending the school of the holy order within the Gorgon embassy of Mire while he remained on Gorgon in service to the Emperor of the solar system… That means our particular group of planets, and he owned them all. That's what it means to be an Emperor; to have power over all things…" Adam begins the story.

Cain continues to stare into the flames of the fire and images begin to form in his mind of all that his Father is telling him. He can see the solar system as is being described to him; full of space ships and planets full of people. Machines are all over the place doing all sorts of things in the service of their human masters. His Father's tale is being played out in his mind like a dream, and his imagination is holding nothing back. "I guess it all really began to change just after that semester at the school… That semester that ended with a Trial…" Adam carries on and Cain continues to imagine all his father is telling him…

CHAPTER 1

SCHOOL OF THE HOLY ORDER
Location - Planet Mire - Capitol City "Opeyka"

The sound of the clock on the wall behind him along with the droning voice of the teacher at the head of the class begins to put Adam in a sleepy state. His thoughts drift off to memories of his home back in Olyra Valley where his girlfriend is. Well, actually she's his step sister. "Not even blood related." Adam argues in his mind to justify the feelings he has for her.

Suddenly the teacher of the class calls out his name. "Adam!"

Adam forces himself back in the moment and looks at the image on the holo-screen behind her. Her name is "Miss Torrens" and she is serious about teaching these students the ins and outs of the spiritual nature of human beings.

She's five feet nine inches tall with brown hair and a slim, athletic build. She's a High-Priestess of the Holy Order of the tree of life. A mouth full for sure but still a high rank among the faculty of the school and to be respected; she once tossed a cocky student right through the classroom door, breaking the hinges right off of it. "Adam, are you going to give me an answer? Where is the conscious center of our minds?" She asks as she points to the hollo-screen image of a human body as though looking at it on the inside. All the veins, bones, organs and arteries on display for one to see.

"That would be in the brain at the cerebral cortex miss Torrens…"

"Very good Adam, but can you tell me this? Where does our soul's energy emanate from the strongest?"

Adam freezes trying hard to recall all the chakra points on the body. "The Pineal Gland in the brain?" He answers.

"Sorry but that's incorrect. Anyone else?" She asks the rest of the class. A Young class mate of his eagerly raises her hand knowing she has the answer to the question. Adam is relieved to let her take over.

"That would be at the base of our spine close to our navel or belly button." Says Lyanna from the right side of the class. Lyanna is a fifteen year old in the same class as Adam, a twenty two year old. Classes in this school don't go by age but by intelligence and ability.

"That's right Lyanna. And can you tell me why it's important to know the difference between…"

Adam begins to drift off again as the teacher shifts her focus from Adam to Lyanna and the rest of the class; twenty three students in total. He can't explain why but for some reason, this teacher reminds him of Eve and he just can't seem to focus on what she is saying. Instead his thoughts drift to images of Eve. Memories of when he had her sleeping in his bed because she got scared of some shadowy images outside her bedroom window. How he felt with her body next to his; the smell of her hair, and softness of her skin. He managed to keep himself from getting too excited beside her with memories of his father. "Corso is his name and he was always on me about my future; telling me that the key to love is patience, and the key to patience is to focus… 'Focus on what?' I'd ask him… 'Anything but the one you love.' He'd answer." Adam recalls his dad saying that once.

The school of the holy order is built in the shape of a large rectangle with three story high, blocks of buildings on the north, east and south vectors of Mire while the west face of the school is left open as a large tiered staircase that provides access to the wings of the school and access to the central courtyard. The central courtyard serves several purposes; one of the main ones is as a battle arena. Other purposes for the courtyard are the obvious ones like meeting with people at break times and having big school lunch or dinner events.

As Adam daydreams about Eve and his home, a loud horn sounds out interrupting the teacher in mid-sentence and Adam in mid fantasy. All the students cheer in excitement and get out of their chairs that are attached to their desks and scurry over to the windows that cover the south wall. Adam comes to from his little trance and joins the students of his class. Every time the horn sounds, it means another student of the school is about to advance to the status of High Priest or Priestess. Only through the last trial of the six trials of the right to consume, will a student be allowed to eat of the sacred fruit of the tree of life that only grows on the surface of the planet "Pangaea". The school encourages its students to observe the fights between students and high priests or priestesses so that students have an idea of the challenges they face just to make it to the ritual. The martial arts contest is called the "Yannobi" meaning "Proof by combat" in the ancient tongue of the founders.

Adam walks over to the window of the classroom; he has short cut, brown, wavy hair and bright blue eyes, his skin is tan white. He's six feet, two inches tall and looks exactly like a younger version of himself. His school uniform is a nice blue "V" collared shirt and dark blue dress pants. Standing next to him is a fellow student named "Squire." They are watching from the last window along that wall, Adam being the last to show up at the window, is the last at the line of students glaring out to watch the fight.

"Hey Adam…" Says Squire as he quickly glances at him then back out the window.

"Oh look! I know that guy; he tutors me on Physics. It's Lucas Bel… Something, I can't remember. Anyway, he's a good fighter… He told me he would be up for graduation soon. I hope he rocks this Yannobi… Do you know Lucas?"

Adam sighs and then responds… "Yeah, he's my cousin… His mom married my dad's brother Morris… Son of Morris and Martha; my uncle and aunt."

"Really!? That is so cool… Your cousin is about to graduate man… Maybe… I wonder who they have picked for his opponent." Squire says as he continues to stare out the window at the gathering of robed High Priest and Priestesses that have come to watch the fight and some have come to score it.

Lucas stands at the edge of a raised concrete platform of sand in the middle of the courtyard wearing a grey, hooded monks robe. As the progression of high members of the school fully files out into the courtyard and then stops; Lucas's opponent steps out of the doors of the south wing of the school.

"Ooh… I know that High Priest too… That's the renowned Darius Siscerelle! Sorry buddy but I suddenly don't like your cousin's odds." Says Squire.

The student next to Squire hears him say "Cousin" and now Adam hears the murmuring of students down the line saying who the fighter is down there.

(Pantera – "Where you come from")

"His odds are just as good as Darius's odds… I have fought Lucas in sparring sessions and I know how good a fighter he is… He can do it."

"I don't know man, Darius has been a High Priest for eight years now and every year he's put into a Yannobi and he has bumped down every student he has faced. Eight for eight; he's practically unstoppable." Counters Squire.

Adam chuckles at the thought and replies. "Well, I'm thinking his record is about to take a hit today."

Darius is wearing the tan white, hooded robe of the High Priests and steps up to his place at the opposite side of the sandy fighting platform as Lucas. They pause for a second and bow to each other before undoing the robe's belt and throwing the garment off behind them at the same time. Lucas is now wearing only light grey shorts; Darius is wearing only white shorts. Both men are very muscular and stand at about the same height of five feet ten inches tall. Lucas is younger by a bit with blonde hair while Darius has dark brown hair. The two of them enter the sandy platform at the same time and begin to do stretches while an elder High Priest says the initai for the fight.

"Yannobi da ma banuta der cri… So da sputa ma delanted… Da ma bala Yannobi ma initai!" Says an old man at the edge of a crowd of hooded High Priests and Priestess.

Adam knows the translation of it to a sort. ["Combat prowess must be proved to move on. It will be fair and with Honour. Let the test of combat prowess commence now."]

Another horn blows in the back ground and the two fighters stop their stretches and move close to square off. Darius takes a stance with his left leg and arm out in front of him while Lucas takes a changing stance mode. He begins moving around Darius in different stances every few seconds. Lucas test jabs at Darius with a left, he takes the bait; Darius leans back from the jab and comes at Lucas with an instant counter of two left jabs and a right hook which Lucas leans just out of the way from contact with his nose. Now Lucas leans in as Darius is pulling back and spins as he closes his body distance with a spinning right elbow. Darius has to duck and spin away to his left and Lucas continues to attack after the missed elbow. He follows up with a right thrust kick; Darius senses it coming and reverses his spin away from what would be a face smasher and thrusts himself up from a crouch and around in a strong left legged spin kick aimed for Lucas's head.

Lucas is in mid thrust kick and sees his opponents counter at the last second; his only move is to duck down and do the splits. He does just that and avoids being dummied with a kick. Now he sees Darius's right leg, the only one holding him against gravity at the moment and decides to sweep kick at it. He pumps his hips up lightly and leans back while shifting the weight of his body to his left and sweeping both his feet towards Darius's exposed right ankle in the perfect striking spot. Darius senses that move too and lifts his right leg just in time while he's still recovering from his missed kick.

Darius is forced to brace himself with both arms as gravity takes his body down to the sand without any sturdy footing.

Lucas springs into action first using his strong arms to shift his body into a low somersault move where his right leg is coming down right where Darius's face should have been but Darius does a springing push up off the sand at just the right moment and avoids it. Lucas springs back up on to his feet and blocks a kick as Darius wastes no time from evading to attacking. Lucas is forced to block a right legged up kick and then dodges a big left overhand swing, giving Lucas his opponents whole back side. Lucas shoots in to tackle and as soon as he contacts Darius's body, he knows that Darius is stepping into the move with preparation for a flip over his own back. Darius does just as Lucas thought he would leaping up and over him, all Lucas can do is halt his momentum and turn around quickly to face his opponent. Darius lands his back flip and faces Lucas on his feet and in stance right as Lucas turns to face him.

"Wow! Did you see that Adam!?" Squire asks excitedly.

"Yeah Squire, I saw that. Looked like Darius was about to get planted."

"Well Lucas almost got clipped too… This is going to be a close fight."

Adam just nods once in agreement with his classmate and continues to look out the window in anticipation of the outcome.

Darius and Lucas now circle each other in search of an opening to exploit. A weakness to attack and gain an upper hand. Lucas leaps toward Darius so fast with a jumping left spin kick it almost connects; Darius ducks and shifts his body sideways with the kick he avoids. Lucas knew he would do that and continues the spin, using the momentum he already has to spin again as he lands and crouches down for a sweep kick that Darius just barely jumps over. Lucas thought he might hit the sweep but as he feels the miss, he decides to continue the spin again while pumping his legs and raising himself in a strong left uppercut that Darius has to block with both arms braced out in front of him. Lucas doesn't quit pressing; he comes down from the uppercut with a fake head-butt to thrusting his right elbow at his opponent. The elbow hits Darius in the right pectoral muscle and spins him sideways. Darius uses the momentum and throws out his left leg, it catches Lucas in his abs. Just a quick thrust kick as he reels over from the elbow and Darius has bought himself the space he needs to halt his opponents attack. Both fighters back away from each other feeling the sting of each other's hit. Darius now realizes his moment and leaps in to press the attack.

Darius fakes in a right leg kick, dykes to his left and shoots in with a big left hook that Lucas senses coming and shifts his body left and forward so that Darius's hook goes behind his head. Lucas grabs at Darius's neck being so close to him. Darius is forced to do the same and now both of them are in a clinch. Arms wrapped around each other's necks as they twist and pull, both trying to control their opponents neck and thus body. Lucas spends extra energy to push Darius back enough to do a small leaping knee that lands on Darius's right rib cage. He takes the hit so that he can pull Lucas's neck down as he lands from the knee, and quickly deliver a left elbow to Lucas's head and quickly move back to clinch. Lucas is un-affected by the elbow and pushes on Darius so that Darius is pushing back with equal force; Lucas suddenly reverses and pulls back with Darius's momentum spinning to his right as a tossing move. Darius is lifted off the ground unexpected but he knows that if he can hold the clinch on Lucas through the whole toss, both of them will hit the ground equally and then…

Darius does just that; holding Lucas's neck the whole way, a whole two seconds that seems like thirty to them both. They land on the sandy surface of the fighting square side by side and begin to roll, one on top the other and then reverse. Lucas ends up stopping the roll by bracing hard and lifting off of Darius at just the right time. It looks like he has Darius pinned and is about to lay him out with a few good hammer blows from above but Darius knows a few things. Right as Lucas winds up for his first blow, Darius thrusts his hips to lift Lucas up and then with incredible speed he pushes his upper body off the ground and strikes Lucas in the mid-section with a double open palm thrust punch. Lucas is tossed back to standing so he is no longer on top of Darius and watches as Darius quickly lifts his legs back in a slick little back roll to get him back to his feet before he can react to the move and force the fight again… Both of them are back on their feet and in stance, neither of them gained any advantage and so they circle around looking for a way to attack again…

A horn is blown by one of the spectating High Priests and the fight is stopped. An elder stands up from the crowd of robed people. One of the judges of Yannobi and oldest member of the order; a High Priest Renaud, stands up and steps forward.

"We have witnessed your fighting ability Lucas and recognize your strength. There is no need to take this contest any farther. This one ends in a draw of student and High Priest and therefore the student is allowed to perform the ritual of consummation of the sacred fruit."

Cheers break out in the courtyard and in the classrooms as everyone watching commends and celebrates the student's graduation. Darius grabs Lucas's right wrist and raises his arm up to the air in a friendly gesture of congratulations. The cheers and clapping slowly subside and the students watching out of the classroom windows return to their desks, books and holographic displays of anatomy and other subjects.

Adam carries on watching the teacher lecture and ask questions to different students. He can't help but replay the fight he just watched moments ago in his mind. He thinks of both Darius's and Lucas's moves and thinks of ways he could have straight up won the fight at any moment with this move or another. Ten minutes in to class and out of the blue, another horn sounds out through the entire school with a higher pitch than the fight horn. It's the horn that signals the end of the school term for all the student and teachers. Also meaning, after three long months of studying and training they all get to go home and take a break. The three month term is ended with a three week break and it always gets everyone excited.

Adam stays seated for a moment and watches the mayhem as all the students cheer and get up from their desks collecting their books and computer tablets to file out the door like herded cattle through a gate. He sits and waits till there's five students left at the door and then gets up, collects his stuff and makes for the door…

"Adam!" Miss Torrens says before Adam can leave; he stops and turns. "Tell your cousin congratulations for me. He fought well and I know he will make a great High Priest."

"Yes Miss Torrens; have a nice break and see you next semester."

"You as well Adam. Have some fun out there… Until next semester." She replies.

Adam nods and turns away and leaves the classroom. In the hallway now, he pauses to adjust to the flow of students rushing past him then picks his spot and joins in with the moving crowd… He reaches his locker down one of the lower halls; placing his thumb on the print pad lock he opens his locker and retrieves his back pack then stuffs in the book and tablet in his other hand. Shutting the locker door, he rejoins the slightly depleted crowd still in the halls and makes his way to the exit doors. Now outside the school with his backpack secured, he makes his way down the tiered concrete steps of the schools main entrance and like most students he heads for the embassy's main hub of transportation.

The Magnarail is Mires largest train system and runs from Opeyka capitol city all the way to Tartuga mining city at the outskirts of Olympus, Mires largest and most violent volcano. The distance from one to the other is forty one thousand kilometers and has many stops along the way. The entrance to the hub is only three hundred paces from the school's main stairway entrance so it's an easy choice for people when choosing a mode of transportation. Adam walks the short distance and climbs the large metal/chrome staircase to the ticket purchase terminals. Adam waits in line at one of the terminals; five people ahead of him. Looks like each other line up has more…

"This is gonna take forever." He thinks to himself… The line moves up and he gets his turn to put in his royal credit card into a port in the machine. He hits a couple of window options on the terminals screen of where he wishes to go and presto. The machine spits out a paper receipt and pushes his card out of the slot. Adam takes the slip of paper and his card back then turns toward the scanning doors. He walks through an open framed passage but the frames are equipped with scanning sensors to detect weapons or explosives. Adam gets the "all clear" tone as he walks through. He proceeds down a hallway that splits off to three hallways; signs in the middle read: Up to go east- Left to go north- Right to go south. Adam looks at his ticket to make sure; it reads "south- west to Olyra Valley". Adam walks up that hall and reaches the platform sixty feet above the ground where a magnetically powered train will stop soon to pick him and many other people up.

(Bassnectar – "Timestretch")

Within five minutes of Adams arrival on the platform, a smoothly curved, metallic train pulls up to the station. It's ten carts long and has a capacity of two hundred and ten people. Inside the train Adam takes a seat on one of the red velvety upholstered two seating benches. He watches as people take seats up and down the cart; a scruffy, dark haired man sits in the seat in front of him. He smells of some type of varnish, he must be a painter. Adam looks away out the window to see the metal beams that support the glass roof of giant hub. Moments later the doors close and the train quickly gets up to speed. Looking out the other window he sees the train hub slowly disappear and same with the school of the order and the embassy that houses it, all blending into one big sea of suburbia. A hollo-screen on the roof of the train cart starts to play advertising messages to distract the passengers of the train. Adam doesn't want to watch them so he looks out the window instead and watches the blur of landscape go as he and many others are being propelled up to four hundred and twenty kilometers per hour.

One of the advertisements catches Adam's eye.

"Come explore the island colony of Ehdon!"

The advertisement begins showing clips of people riding on the backs of large docile dinosaurs and cliff jumping into crystal blue pools of water.

"Adventure awaits you; for a limited time you can get an all-inclusive three night stay at the prestigious Cobalt Palace Hotel for two; now only fifty five imperial credits."

Adam thinks to himself. "That would be a nice vacation to take Eve on and finally tell her how he feels about her."

The commercial changes to a "work wanted" add at the Tartuga ore mining camp which really is just a good one third of the entire city of Tartuga… Adam tunes it out and looks out the window again, imagining his upcoming arrival to his home in the beautiful Olyra valley. His heart races at the thought of seeing her again after a three and a half month absence. His mind races with ideas of what he might say; circumstances he could create to get her alone and say it… But say what? I love you? She will just think you mean as a sister and giggle and move on thinking nothing of it. She will not see the love in his heart he has for her… As his mind wanders deeper; the train speeds on down its magnetic track.

Time passes quickly and before he knows it the computerized voice of the train's computer is speaking over the P.A.

"We are now approaching Olyra station. All passengers with this destination, please prepare to dis-embark."

Adam snaps back into reality and lifts his pack from the floor to sit on his lap in preparation to get off the train. It slows and comes to a stop; doors open and Adam gets out from one of the three doors of the cart. The Olyra station is plain compared to the capitol's station. This one is a plain concrete platform only two feet from ground level outside. It stretches out about fifty feet long and half that wide; twenty or so feet from the tracks to the three ticket terminals and another five to the outer doors of the little hub of a train station. Adam spots two security personnel off to the side of the outer doors as he exits the terminal. Several people rush past him and get into hover-cars waiting at the terminals parking/waiting lot. Night has fallen over Mire as he was day dreaming in the train cart, but it's a warm early fall night. He doesn't mind taking a walk through the town and slightly through the country side as he hasn't been here for some time now and just wants to take in all the old familiar sights.

He passes the old convenience store on the corner of Barns and Lupil Street and remembers the first time he stole a candy bar from that store and got caught by a fellow customer who let him off the hook after bashfully replacing the item to the shelf. He then walks by the sports field where he once played a crucial game Relay ball and scored the winning goal; his team mates hoisted him up on their shoulders and cheered, chanting his name for a moment before letting him down and dousing him with sprays of champagne from a couple different bottles. He was happy then and can't seem to come to grips with this whole training regimen his dad has him going on with the whole school of the order. Why wouldn't he just get him a post in the Empire somewhere; like a facility guard?

Adam walks onward down the town's main street "Barnes St." As he goes the scenery changes from buildings to fields of wheat, corn, and oats. His little Olyra valley is a productive one and he is proud of that; his skin tingles with excitement. He realizes he is only moments away from his driveway and a two minute walk down that driveway to his front door. His mind begins to focus on Eve again…

Adam opens the stained wood door to his mostly stained wood house. The home is quite large with a main level, basement, upper level and then a couple of bedrooms on a third level with a nice porch out front and a greenhouse and garden section in the back yard. Upon entering the house, Adam looks up the stair case to his left and sees nothing. He takes his shoes off and lays his backpack against the wall of the foyer. Two feet ahead of him and to the right is the door to the living room; he looks in there and sees a bunch of familiar furniture but no ladies. He continues down the hall. The stair-case wall to his left opens up to the kitchen slash dining room combo, and that's when he sees them. His mom and Eve sitting at the dining room table talking with each other as they sip on tea and slowly work on a virtual puzzle spread out over the surface of the table. The two of them look over at Adam at the same time ("Adam!" they say simultaneously) and pop up out of their seats to give him a big hug.

"How are you?" Asks Lynn; Adams mother.

She is a tall and strong looking woman with flowing black hair and fair features for a woman in her mid-fifties. She is wearing a one piece, long flowing, blue dress. Eve is slightly shorter than Lynn and has long, flowing black hair as well. Eve is only twenty one and is slightly more beautiful than Lynn which you could blame on her youth, but Adam knows she is an entirely different person than his mom. Yet some things they have in common and maybe that's what makes her lovelier to him than anything else could. Eve is wearing skin tight, black work out pants and a skin tight, white work out top.

"I'm doing good; you know…It was a long train ride and wouldn't mind some of that tea."

She says "Of course son. Come on over and join us at the table, I'll put the water back on."

"Thanks Mom."

Adam follows the two of them into the dining room right next to the kitchen; no walls to separate the two. Adam sits at the seat directly across from Eve.

"Tell me Adam… How's the training going at the school?" Asks Eve.

"It's going good… I'm close to graduating, I can feel it… My cousin graduated earlier today…"

"Are talking about Lucas? He graduated?" Asks Lynn from a few feet over in the kitchen.

"Yes Mom. He graduated after he won his Yannobi today." He answers.

"That's great!" Lynn says as she turns on the tea kettle, then joins them at the table pulling out a chair, she sits on it.

"Remember when Lucas use to visit us and you two would get to joking around about who was the stronger out of the two of you? And then you'd toss him around the back yard for a while until he gave up." Lynn recalls.

"Yeah Mom, I remember." He answers with a big grin on his face.

"They must have put him up against a wimpy High Priest." Lynn says.

"No Mom, they actually put him up against one of the recently graduated and undefeated High Priest Siscerelle. A real good fighter; they ended it with a draw." Adam replies.

"Well I guess all that fighting in the back yard with you paid off for him." Lynn says jokingly.

"Hahaha." Adam laughs. "Maybe you're right Mom."

The kettle begins to whistle behind Lynn; she excuses herself and returns quickly with a hot cup of tea for Adam.

They sit around the table and talk about the past; when Adam and Eve were just kids. "Remember the neighbour's kids?" Asks Lynn.

"They were kind of an odd couple right?"

"We may have had something to do with that Mom." Adam answers. "We were just kids and horsing around…"

Adam looks to Eve; she gives him the nod of the head and he

continues. "We were chasing the chickens around; me, Eve, Cara and Maliki. We chased those chickens over to Balch Creek and then they fluttered over to the other side and clucked along the bank of it like they were mocking us."

"So they crossed over the property line huh? That creek is the most disgusting creek ever... How did you get them back across?" Lynn asks.

"We didn't..." Eve cuts in. "But we convinced them to try. There's that willow tree at the far north corner of the property where some of the branches go half way over the creek. We tied a rope to one branch and convinced Maliki to go first to swing across."

"He grabbed the rope and gave it a good run but couldn't let go until it was already coming back to our side of the creek. He splashed down hard into the murky creek." Adam carries on.

"He swam back over to the bank and tried to get his sister Cara to help him out. She stood at the bank and tried to pull her brother out but he was heavier than her and pulled her into the mucky water instead... It was so funny to see them crawl out covered in mud. They couldn't wait to get out of their gross clothes so we both stood by the tree; me and Eve, and told them we would look the other way while the two of them undress and ring out their clothes."

"Yeah but we peeked." Eve picks up on the story. "And as we looked we saw Maliki push his pants down and bend over. He had a leech attached to him on his... Umm you know that part..." Eve leans over to Lynn and whispers the rest in her ear.

"Oh my god! There! That's horrible..." Exclaims Lynn. "Did you guys tell him?" She asks.

"We didn't have to. Cara saw the same thing and freaked out because she thought the same water bug would be on her in a similar spot." Eve answers and continues. "Maliki found and ripped the bug off of him but it made him bleed there pretty good." Adam is chuckling as Eve tells the rest. "They rung their clothes out the best they could and took off to their home. We didn't see them for like a week after; they were quite embarrassed."

Lynn is smiling but shaking her head at the same time at the grossness of the image she saw in her mind upon hearing the story. Adam thinks of another time they were visiting them at their house.

"Did we ever tell you about the time we went to their house and played in their yard with the ring around the Rosie game?" Asks Adam.

"No actually I haven't heard about that one. What happened there?"

"We were in their yard; just me and Eve, while their dog their dog Roxi took a huge dump in the thick grass. They came out of their house to play just after…"

Adam is telling the story but suddenly hears the hollo-computer ringing in the office past the kitchen and down the hallway a few feet. "Doot dooot doot."

"I'll go get that… Eve; you know the rest, keep going and I'll be back in a moment." Says Adam as he gets up and goes to answer the call.

Walking down the hall he turns left through an open door way to his dad's office. The office is of a nice size with a large desk against the left wall and book shelves full of books on the right wall.

On the wall across from the door is a window wall that looks out on the west side of the property. Adam sees the name on the hollo-screen; 'Lucas' and answers the call with a wave of his finger over the answer window. Lucas's face appears in the hollo-screen.

"Adam! Just the man I was hoping to catch. How are you doing cuz?"

"I'm doing great. I saw your Yannobi today and man; I'm impressed. You fought well against Darius; gave him his first draw." Says Adam.

"Thanks Adam, he was a tough opponent; there was a point where I didn't think I would beat him."

Back in the kitchen/dining room; Eve continues the story that Adam began, about the neighbour kids Cara and Maliki.

"So we were all in the front yard and Adam got this idea to play ring around the rosie. We all joined hands and started spinning around and singing the song. When it got to the part, 'We all let go!' Adam let go of Cara's hand at just the right moment so that she fell back on the freshly laid pile of dog crap. She got up and was slightly confused at first; she started sniffing in the air and trying to reach behind her to touch her back. Well she did touch it and she pulled her hand to her nose to smell it and then she started to puke."

"Oh my gosh… Adam did that on purpose?" Asks Lynn.

"Yeah, I guess he did and he was laughing his ass off and I kind of was too." Admits Eve and chuckles at the memory of it.

"I guess that is pretty funny." Lynn admits and begins to chuckle a bit. "What about Maliki? What did he do?"

"Oh that's even better… He felt sorry for his sister and tried to help her get the poop covered shirt off of her but the more he smelled it the more it set him off and he ended up puking on Cara's head for a second… You know; because he turned away from her right after the puke effect hit him with force but because he puked on her head, it caused her to puke a lot more." Both of them break out in laughter at the thought of that.

Back in the office Lucas continues the conversation.

"I just kept thinking about what I'd do if I was fighting you… I know that sounds strange to you but from my perspective that's an honour. Sparring with you gave me the added skill to win my Yannobi today and I want you to know that I'm grateful for that. Grateful enough to name you as one of my two acolytes. Will you come to Ehdon with me the day after tomorrow?" Asks Lucas.

"Of course Lucas, I'd be honoured to be your acolyte at the ceremony and thanks for that bit of credit towards your win… I guess your glad then that it wasn't me facing you on that platform." He says with a big grin.

"Real funny Adam. I'd have whooped your butt." Lucas says smiling back.

Adam suddenly thinks to ask. "Do you think it would be ok if I brought Eve?"

"I don't know Adam… you know how women can get sometimes… Besides she's your sister and that's like a request you make to a girlfriend or something."

"No, I know that… I meant both Eve and my mom to come along. I'd pay for their tickets. We've just been cooped up a bit I guess; me at the school and the ladies here at home. I feel like we just all could use some time in paradise and away from all this… Normal living."

"Ok Adam, it's very thoughtful of you. They can both come along on the basis that the school doesn't pay for them. You on the other hand are in the schools expense book; you pay nothing. The return flight is booked for three days after the ceremony; lots of time to enjoy the islands finer pleasures."

"Ok Lucas you got yourself an acolyte. Where do we meet?"

"Be at the Onydath station at O four hundred hours on Tonos evening and I'll meet you there as you get off the inbound train and we'll take the O six hundred shuttle to Pangaea." Explains Lucas.

"Why not go from Opeyka? You're there now right?" Adam asks.

"Yes but I'm heading to my home in Onydath tomorrow morning to tell mom and dad the good news in person and collect a few things before going… So I'll see you there?"

"Sounds good cousin; see you there." Says Adam and swipes the bottom of the hollo-screen to hang up the call.

Adam re-enters the kitchen smiling from ear to ear. Eve and Lynn notice right away that there's a change in Adam.

"So what was that all about?" Asks Eve.

"Lucas was on the line; did I mention that he graduated to High Priest status today? He will undergo the ceremony soon and the flight leaves Onydath station in two days. He has asked me to be one of his two acolytes!" Adam answers. "I accepted the offer and asked if I could bring you two along; he said yes! So how about it? You two want to go to Ehdon on Tonos?"

Eve and Lynn light up with excitement. "I would love to go to Ehdon with you." Says Eve.

"And so would I." Says Lynn.

"Great! It's settled then. We're all going to Ehdon."

"Oh I can't wait!" Eve shouts and goes to give Adam a big hug.

"You're the best brother a girl could have. I'm going to my room to start packing; I'm so excited!" She practically shouts in Adam's ear, then let's go of him and dashes off to go upstairs to and begin packing her two large suit cases.

Adam's sight goes slow motion as he watches her sprint towards the staircase noticing the way her butt wiggles slightly with each step she takes. He almost forgets his Mom is standing right there watching him. He turns calmly to face her.

"She gets so excited at the chance to go to Ehdon… Remember the first time we went there? She was so scared…" Adam says.

Lynn glares at him suspiciously for a few seconds and then dismisses her thoughts. "That's because she was 9 years old and never been off world before."

"Yeah, and look at her now…" He decides to change the topic suddenly feeling very uncomfortable. "So how's Dad doing? When is he done his current rotation?" He asks and the change in topic works.

"Dad is doing fine. His next break from duty is in four weeks and two days from today… He misses us; he told me when he called a few days ago."

"Damn it; I'm back in school in three weeks mom. We're not going to see each other again, for the third time in a row!"

"I know son… Hush and be calm… You'll see him again in the future; you'll graduate soon and then you can book your own schedule at the school or leave the school and work within one of the cities close by and then you will see him every end of rotation." Councils Lynn.

"Ok mom; you're right. This absence won't last forever." Adam says and calms down.

"That's my boy, or I mean man. Look at you, all grown up now… You must be hungry after that long journey from the school, I'll make you something to eat. Come, sit down and tell me about your last term. Did you make any new friends? Or a girlfriend perhaps?" Lynn inquires as she gets to making Adam some food…

The night progresses and Adam is full with good food and tired from a long day. He tells his mom he's tired and going to turn in for the night; giving her a hug, he then heads for the stairs and leaves his mom in the kitchen. Adam climbs the stairs and pauses at Eve's room to peek inside as the door is open crack. Eve is folding clothes and placing them in a suit case; she moves out of view so Adam leans to follow and his shifting weight causes the floor board to creek loudly. Eve hears the noise and Adam makes like nothing's going on and quickly knocks on the door and says her name. "Eve?"

"Yes Adam come in, what's up?" She asks.

"Oh not much, just wanted to say good night to you before going to bed."

"Ok… Well, good night then Adam. Thanks again for inviting me and mom to Ehdon with you."

"Don't mention it. Besides, I can't imagine going without you two. Remember the last time we went to Ehdon and camped out at that beach front campground?" Asks Adam.

"Yeah I remember that… Those sun sets were just amazing, and we had such a good time. Now we are older and braver… I think we should do something crazy there like base-jump from Calverth Mountain's plateau… Or something like that."

"Sure Eve; we can do that and so much more. I hear the festival of Harvious will start in three days; we can be there for that too. Then the sky's the limit…" Adam says enthusiastically then calms down a bit with. "Well I'm gonna pack a few things and then fall asleep, good night Eve."

Eve replies in kind and Adam leaves the room to find his own room two doors down the hall from hers. He opens the door to find…

(Deadmou5 – "Closer")

Nothing in his room has changed; there's his bed against the wall in the far right corner. A night table beside the bed with a lamp and then there's the one window right across from him at the door; his desk sits against the left wall and a dresser next to that and then a closet on the same wall as his door that stretches the four feet to the corner. All crammed together and all alone. He opens his dresser drawer and moves some shirts aside to get a small stash of pictures that other people have taken of the two of them together. He fumbles through them and finds the one with the two of them on Ehdon. They were wearing straw hats and Eve was in a 2 piece swim suit, while his younger self was in shorts. They had just been walking along the beach with dad when Eve found a star fish. Seconds later he found a crustacean called a silver dollar. They both were close in the shot, having his arm over her shoulder, hers over his shoulder. Both holding out their prize for their father to capture in this picture.

"We were only thirteen and fifteen years old in this shot and it all looked so innocent. How would she know what she does to me when I have learned to hide it so well?" Adam thinks to himself and ponders his dilemma. "We aren't officially related so in my heart I know my feelings for her are not perverse. But my parents would freak out; Dad for sure would disown me… How can I tell you how much I love you Eve?" He thinks as he stares at the photograph.

Adam lays back on his bed and sinks into a comfortable spot as he looks at the photograph a bit longer. He drifts off to sleep with the picture on his chest, and has a dream with her in it. They are running through a forest together; deadly creatures are chasing them. Then they are flying through the sky; he goes deeper into the dream world and sees scattered images of people fighting… Then images of him holding Eve in his arms on a clear starry night; both moving in for a kiss…

Morning comes to Olyra Valley and the ladies of the house are up early, but Adam stays asleep. Eve comes out of the washroom after her shower and sees Adams door open slightly and hears him snoring slightly.

"How can he still be sleeping? Doesn't he know how much prep it takes for a trip like this? Like how much packing could he have done in one night?" Eve thinks to herself. "I'll just open the door and take a peek."

Eve slowly swings the door more and more open until she sees Adam sleeping in his bed (clothes still on) with a big bulge in his pants. She stops and backs away into the hall feeling embarrassed. "I heard about men and their morning bulge, so why am I so shocked to see he has one?" She asks herself. She listens and hears no change in Adams breathing, or any other movement. "Why do I suddenly want to see it again? Does that make me sick? I mean I know I'm attracted to men but my own brother? …Well, he's not really brother by blood… Just another quick glance…"

Eve inches back over to see Adam in his oblivious state of excitement and then notices a picture laying face up on the floor; a picture of the two of them together back when they were young. Adam stirs in his bed and Eve backs away completely to go back to her room. "Is he fantasizing about me in his sleep?" She wonders. "What if he is? No, he wouldn't… He's my brother and I'm his sister and that's that."

"Adam! Eve! Come down for some breakfast!" Lynn shouts from the bottom of the stairs.

"Ok mom, just a minute!" Eve shouts back and then shouts down the hallway to see if Adam woke up to that. "Adam? Are you awake yet?"

"Aahhh. Yes Eve! Be out in a minute!" He shouts back.

Time flies by on this day as Adam, Eve, and Lynn all get prepared to leave Mire for some time on Pangaea's one and only island colony. Ehdon has become the solar systems premier destination for vacationing as it has the most amazing plants and animals living on it as well as a natural beauty unlike anything found on Mire or Gorgon. Adam finishes packing his large travel bag and suit case as dusk comes to summon another night on Mire; tomorrow is their departure day, "Tonos".

Eve, the whole day through, successfully hides her embarrassment of her morning peep show, as well as her new found attraction for her step brother. Which she tries to convince herself is nothing more than a sense of curiosity and a what if? And nothing more. They turn in for the night and night quickly gives way to the morning and a new day… The big day…

Adam is coming out from his dad's office and turns to enter the kitchen/dining room where Eve and Lynn are sitting. Eve is now wearing blue jeans and a white t-shirt to go with her light white summer hoodie. Lynn is wearing pink sweat pants, a light blue shirt with a pink and white striped button up dress shirt over top; hair braided into a long pony-tail. Adam is in blue jeans and a black dress shirt with tribal patterns embroidered on it in white.

"The Hover Shuttle will be here in a few minutes to take us to Olyra Station. We get tickets from there to Onydath Station and from there we get the tickets to Ehdon." Adam says.

"Well I guess we should wait outside then." Suggests Eve.

"Good call, let's get our luggage outside the door." Within minutes of them waiting, the jet black Hover Shuttle arrives, kicking up a bit of dust off the paved driveway where it comes to a stop. The rear hatch of the vehicle opens and Adam assists the ladies in tossing the luggage into it. With that task done, he closes the hatch and opens the left side door for Eve and Lynn to enter. He closes the door behind them like a gentleman and goes around the back side to the right hand passenger door, opens it, takes his seat next to Eve and closes it.

"Oh yeah… This is gonna be great!" Eve says with excitement as the Hover shuttle picks up off the ground and speeds away down the road to deliver its passengers to the train station.

At the front of Olyra Station Adam again helps with the luggage, handing each piece to the proper owner before taking his out last and closing the hatch of the Hover shuttle. The three of them enter the ticket booth room; Adam goes up to one of the electronic booths and with his credits card he purchases tickets for them. Eve walks through the scanning doorways first Followed by Lynn and then himself. The scanners beep a nice beep and a light by the door blinks green for all three of them to signal the all clear. They walk the fifteen paces further in to stand on the docking platform and wait with about two dozen other people. An electronic display on the rear wall just left of the scanners shows the estimated time the trains will arrive. Adam sees the one they need to board.

"NORTH EAST BOUND TO ONYDATH – TWO MINUTES AWAY – 0: 1100H"

Like clockwork, the train shows up from the east and stops perfectly in line with the markers painted on the concrete floor for where the doors should be. The doors of the train slide open; some people come out from the carts and pass by them, then they go in and find a cluster of four empty seats which they claim and use the fourth seat for their luggage as well as some of the ground space close to them. Within a few moments everyone boarding has found a seat.

A pleasant, automated female voice speaks from the trains P.A. system. "All passengers please be seated."

The doors of all the carts close at the same time and an electric crackle can be heard from underneath their feet as the train powers up to get moving.

"Next stop Ogyllias Station."

Bassnectar – "Parade Into Centuries"

Eve spends most of the train ride listening to music with personal headphones and reading an e-book on her tablet while Adam talks more about his time in school and what he's learning about; explaining things to his curious mother. The trip from Olyra to Onydath has five stops in-between and takes the trio a little over two hours to complete. They step out of the train among a throng of people onto a much better docking platform. Fancy light posts project shadowy images of all kinds of things like fish leaping out of water to dragonflies with fluttering wings of light. Some flash by on bare sections of wall and some on the glassy concrete ground of the station. Clothing shops and cafés litter the long back wall of the docking pad; Adam looks at his smart phone screen for the time.

"Well we have at least half an hour before Lucas gets here… We should get something to drink from that café over there and sit there until he gets here. Sound good?" Asks Adam.

The ladies agree to the plan and make their way to the café. Adam holds his phone close to his mouth as they walk.

"Text Lucas." He says to it…

It beeps once to signal that it's ready. Eve glances back to see him wheeling his luggage along and using his phone with his free hand. "Hey cuz, we got here a bit early so we're going to hang out at this 'Wild Bean Café until you get here."

He hits the send button and joins the ladies at the line-up of the café.

While the three of them are sitting at a round glass table just outside of the café, Adam is distracted by an obviously homeless man dressed in what he'd call filthy old rags. He is ranting about a coming apocalypse and the end of life in the solar system. People walk by him and give him weird looks as well as keep their distance like his long, greasy hair has lice or something. He listens closer by filtering out the background noise; a trick taught by the school he attends.

["From the sky he will descend and sow the seeds of destruction! The dark one lives as a man and will soon establish his kingdom of corpses. And darkness will rule the worlds of man forever!"] Is what he's yelling and then two security guards approach him.

Eve and Lynn follow Adams gaze now and see what he's watching unfold.

Eve turns back to Adam and says; "I heard about these mentally unstable people. Every once in a while they slip into places like this and rant about stuff and security throws them out. It's so sad…"

"Yeah, it really is." Replies Adam.

"It really is what?" Asks Lucas as he blind sides the three of them sitting at the table.

All three of them look behind over his way at the same time.

"It really is nice of you to allow me to be your acolyte is what I was saying. Thank you." Adam says with a smile and gets up to shake his cousin's hand.

Lucas is wearing a nice white dress shirt and beige dress pants, his hair is cut short and spiked up with some sort of styling gel.

"You're most welcome Adam… Aunti Lynn; so good to see you again." Says Lucas and gives her a big hug.

"You too Lucas… My how you've grown in the last few years… You're bigger than Adam now."

"Thanks Aunti; just been living well at the school… Eve, I'm glad you could come along."

Lucas releases his Aunti and gives Eve a hug then turns to introduce his other acolyte and two seniors who are to be present at the ceremony. They were standing off to the side but now approach the table.

"This young man here is Will Duncan and is the other acolyte. This man beside Will Duncan is High Priest Gary Ulrich and on his side is High Priest Darius Siscerelle." Lucas introduces and watches as they all shake hands.

"Will, Gary, Darius; this is Adam, Eve and Lynn… Now that we're all introduced, I suggest we make our way to the space centre. It's just a ten minute walk from here so if we go now we'll have a few minutes to get settled into our seats before launch."

They gather their luggage and make for the space station which is attached to the train station through a series of corridors, hall ways and escalators full of people. They finally make it to the ticket booths; Adam quickly buys tickets for the ladies and then is handed a ticket from Lucas for himself. They drop their luggage on the luggage conveyor just before the boarding gate that is secured by guards and flanked by scanners. They pass through unhindered and make their way down the corridor that connects to their shuttle.

They are now aboard the shuttle which is basically a large triangular aircraft with a set of powerful engines. Once the loading process is done, the hatch is closed and magnetically sealed. Engines fire up slightly and on three sets of wheels its pilots move the spacecraft into position underneath a gigantic "O" shaped Air balloon launching platform and kill the engines. A series of notches have been included in the design of the hull of the ship for super strong steel cables. Once in position on the platform, computerized mechanical arms deploy from their stationary positions and attach the cables that hoist the shuttle into position on the launching ramp in the centre of the large helium/Argon gas filled balloon. The entire structure has to be tethered to the ground by a couple of very lengthy rolls of high strength steel cable or it would float off into the atmosphere and not come down. Once the Shuttle is loaded in the middle ramp of the floating launch bay and secured to a super strong steel buckle designed to release after the launch, the tethering cables are un-raveled allowing the structure to rise up into the sky. Once it reaches the upper atmosphere (which takes only a few minutes) a large canister of compressed air on the opposite side of the ramp and attached by the same buckle to the belly of the shuttle is punctured by a mechanical pin and "Boom". The shuttle is thrust upward ever so quickly on a perfect angle to clear the entire structure in a matter of seconds. At the top of the ramp is a strong steel blocker for the CO2 canister and attaching buckle yet the shuttle is free to rise with the gained momentum that throws them up two hundred feet before the pull of gravity wants them to come back down. Plenty of time for the pilots to fully fire up the main engines and boost away to complete the distance needed to enter space. Once in space, the shuttle hooks up to a hyper drive attachment and launches the shuttle towards its destination at super-sonic speeds.

Several hours later the shuttle blazes through Pangaea's atmosphere and soon after that it lands on Ehdon's runway located on the eastern edge of the island colony. The Island spans four hundred and fifty kilometers from west to east and six hundred and twenty kilometers from north to south and is situated just shy of three hundred kilometers off the coast of Pangaea's mainland (eastern seaboard). Pangaea's mainland is off limits to all humans for obvious reasons, but the island had long since been cleansed of any harmful creatures and deemed safe and livable for humans by the Imperial board of planetary standards… The shuttle slows to a snail's pace as it approaches the docking platform for Ehdon's space station. Built in an oval shape where the large area receives and loads ships and the slimmer end is where the station meets the city streets. Hover cabs and Daxaur carts are lined up along the street outside the stations main doors. Right outside the doors of Ehdon's space station is a large section of the cities down town core, full of shopping malls, restaurants and hotels. Eve convinces them to take the Daxaur cart which is a fancy coach on wheels that is pulled by four strong, well trained dinosaurs (much like a duck billed platypus). The lights of the inner city stores subside as they get farther out and get replaced by lights of driveways of people's homes. Fancy and extravagant homes they are, that only the super-rich could afford to live in. People like athletes, actors and artists of home and fashion.

"Adam; we're going to have to drop the ladies off at the hotel. I need you to come with me to the temple where we must prepare for the ritual. You acolytes need to perfect the pitches of the séance or I could end up lost in the other realm." Lucas says as they sit together.

CHAPTER 2

WINDS OF FATE

Sub Chapter 1: The Making of a Monster "Lucien Ferradin"
Mire - Secret Military Complex - "Okladore"

A middle aged man sits at desk; drafting papers are strewn about in front of him. A pencil moves rapidly in his hand as he finishes up the final touches on a sketch. The room is twenty feet by thirty feet squared; ten foot ceilings and all made of metal panels bolted together at the seams. Against the right side wall from the doorway is a comfortable looking bed with black, silk blankets and pillows. His name use to be Lucien Ferradin; he's wearing a black, long sleeve silk shirt and black silk pajama pants. On the wall opposite to the door is his desk and in the space to the left is a matt with the infinite pattern woven on it in white and an altar structure with a human looking skull on the top of it but made of pure crystal. He gets up from his desk and opens a drawer of it to retrieve some kind of a smoke and a torch lighter. He puts the smoke to his lips; lights it up with the lighter and takes a large puff. He sits on the end of his bed and looks across his room to the crystal skull. His jet black hair curls down over his forehead and stops at his eyebrows; his eyes are dark hazel set in a ring of blackness. Wisps of smoke pass by his vision as he exhales the smoke slowly and stares at the skull.

"How is it that we know each other again Dai'Alzan?" He asks the skull.

"Right, you betrayed your own kind to save our race and your kin abandoned you and eleven others to die on this planet and I was there…" He says and then takes another big puff from his herb smoke. "Corba was so easy to enter, his soul was so beat down and vulnerable; much like this one was before joining with him. Corba felt responsible for not including the dark matter algorithm in the flight plan after the last space jump. Hitting that chunk of dark matter was his fault and it ate him up allowing me to enter his mind after a time. Creating humans was the only way to create a work force capable of repairing your ship in time, because so many of you died upon impact those thousands of years ago. Only fifty two out of two thousand, one hundred and eight survived. But little did we as humans know that you don't really die until you enter the power of a star. You can just go home to your word's robotics facility and build yourselves another body. But only if you make it back."

"Screw you Lucifer." The crystal scull replies in his thoughts.

"Oh no my friend; it's you who are screwed… All my knowledge came from you because you are obliged to answer any question asked of you. It's your curse and our blessing as humans."

Lucien puts his smoke down in an ash tray on his desk and sits back down on his bed; closing his eyes he lets the colors swarm together and create whatever images they may create. "Only someone as spiritual as I could talk with you. Other humans are too weak."

"Other Humans?" Asks Dai'Alzan the skull…

"You are no human. You only found a human host to infest… I can see back in your mind Lucifer, or should I say Lucien; before the Dark Lord took you… You were innocent; free from sin."

"I was always there Dai'Alzan; deep in the souls of each and every one of them… Lucien was weak; eager to join with me and become strong… Let me show you now, look now into my mind; see the truth of these humans you helped save." Lucifer answers in his mind and then he falls back on his bed and goes into a trance like state.

His earliest thoughts go back to when his name was Lucien

Ferradin; a four year old kid living on Mire. His older brother (by two years) Gabriel was playing with a toy car that has lights that flash. Lucien is fascinated by it and can't stop watching as Gabe pretends to race the thing around the living room floor. The House is a typical one level, three bedroom with the living room next to the kitchen and dining room, the two being separated by a wall and short hall way. Lucien's Mother Verra is home and calls Gabriel into the kitchen; he looks over and sees his mom ask Gabe to help his baby brother Michael into his high chair for feeding time. The toy car sits in front of him un-used so Lucien decides to pick it up and play with it himself. He gets carried away with the lights of it and his imagination of this car being in a chase with other cars. He zooms it in a circle and sees Gabe's sock covered feet suddenly in front of his nose. He senses that Gabe is angry with him so he offers the toy back to him. Gabriel rips the toy car out of his hands and looks at Lucien for a moment before smashing him in the face with the toy car. Lucien's vision goes dark…

(Billy Tallent – "Covered in Cowardice")

Flashes of memories go by until his next traumatizing experience; three years of memories play out in the span of mere moments. Lucien is seven years old now and has gone through a couple grades in elementary school and is about to start the third grade. Its summer break for those living on the main continent of Mire called Olympus. The kids are enjoying a nice hot day playing in the sprinklers, chasing bugs and riding bikes. Well the older kids are riding bikes. Gabriel is hanging out with his friend Miles. Both of them are nine years old and big boys for their age. The two of them have set up a ramp using old boards they found in the back yard by the shed. They set it up in the middle of the yard and have it so it jumps the small, inflatable kid's pool. They also both have nice bikes where all Lucien has is a banana bike with training wheels; it couldn't jump a pebble.

Lucien remembers being jealous of the two boys, wishing that he could take a turn hopping a bike over the pool to the other ramp and landing it all cool and pro like. How that would impress his older brother and his friend and make them like him so much more, because at the moment they don't like him so much and they have made sure he knows it. After completing one of his jumps, Gabriel looks over at Lucien and sees the fascination in his eyes. He rides over to Miles with a twisted idea that might reward them both with some entertainment.

"Hey Miles... I'm gonna let my little brother try the jump." Says Gabriel quietly even though Lucien is half the yard away and wouldn't hear a thing.

"Are you sure Gabe? He's kinda small for these bikes." Miles replies.

"I know man, that's the whole point. He's gonna bail right before he hits the ramp and make a big fool of himself. Trust me, this is going to be hilarious." Gabriel insists.

Miles agrees to the plan.

"Hey Lucien!" Gabriel yells as he rides up to him sitting on the step of the porch. Lucien had zoned out on little three year old Michael playing in the sand box with Jordan (Miles' little brother of three years old) off to the left of the porch. The back yard is a nice level continuous piece of lawn forty feet long by fifty eight feet wide from fence to porch. Exception being the shed in the far left corner and the sand box on the near left corner of the yard. Gabriel skids to a stop right in front of him.

"Yes Gabriel?" Asks Lucien.

"I was talking with Miles and both of us think you're old enough to try the jump." Gabriel tells him with a serious look.

"I don't know Gabriel... Your bike is so big, I can't get on it."

"Sure you can Lucien; here, use the porch steps." Gabriel says as he hops off his bike and positions it a foot away from Lucien and right beside the porch step.

"Come on Lucien, we all have to put our big boy pants on at some point... I'll hold you up while you get used to going and grab you when you slow down enough to stop."

Courage begins to build inside of him as he sees the opportunity in front of him to be a big boy. Lucien agrees to try ride his big brothers bike and climbs up onto the seat as his older brother holds it steady.

"Ok, I'm going to push now and you have to start to pedal at the same time ok." Gabriel instructs his brother. (Their mother Verra looks out the glass door of the house that goes to the porch and sees them playing. She smiles and thinks nothing of it.)

"Ok Lucien, I'm going to let go now!" Gabriel shouts from behind him.

"Remember to steer around the yard with the handle bars!" Gabriel shouts just as he realizes that he's heading right for the neighbours fence made of sturdy wooden planks.

Lucien leans hard to his left and steers clear of impact just in time. He's so excited that he's now riding his big brothers bike he shouts with joy. "Woo Hoo!"

After a few laps around the back yard, Lucien is feeling pumped and ecstatic about his graduation from small bike to big bike.

"You got this Lucien! Take the jump brother! You got this!" He hears Gabriel shout at him from the porch.

Lucien eye's up an approach and turns into it picking up speed as he pumps his legs hard and works the pedals to gain speed. Before he can react he realizes that he's screwed. He hits the ramp with speed but has no idea about how to lift the front tires and raise the bike in a jump. It happens in slow motion to him… The front tire drops off the edge of the top of the raised ramp; his momentum thrusts him head first towards the hard wooden edge of the opposite ramp as he instinctively lets go of the handlebars so he doesn't break his neck underneath a heavy bicycle. The bike lands upside down in the kiddy pool between the ramps while the back of Lucien's head connects hard with the edge of the opposite side ramp as he completes a twisted death flip over the pool. Lucien blacks out but can somehow still see in his current state of subconscious thought, his body slides to a stop at the bottom of the ramp; a trail of blood left behind him. Gabriel runs up to him as his mind and sight hovers above.

"Mom!" Shouts Gabriel as he runs to his brother's side. "Lucien's hurt bad! Call for help Mom! Call for Help!"

Verra hears the cries of her oldest son and comes running to the porch to see Lucien laying on his back at the foot-step of the bicycle jumping ramp Gabe had made with Miles. Lucien hears his little brother crying from over in the sand box and then there's darkness…

Lucien feels the softness of blankets at his fingertips and smells the familiar scent of his bedroom.

"It was all a bad dream." He thinks to himself as he slowly pulls the blankets down over his head so that he can see around his room.

His eyes adjust to the light of the lamp on his night table next to his bed that's pressed against the right wall of his room. His clothes closet is right across the room from his bed and he takes notice of how its doors are left wide open; he never leaves those doors open. The door to the hallway is just to the left of his closet and he thinks to make a break for it to his mom and dad's room to find out what happened and why his room looks so dark, but finds that his legs don't work as he tries to move off the bed… Now he is worried.

"Why don't my legs work?" He asks himself.

Something from within his closet moves and he hears sounds of clothes ruffling together. Lucien freezes for a few seconds; his heart is beating a million beats a minute he's so frightened. He flops back onto his bed and covers himself again with his blanket and hides there, pretending to be asleep.

"Luuccciieenn."

He hears his name being whispered by some sort of creature from over in the direction of the closet. Chills run up his spine and he is afraid of whatever exits within that closet.

"Fear not child, for it is your Father Morrick." Lucien hears next.

The voice of his father causes Lucien to doubt his own mind. His father could have been hiding in the closet for some reason. He's not sure why but he's sure that the voice he just heard is that of his dad's.

Lucien pulls the blanket back down from over his head to see a man that looks just like his dad standing in the middle of his room.

"Father? Is that you? … Why are you here in my room so late?" Asks Lucien.

The man appearing to be his dad just stands there and stares.

"Dad? Why aren't you talking?"

A few seconds after he asks this the man's face shifts out of focus and becomes distorted to his view, then returns to normal but for his eyes. His father's eyes have become orbs of pure darkness.

"You aren't my dad." Says Lucien.

"No I'm not; I just knew it would be easier for you to see me this way…"

"I'm dead then." Lucien thinks. "I'm dead and this is the Nether-realm and you are…"

"No Lucien you are not dead; you are but in a deep sleep that comes when close to death… I am the keeper of this realm; I call it Shadow Land and my name… Well, you can call me Shadow Man."

"You just read my thoughts."

"So this is just a dream then? And I can wake up right now if I want to?" Asks Lucien.

He hears deep raspy breaths from Shadow man as he waits for an answer.

"No you can't… Your mind or brain has suffered a hard hit and will take time for it to repair… You were suckered by your older brother to take a jump that you should never have attempted at your age… Look at the ceiling of your room…" Shadow man tells him.

Lucien sees a dimly lit spackled white ceiling but wait… It's changing before his eyes into a full blown 3D image of the universe full of star clusters, galaxies and even meteorites floating across the ceiling at random.

"That is amazing… We usually have to go camping for this kind of a view of the heavens."

Lucien has no idea how this is happening but he likes it.

"Lucien; you are about to live a life of misery at the hands of your brothers, especially the older one Gabriel…"

The vision of the universe changes as he glares at up at it into a sort of living 3D projector. Now showing; "Lucien's future". Flashes of moments go by in a kind of picture book style. Three to five second frames that jump forward in time by days, weeks, even months. The moments are painting a picture of his utter humiliation and infinite torment at the hands of his brothers until Lucien is overwhelmed with the most destructive feelings. There's images of a beautiful woman who he has feelings for and gets to know over time and then watches, no scratch that. Lucien practically experiences the events of his future twelve years until it happens. The day that that ends it all for him… Lucien, one day finds his two brothers raping the woman he loves in his apartment. Lucien loses his mind and tackles both his brother's right out the main living room windows and then watches himself fall ten stories out of an apartment building with them, to land on the cold, hard cement with a "splat"!

"Aaahh! Why!?" Lucien screams and covers his eyes with his blanket. "How?"

He slowly uncovers his face to see Shadow man still standing where he has been the whole time. "How was it that I felt her? Andreah… How is it I know her name… How can you… You tell me this is my future but I don't believe you. It just can't be."

"Oh but it is…"

Shadow Man is an ancient dark angel named Azazel, and was present at the dawn of creation. He can travel through time and space at the speed of thought and is drawn to life to instill in it the need for the antithesis… Death…

"Your own family torments you to the tipping point where you end all their lives, including your own… That brings me to why I'm here Lucien. I don't usually offer alliances with your race but your life… Your future has caused me to want to interfere."

"And what could you possibly do to stop it? If that's to be my future; how can anyone stop it?"

"Not anyone; not just you or I… But Usss." Shadow Man says. "Together we will change the course of your life." Lucien stares at him and thinks for a moment. "So together we can stop my brothers from ruining my life, is basically what you're saying."

"Yesss Lucien. Together we can do ssso much. We will not only stop that time line but together we will create a whole new one with us at the center of everything… We can show humanity a new way of life, a way of infinite peace. Would you like that young Lucien?" Shadow man asks him an undeniable question.

Of course he wants to be a part of everlasting peace for mankind; who wouldn't?

"Yes, I would like that a lot." Answers Lucien.

"Good… Rest now Lucien… We will be together again soon enough." And with those words, Lucien's vision goes to a blur and he can't help but fall back on to his pillow and falls asleep…

He sees a sliver of light and hears a bunch of noises. Focusing harder on opening his eyes, he manages to get them fully open and sees that he's in a hospital room with tubes full of fluids hooked into his arms and a heart monitor patch on his chest. He is confused because he can't remember why in the world he's in here. "What happened to me?" He asks himself in thought. As he tries to lift his body off the hospital bed, a sharp pain at the back of his head stabs through his core and paralyzes him there. Fear grips him and his heart rate monitor start to beep in a rapid pulse much like the way his heart is going at the moment. Two nurses come rushing in to console him and add some dopamine's to his I.V drip to calm him down. "It's ok son. We're here to help you. You're in good hands, just relax Lucien and everything will be just fine."

Back in reality now; a thirty five year old Lucifer sits strait up from a laying down position. Staring right across the room to the crystal skull with eyes as black as the middle of a black hole.

"So do you understand it now or do you need to see more?" He asks the skull using his thoughts.

"Do I understand!? It is you my misguided counterpart, which fails to understand. We had no choice but to create a work force or die on some desolate planet. We had no idea our offspring would be perverse. From what I saw, humans were good, kind and honest. The ones I knew meant no harm to anyone." Dia'Alzan counters.

"So you wish to see more…" Lucifer says without speaking and slams back down hard on his bed; his body shivers and convulses several times before laying still.

In Lucifer's mind the drama unfolds quickly from being brought home from the hospital to his recovery several years later. Images of Gabriel questioning him about the bike accident. Lucien keeps saying that he remembers nothing, but every time he said it, he was lying. Gabriel bought the lie hook, line and sinker. He see's flashes of himself hiding around the living room wall, listening in as his mom and dad talk about their son's amnesia. His father is enraged and blames her for being a negligent mother… A couple years pass by in his dream like state. He is now twelve years old and getting strong for his age. Gabriel is still bigger than him by five inches in height and about thirty pounds of mass. He is in his room with his bed pushed against the wall and everything arranged for him to have maximum open space in the middle where he is practicing a form of martial arts secretly and subconsciously being taught to him by Shadow Man. It's night time so he has a couple of lamps lit within the room. He has a large mirror on the end-wall of the room for him to see his form as he moves. Lucien holds in a scorpion like stance with his right foot extended in front of him and his left bent to a low crouch; his left arm over his head and his right arm down close to his side. In the blink of an eye Lucien leaps up with a back flip, kicking up his front poised leg in a flash kick. He follows up from a perfect landing and leaps toward the mirror with a spinning right roundhouse kick and a three punch combo ending with a heavy right uppercut and back to stance. This is a twelve year old with some serious moves.

It was at this moment when he was practicing that Gabriel happened to walk by his door and hear his brother doing some sort of work out. He busts in and sees Lucien in his pajama bottoms with his room all re-arranged and engaged in some kind of work out.

"What's this little Lucy? The girly boy thinks he can make himself a man with some little fight routine? And perhaps little Lucy thinks he will be able to use it to beat me up?" Gabriel taunts.

There's an awkward silence in the room and then he hears his parent's car start up.

"That's Dad leaving for his Backrama Club… Mom's in the living room watching the Holo-com on loud… No one can hear a thing… So how about you show me those fancy little moves Lucy?"

"Get out of my room Gabriel! I'll hurt you if you force me to!"

"Punk! You haven't been able to hurt me since you were born. This will be no different."

And with that, Gabriel moves in on Lucien. Lucien suddenly panics now that he's confronted by him and freezes. Gabriel takes advantage and grapples Lucien by the neck, then lifts him off his feet and throws him back across the room. The bottom wooden leg of his propped up bed frame, connects with the back of his head as Lucien lands from the toss. His eyes close and his body stops moving; his conscious mind drifts off to a point on the ceiling of the room and he watches as something else takes control of his body.

(Alice in Chains – "Them Bones")

Gabriel freezes in terror as he once again believes he has killed his younger brother. He steps closer towards him seeing no sign of life and places his face close to Lucien's face to hear if he's breathing or not. Lucien's eye's open as dark as the eyes of the dark angel that is now in control of his body. Both his hands grip Gabriel's throat with the strength of a fully grown man. Gabriel reels back in total shock and uses his weight to fall all the way back and then roll on top of his brother. Now Gabriel tries to get a grip on Lucien's neck but Lucifer senses the danger and switches strategy to all out dirty. Struggling for a good grip on the neck, Gabriel places his hand close to Lucifer's mouth; that's right. It's not Lucien in control of this body, it's the combined might of them both and their name is Lucifer. Lucifer bites down hard on Gabriel's two smaller fingers on his right hand. Gabriel screams with pain and pulls back to see that the two finger tips have been bitten right off.

"Aaahhh!" He screams and watches the blood squirt out.

Lucifer rolls and pushes a stunned Gabriel off of him and spits his finger tips on the carpeted floor. Gabriel rolls back over on to his knees and Lucifer jumps to his feet.

"Now it's your turn to suffer Gabriel!" Lucifer says and lands a left, right, left punch combo.

He pauses to wind up for a roundhouse kick that he delivers to the right cheek bone on Gabe's face. Gabriel falls to his stomach and writhes in pain.

"Don't worry Gabriel. I won't kill you… Not because I'm your brother or any other reason other than the fact that I will have use for you in the future… You have caused me a lot of pain…" Lucifer says and kicks Gabe hard in the face as he tries to get up. "Pain enough to kill you over, but what I have in store for you will be much better than death."

Lucifer walk over to his dresser, pulls a drawer free from the unit and dumps the clothes out on the floor. He grips the solid wooden structure firmly in his right hand and aims to smash the front facing corner of it on the back of his wounded brother's head. Gabriel struggles to crawl to the door and escape his evil brother's room. Lucifer walks over to him and takes an even closer aim on the back of Gabe's skull with the sturdy wooden dresser drawer and "Crack!" Gabriel's lights go out.

Lucifer drops the busted drawer beside his comatose brother and walks calmly out the door of his room. His next atrocity is killing his mother with a kitchen knife and placing her at the front door for when his dad comes home. A half hour goes by and Lucifer sees the lights of his father's car pulling into the driveway. He grips the sharp knife and hides it under his mom's body with his left hand and then curls his right arm around her neck and pretends to cry over her.

Morrick walks in the door and sees his son crying over his wife's bloody body.

He runs up to their side and asks his son. "What happened here Lucien!? Verra! Wake up Verra!" Morrick says in a panic and pushes Lucien aside as he looks for the wounds on her body.

The knife comes out in the open as Lucien/Lucifer is pushed aside. He looks at his mortal host's father as he frets over a dead woman. Disgusted by the sadness he sees in him he plunges the knife in his hand deep into his father's neck.

"Yes!" Lucifer shouts from the amount of joy and excitement he feels from watching the life drain out of the man's eyes and the shock within them for being his own boy to do it…

Lucifer looks around the room and thinks.

"What now? …Fire! Fire cleanses all. But first the brothers must be allowed to live." He thinks to himself.

Lucifer finds Michael playing with some toys in his room and tells him quietly and in a sort of panicked state.

"You have to leave Michael; there's a couple of robbers in the living room. Go out the back door and hop the neighbor's fence and have them call the police."

Michael nods and quickly makes his way out. Lucifer watches as he slowly slides the porch door open, runs across the yard and then hops up and vanish over the fence. Lucifer goes back to his room and grabs his unconscious big brother by the leg with ease and drags him over to the porch door and leaves him a few feet out the doorway. Now Lucifer goes to the garage and grabs a few cans of an aerosol paint and returns to the living room to toss a chair and some small couch cushions in the middle of the room and two of the cans he places carefully on the side of the pile. He now grabs a magazine on the coffee table, tears out few pages and walks into the hallway that leads to his parent's bedroom. In the middle of the hall built into the left wall is a closet door that houses the furnace and water boiler. Opening the closet door, he sees the light he needs behind a flimsy steel panel and rips it away to expose the pilot light flame. He holds his crumpled magazine pages up to it and watches the eager flame hop onto it and rapidly grow with the fresh source of fuel. Lucifer calmly walks the burning paper back to the living room, retrieves his can of flammable paint from a nearby shelf and wastes no time hitting the flame with the spray paint aimed for the small pile of furniture he made for this reason. A large hot flame blasts out and ignites the consumable things; the fire spreads quickly and Lucifer abandons his tool of destruction for the back porch door and stops to go turn the pilot light off and rip the gas line off from the wall, then runs for the porch. He pulls Gabriel farther away from house and into the back yard; he gets to the shed and hears his neighbors from over the fence crying both their names.

"LUCIEN! GABRIEL! Are you guys there!? Police are on their way! Just stay put until they arrive!" Shouts a woman's voice.

Lucifer looks around and thinks of where to go… "The elementary school has a box of lost and found clothes and stuff; plus a washroom to wash the blood off my face and hands… They will find homes for the two of you."

He looks down at Gabriel. "Not that you will know being a vegetable and all… But don't worry brother; I'll make you right in a few years." He whispers.

He looks to his old home as the flames inside begin to grow and smoke billows out from any and all exposed cracks and openings of it. Sounds of sirens begin wailing in the distance and slowly are getting louder.

"Time to go!" He says to himself and hops the side of the fence into the other neighbor's yard; dashes across that yard and hops the parallel fence into another back yard and disappears into the shadows.

Two police Hover-cars pull up to the front of the house and a pair of cops step out from each one. One of them gets on a digital radio transmitter attached to his right sleeve and asks dispatch to send the fire suppression crews to his location immediately. Another takes a scanning device out from inside his car and now points it at the house. A thin, flat screen attached to the scanner shows an x-ray image of the house. The fire in the living room lights the screen up with colours of yellow, orange and red and then it scans through to the back yard.

"Looks like we got a live one in the back yard; barely any life signs."

The other officer gets back on the line with dispatch and request them to send EMT units as well. Two of the officers are about to attempt to go in the yard and try get the wounded person in the back yard when the fire in the living room ignites the gas from the furnace room. The resulting explosion blasts out the glass windows and sends balls of fire all over the place. The cops back up to the safety of their Hover-cars and wait for back up…

Balls of fire is what Lucifer sees as he slowly comes back to reality; opening his eyes, he gets up to sitting position at the end of his bed again and stares at the crystal scull once more.

"You see now? We wanted to kill… We wanted to destroy and burn… Give us humans a taste of true power and each one will love it and crave for more… The power to instil fear in others is an intoxicating thing; most aren't even aware they do it." Lucifer says to Dai'Alzan.

"You're right Lucifer."

"What?" Asks Lucifer, clearly taken by surprise by the answer.

"We were going to come back to Gorgon to teach and mentor you humans. Teach you all the power of love and the feeling of goodness when you help others unselfishly. We would have won the battle for human's soul's right there, but then you 'spirit of Darkness' found a way inside our most vulnerable brother and convinced him to betray us. We quickly hid <u>two</u> families of six; five of them were male and seven were female, enough to start the race again. Two families out of the ten families we had originally tried to save; then the council of nine arrested us. They charged us with treason and as the repairs to the ship were done; they exiled us from the ship and the return flight home. Before leaving they killed the twenty two human families we couldn't save then left us on Gorgon to die… We found our stashed away humans after the council was gone and watched them flourish as the years passed, but evil was always there. We constantly had to punish them for offences made against each other; it was close to the time of my body's death when I realized that humans will never change. We should have never let a single one live, but they were our kin and we couldn't just destroy them; not after befriending so many of them."

Lucifer stares at the skull taking in his reply. "You loved them, a weakness I don't have… Don't worry Dai'Alzan… I will fulfil the path that was taken from you… I will bring these humans to a new understanding of life and peace. They will soon stand tall with pride and honor, but first they will learn to kneel in humility and pain."

With that said, Lucifer walks over to the drawstrings that hold back a dark purple curtain. It falls over to cover the crystal skull; he walks back over to his desk and is about to continue on one of his drafts on it when a "deet doot" sounds out from the speakers built into the ceiling panels (of every room in the base). The sound is basically a doorbell, someone is out in the hallway to see him.

The base is safely hidden underground in what was an old mine and then expanded into the field just in front of the mines main entry point; now a heavily guarded gateway. The complex is so extensive that it takes Chief Doberlin of the Mirosian high guard forty-five minutes to walk through to get to Lucifer's private quarters at the north east quadrant, two levels below ground. Max Doberlin is the President of Mire's High Chief of war and has lived through two major skirmishes with the Empire. He is wearing his flashy white and silver officer's suit as he stands six feet five inches tall at Lucifer's door. The door opens and Lucifer is standing there to greet him.

"Chief Doberlin! I wasn't expecting to see you until…" Lucifer pauses to think about the date.

"Until Munari the fifth and today is Munari the fifth." Doberlin says dryly.

Lucifer looks at him closely and scratches at the stubble on his chin. "Is it really? Because I thought today was Sanzana the third…

My mistake… Anyhow, I bet I know why you're here!" Lucifer says loudly and points at him. "Same reason you're always here Munari the fifth of every month… To check up on me and my science projects and hassle me for an update on his wife and daughters condition. Well I assure you once again the science projects are nearing completion and that the President's family is alive and well, living in a dream chamber aboard my militia controlled mining ship the Pey'Agus, posted out near Titus the moon. Not to confuse it with the theme park…" Lucifer tells him trying to be funny.

Doberlin doesn't even blink.

"They have no idea that they have even been in my custody."

"I'm afraid I'm going to need proof…" Doberlin says and stares back at him.

Lucifer thinks of killing him right now but then has a better thought. "Come then Chief Doberlin; let's go see with our own eyes and then I'll have a message for you to take back to your president along with your proof." Lucifer says and gestures for the good Chief to begin walking down the hall beside him.

As they walk, Lucifer talks a bit. "Didn't the Empire kill your wife and son in the quelling of the rebellion in Saymercos city?"

"Yes; they were gunned down among the crowds trying to escape the Storm-guard troops. Sent by the Emperor of course and for that I will hate him until the day I die."

"Emperor Kattan is a hot-headed war monger and will pay with his life for his crimes… Down this way." Lucifer directs him through the base as he talks.

"President Kephness wishes to see a Mire free from Imperial control; had you simply confronted him and talked to him about your plan, he would have listened and helped you without the need to kidnap his family and hold them against his word." Says Doberlin.

"You're wrong Chief; Steven is a puppet of the Emperor and wold go against me at the last minute out of fear. Fear that too many people will suffer on both sides to give in to all-out war."

"And you're sure all-out war is what needs to happen to free us from their grip?" Asks Doberlin; Lucifer simply stares back at him with a get real kind of look. Max recognizes the look and knows that he just asked a stupid question.

"I get it Lucifer and I can't wait to see a truly free Mire as well as these projects of yours in action against our enemies… But the President is just a simple man with a family who never asked for any of this. You could return his son to him and still hold his wife until the term is over." Pleads Doberlin.

"I'm sorry but that can't happen…"

"And why not?"

"Because I'm going to reunite the whole bunch of them real soon. It was going to be part of my surprise message for him but you just can't wait when it comes to good news huh Chief?" Lucifer teases.

"He will be pleased to hear that Lucifer… How much farther do we have to go?" He asks.

"Here we are Chief." Lucifer says as he stops them at a steel doorway; one of hundreds that line the sides of the bases halls.

Doberlin looks at the door marked with a big white "SP-2" stamped on it. Lucifer gestures to Doberlin to hit the button on the wall panel that opens the door. He does as suggested and follows Lucifer into the room. The lab is quite big; three times larger than Lucifer's room. Inside are what appears to be large metallic egg shaped devices that are open at certain ports with wires hooked up that run to computers that sit on desks against the fall wall of the lab. Doberlin is taken back for a second as he questions if he is awake or dreaming at this point; it's a surreal picture that one would expect to see in a cartoon.

"So these six… Giant egg looking thingies will bring the end of the Empire? It's so hard to believe that the technology we have can do more damage than…"

"More damage than the Gods?" Lucifer asks rhetorically and then thinks to show him the other.

"Come with me Chief; I want to show you another one of my projects that will clear things up for you. Once you see him then you'll understand." They leave the lab and walk down the hall again.

"Understand what?" Asks Doberlin.

"That we are the Gods. All you have to do is want it hard enough. To do anything at all to get it."

"Get what?"

"Anything at all. Whatever your heart wants."

After walking in silence down the inner halls of Lucifer's main base for several minutes, Lucifer stops the Chief at another steel paneled door; this one marked "SP – 1". This time Lucifer hits the button on the wall panel beside the door and opens it. Doberlin scrunches his eyes and moves his head inquisitively as he walks into the science lab; wondering what exactly it is he's looking at. Lucifer follows behind Doberlin and the door to the lab closes behind him. "What is that?" Asks the Chief.

"That is a fully operational Cyborg named Gabriel." Says Lucifer and walks past a stunned Chief.

The lab is full of computers on tables that span the whole left and right wall from the door. In the middle of the room is some sort of large, steel framed medical chair and sitting on it is a very big looking man. Except that it's not a man; Lucifer turned his comatose brother into a Cyborg over the span of a few years. His back is turned to them both but Doberlin can tell just from looking at his back side that Gabriel is Huge and wouldn't want to try fight a thing like that. He lets it sink in for a moment then turns to face the Chief.

"Usually I don't let anyone in here without first being sanitized and changed into a medic's smock. Our sensor diodes and other equipment is very sensitive to alien particles. We should leave…" Lucifer says and gestures his hand towards the door.

They leave the lab and pause just outside the door. Lucifer wondering what to say now and Chief Doberlin wondering what exactly Gabriel can do in a fight.

"Perhaps you'd like to go to our hanger bay and see the magnificent Mir'Denack?" Asks Lucifer.

"Um, yes…"

They start walking down the bases extensive hallway system. "I'm curious though. What can Gabriel do in battle?"

"I could tell you but you wouldn't understand things like kinetic relay nodes and positron force shielding. I'll have a soldier film him when I throw him into his debut battle and send you the footage." Answers Lucifer.

"Sure, that would be most... Entertaining... How is our re-commissioned science ship, the Mir'Denack?" Asks Doberlin.

"Ninety six percent complete; we have her scheduled for launch in approximately sixty five hours." Answers Lucifer.

"It's a shame really... She would have made one hell of a science ship; she was supposed to make it past the outer rim and collect images and data on some of the larger planet like asteroids stuck in far orbit of."

"All so fascinating Doberlin." Lucifer cuts him short.

"But she's now been turned into the most powerful warship in the system... You know the Empires main weapon systems for their ships?" Asks Lucifer.

"Yes, of course; it's the Voltrax Coil. Fires out a super charged bolt of raw energy; a lightning cannon essentially." Answers Doberlin.

"Right, well I've found the shield frequency... It emanates a similar frequency as the weapon, but on many layers pancaked together and vibrating at varying mili-amps... I've lost you haven't I?"

Doberlin doesn't answer right away, he thinks about his next words. "Like many of us Lucifer, I don't need to know how it works just that it does work. If it does what you say then that's great. What about weapon systems?" Asks the Chief.

"My own design; I call them 'Knalk Cannons' and they use a compressed ball of an aluminum alloy as ammunition. The ball is then electrified and shot out using a magnetic accelerator that propels the ammo up to Mach six speeds."

"That's an unheard of speed for a projectile, fired from a gun with no chemicals..." Says Doberlin.

"It's a devastating weapon and she has twenty three of them in total… And here we are." Says Lucifer and gestures to a larger than usual, sliding steel door marked with a "Hanger Bay" in yellow paint. Using the wall panel, Lucifer opens the door and they both walk through…

"It is quite impressive…" Says Doberlin.

The two of them are standing on a short steel panel balcony that overlooks the entire hanger bay. To the left and right of the entrance are a flight of stairs, seventy five of them to the bottom floor. From floor to ceiling is just over sixty meters and from front to back wall is one hundred and twenty-five meters. The hanger is huge and is being occupied by a very large space ship; all shiny and new looking. With multiple levels that curve gently into the next level giving the ship an overall appearance of a giant layered oval. Like a stretched sideways egg but huge and made of steel. Technicians and tradesmen are all over the ship and hanger; all wearing identical black uniforms with the triangle symbol of Mire's main monument. "Olympus' Mons" the mega-volcano has long been the symbol of Mire's army, but it's a red triangle with two half circles (representing moons) flanking it, one on each side.

"Come, let's take a walk." Says Lucifer. "I'll show you the captain's deck."

Doberlin nods his head and follows Lucifer down the stairs. All base personnel stop and salute Lucifer as he passes them by. He ignores the base personnel as he's talking with Doberlin the whole way.

"The presence of so many of these Imperial serving Gorgonite's on Mire disturbs me. If our liberation is to be a success I'm going to need all of them detained…" Lucifer lets that sink in and continues. "Remember the project "Over-Lord" that I had pass in the senate? The project of constant surveillance of all Gorgon serving families living on Mire?"

"Yes, I remember that I even voted in favor of the project." Answers Doberlin.

"What you all failed to realize is that phase 2 of the project includes in order twenty six, rounding up all Gorgon born or Empire serving people currently on Mire in the event of an all-out war, and placing them in detention camps so they can't be used as spies or suicide bombers."

"I realized it right away… If total war breaks out; we will be ready to execute order twenty-six." Says Doberlin.

"Good! You read the whole thing through! Come, I'll let you sit in the Captain's chair just up a couple levels in the elevator here."

Lucifer stops him underneath the right middle section of the ships underbelly. Lucifer waves to a camera mounted close to a big round hatch built into the hull. The hatch hisses and clicks as it unlocks from within; it slides open and slowly drops a magnetic interlocking bar that stops a couple feet from the surface of the floor. The elevator comes sliding down the track bar; a glass encased circle with a steel panelled smart-floor that can detect unwanted things like bombs or deadly pathogens. Curved glass doors slide open and the two of them step inside; the doors close and up they go, into the Mir'Denack…

Lucifer completes giving his guest a tour of the base and walks him out to the front gate. He nods to the guard inside the control booth who takes the hint and hits the button to release the locks on the gate and make the motor turn the wheels to open the thing up so Chief Doberlin can leave and take a message back to the president of Mire.

"Remember Doberlin. He needs to be here in exactly thirty-five hours from… Eight minutes ago, and he will see his family again. I'll have them transferred here right away so they can freshen up before their reunion."

Doberlin looks at his wrist-band hollo-comm. for the time and then nods once to Lucifer before turning and leaving the base. Lucifer heads back to his private living quarters stopping a young female officer and asking her seductively to go to the mezz-hall and grab them both some food and return with it to his room. She obeys…

Several hours later he finds himself naked and laying on his back, on his bed, beside the cute young female officer. She has the blanket over her as she sleeps. He slides over and sits up; grabs his black pajama bottoms and slides them back on. He retrieves a half burned smoke of trance weed; the only way he can sleep these days. He lights up and takes a few big puffs, sitting down on his nice office chair. From the desk drawer he retrieves a small I-pod with headphones. He puts the ear-buds in and hits the play button; closing his eyes he lets the music bring back memories…

(FFDP – "My Own Hell")

Colors swirl around in an infinite amount of space right behind his eye-lids. Were we have the ability to dream up and live in alternate realities; see the past or even glimpse the future. Lucifer goes to a time in his past as the colors stop swirling and solidify into a solid 3D world. He's fifteen years old and developing in his growth; growth in size as well as ability to fight and steal. He lived with a bunch of other homeless people in the city of Onydath; the south east end of the city was and still is rife with poverty and crime. A part of the city Lucifer loved as he got to see many acts of violence and even participate in some. Lucifer is walking at night down a dark and dangerous street. Buildings are boarded up, windows are smashed out, and graffiti is everywhere as well as trash. He stops by a park dressed all in black and settles into the shadow of the trunk of a large Oak tree and watches in secret. He's been following this gangster from Arwin street five city blocks away, to this dump where he's about to meet up with some of his gangster buddies and another person; a fence. To the right of him there is broken up foundation of what may have once been a public washroom. A lengthy piece of rebar steel is sticking out of the rubble. He looks back to see his mark dyke into an alleyway and stop…

"Hey yo! Bruno, Buck and Boris. The three B's. What's up gangsters?" Asks Lucifer's mark, street named "Loop Dog" given to him for losing the cops once by doing a couple loops around this one part of town and confusing the cops so bad that he ditched the car by a bus stop and got on, getting eight city blocks away before they found the car parked on the same block as the police station just on the opposite side.

"Hey yo Loop Dog. Just pimpin and dealin man what's up with you? I got the fence here." Says Bruno as he looks behind him and gestures to some skinny small guy wearing a dark brown over-coat and black bowler hat standing behind him. "That's Shorty; been fencing our scores for the last two years… So whatchya got for me Loops?"

"Take a look at these two necklaces." Loop Dog says and gets the five of them to huddle close together; Buck produces a small flashlight to shine on the score.

"Ooh, those are nice." Says shorty as he takes out a digital carat reader and holds it close to one of the many diamonds embroidered into the necklaces.

As Shorty looks closer he hears a loud "Thwap!" sound and suddenly Loop Dog's reeling body is crashing into him causing him to fall back onto his butt. Blood from the back of Loop Dog's head starts squirting out and splashing in Shorty's face causing him to freak out. He drops the necklaces and with one hand tries to shield the spraying blood while crawling away with the other in conjunction with his legs to push Loop Dog's dead weight off him. He hears yelling, profanities and cuss words along with several more loud "Thwap!" sounds. He looks behind him now and sees Buck and Bruno already lying face down on the gravel; neither of them are moving. Boris is trying to flee but his assailant throws the steel bar in his hand in a whipping motion aimed for the legs. It spins a couple dozen quick times and takes Boris in the right knee cap sending him on a short trip to meet face first with the ground in a cry of pure pain… Shorty turns around not wanting to see anymore, and knowing that after he's done with Boris, he's the only one left. Abandoning the jewelry, Shorty runs out the alley and down the street as fast as he can. After a couple of blocks he stops, dykes into another alley and looks behind him to see if that lunatic is following him. He can't see anyone so he leans back against a wall, closes his eyes and sighs in relief. He opens his eyes and there he is. He's standing right in front of him staring at him. Shorty is so startled and afraid that he craps himself.

"Please don't kill me man." He says cowering to his knees.

"You get to live and spread the word… The dark one lives and he's here to claim his throne."

Lucifer pretends to punch Shorty causing him to flinch and cover his face completely. After a few seconds of not being struck down he looks up from his cowering position and sees no one there. Just like that, he's gone.

The next memory he has is a year later. It's a nice sunny day and he's wandering the markets in the upper west end of Onydath for some food to steal even though he has enough money to buy whatever he wants. He comes across a smoked meat vendor who's busy with a customer and so he moves in to steal a slab of smoked meat but stops short as his heightened state of thieving sight and hearing picks up on a scene of bullying about to go down with a group of teenagers close to his age and some strangely clothed boy whose buying a piece of clothing from a vendor and has no idea what's about to happen to him. The boy about to be in trouble turns to walk away. Having what he came to the market for, he makes to leave via the magnet train. He has to travel through a few stairwells and corridors to get to Junction way… They will make a move some time then. Six teenage boys follow this kid dressed in a strange garment and wearing his hair in a braid at the front and cut short all around. Lucifer follows the group cautiously. They go down a stairwell between a couple of apartment blocks and come to a quiet alley-way tucked between the apartments and a roadway fence. That's where they make their move.

(Pantera – "Mouth For War")

"Hey! Prelate!" Says one of the bullies.

The strange boy stops and turns around to face them.

"We don't like your kind around here… We think you should

leave Onydath and never come back." Says the biggest one who is about the same age and size as Lucifer; 16 years old, five feet two inches and a hundred and twenty pounds.

Lucifer stops up short and listens to the rest.

"I am about to leave Onydath right now so... Message received guys." Says the strange boy.

"No, I don't thinks so. Message not received; not until you feel what it'll be like should you ever come back." Says the bully.

Lucifer has to move down a bit to look at what happens next...

The big kid doing all the talking moves in and grapples the prelate while two of the other five kids move to each side and wind up for a spin kick. The prelate lifts up on his opponent and then pulls down with all his might as his opponents jaw rests against the top of his head. He lands hard on his butt and avoids two separate spin kicks by the flanking bullies at the same time he stuns the big one as his chin connects with some force against the top of his head and bounces off. The prelate rolls back to his feet and engages the four other boys. The two that missed their first kick reverse stance and go for a similar spin kick from the other way. The prelate bends back in a reverse cartwheel dodging the kicks and then leaps towards the one on his left with a superman punch from his right and connects on his chin knocking him right out...

The fight gets dirty from here as the two other boys dash in at the same time and grab the prelate's arms and pin him against the fence. The big bully is back to his feet and takes advantage with an unhindered right hook to the boy's face.

(Smack!) "You thought you could take us all on? Ha, idiot!" He shouts as he winds up and lands another hard right hook on the boy's face.

Lucifer decides to make his presence known.

"You know boys, it's one thing to outnumber a weaker opponent... It's another to outnumber a stronger one." Lucifer says as he walks down the catwalk towards them.

The four of them still conscious look over to Lucifer; they have no idea who he is but feel the need to teach him a lesson too.

"You looking out for this punk?" Asks the big kid.

"No… All I see is a bunch of scared little brats who think they had it rough growing up so they gotta scare others but really they have no idea what rough is." Answers Lucifer.

"Is that so?"

The big kid punches the prelate (Meaning an apprentice of a High priest of the order) kid hard in the face again and watches him go limp. The other two kids let go of his limp body while the fourth kid stands by and simply watches. They turn their attention to Lucifer.

Lucifer dashes at the fence and runs up the side of it as he begins his attack. One, two, three big steps up the side of the fence and Lucifer leaps in the air coming down with big left hook on the big bully. He leans back to dodge but takes the hit hard in the upper left shoulder. One of the lackeys leaps in with a right hook for Lucifer's face; Lucifer leans back and watches the punch whip past his cheek. He instinctively reaches for the kids neck (Back to back now) as he spins to avoid the punch. Grabbing the kid at the back of the neck tight to his shoulder and dropping to the ground to land on his ass Lucifer smashes the back of the kids head on his shoulder bone. The kid goes unconscious right away, landing right beside Lucifer who rolls over backwards, over the kids limp body and barely avoids a spin kick by the other kid still in the fight. He senses the big bully behind him who has recovered from the leap-punch he just hit him with moments ago and continues his momentum backwards from his roll as he pumps his legs up in a jump and sticks his right elbow out. He blindly leaps back and connects his elbow across the bridge of the big bully's nose and spins to land on his hands and knees. The two other kids try rush Lucifer but he somersaults out of the way as they go to pile on top of him. They bump heads as Lucifer rises to his feet from the summersault, he whips his right leg back behind him and connects a hard kick to one the two remaining back up kids. He gets the kid right on the side of the head and knocks him sideways and out of the fight; the big bully is bleeding from the nose but still in the fight. As Lucifer is regaining his stance from the roll and reverse up-kick, the big bully cheap shots Lucifer with a right hook to the jaw and the last conscious back up kid grabs Lucifer from behind in a full nelson. The big kid hits Lucifer quickly with two to the gut and one to the face, and is about to go for another punch to Lucifer's face when the strange boy gets him from behind in a running reverse head lock that sends both boys crashing head first into Lucifer along with the kid holding him. Lucifer lands hard on top of the kid behind him and involuntarily smashes the back of his head on the bridge of the kid's nose. The impact also causes the colors to swirl in Lucifer's vision as he hurts a soft spot on his skull, shaking his brain.

Lucifer rolls over to his hands and knees and focuses on the cement ground in front of his face in order to stop the swirl of colors and certain unconsciousness that threatens to take him; slowly he regains control and looks up to see the strange boy standing in front of him. Lucifer looks over to see the big bully and instigator out cold on the ground several feet away.

"My name is Darius…" Says the strange boy. "Thank you for helping me…"

Lucifer nods slowly and gets to his feet rubbing the soreness out on the back of his head. "How'd you finish him?" Asks Lucifer.

Darius gives him a weird look, like a 'why ask that?' look but then quickly dismisses it. "I came up with a strong right knee to his head as he was crouched over from my tackle; lights out… Who are you? And why'd you help me?"

"I don't know." Lucifer's vision blurs as he looks at the boy… His memory is changing from what really happened. His head is splitting with pain; he covers his eyes, rubbing them as if it would help, and as he re-focuses to see the boy, he sees him as an adult.

"I know why Lucifer…" He pauses knowing that this is not what really happened but some sort of premonition. "So that I can stop you!" An older version of the boy shouts as he delivers a hard punch to Lucifer's face…

The imaginary punch knocks Lucifer back into reality, like falling from a building in a dream and going splat right back into your conscious mind. He looks around his room within the base in a panic and begins to realize where he is.

"There's no way… Darius?" He thinks to himself and walks over to his bed; Lucifer reaches under it and procuces a picture album.

He looks through it a few pages and then comes upon it. The picture of himself and Darius; the boy from the school of the holy order of the tree of life… The boy who introduced him to his destiny.

CH. 2 - Sub Chapter 2: It Comes From Within

RIDING IN THE DAXAUR cart, on rout to the hotel, Eve can't help but think about Lucas' last statement. About the acolytes perfecting the pitches of the séance, and that he could get lost forever if it goes wrong.

"Lucas? How long was the longest ascension ceremony?" Eve asks him out of the blue.

Lucas thinks for a moment and then Darius answers for him. "The longest ceremony took two and a half days; the priest and acolytes almost died of dehydration." He says.

Eve gives him a shocked look. "That long!? Well you better not take that long Lucas. Or the both of you will miss the big festival." Eve says with a grin. "And I don't want you getting lost in that realm Lucas, so you better nail those pitches Adam." She says and gives Adam a nudge to the ribs with her elbow.

The Hotel that Eve and Lynn are staying at comes up and the Daxaur cart comes to a halt. Eve and Lynn say their fare-wells and exit the cart with luggage in hand. The door closes and Adam watches out the window as the driver gets the beasts up front moving again. He sees them walk up to the hotel doors and then they are out of view; he sits back in his chair but continues to look out the window at the passing buildings on his way to the small temple at the outskirts of the colony.

Next Day — Pangaea — Ehdon Colony - Path of destiny

ADAM FOLLOWS CLOSE BEHIND High Priest Darius Siscerelle as they make their way down the sacred pathway of destiny to the tree of life where the first colonist use to dwell. His vision is limited by his hood that's attached to his cloak; he must wear it on the journey to the sacred and holy tree where the ritual of consummation will occur very soon. It's a lightly forested area of the island close to the cliffs of contemplation on the north east part of Ehdon. The Plateau of the tree is a twenty minute hike through this forest of old trees, moss covered rocks and ruined buildings of the first Priests at the start of the whole Holy Order. People have steadily been settling the island paradise for the last five hundred years; from the start of humanity's leap into space travel about five hundred and sixteen years before this very moment. In those days was the birth of the Empire of Mankind on Gorgon, the first president of Mire and the founding of Ehdon and the birth of the holy order of the tree of life with the discovery of the tree and all… Adam climbs a flight a stairs and as he reaches the top he sees the opening of the path to the plateau.

(Godsmack – "Serenity")

Exiting the path, Adam looks upon a grass covered, gently rising slope where at the top is the majestic tree. Its trunk is huge; ten feet in diameter and its branching structure grows perfectly with all branches flowing in symmetry from up out the trunk to make an arch back out and tips facing down to the ground. The off chute branches form a perfect canopy and the precious fruit grows within that. What's more amazing is that it appears to glow with the fading light of dusk as they gather underneath it; as though it retains the suns light and uses it during the night to shine. High Priest Gary Ulrich begins the ceremony as the four of them surround Lucas; he starts it by picking a fruit off the tree from a low hanging branch and hands it to Lucas. The three inch round, red/orange fruit is glowing inside as he holds it in his hand; Lucas mutters the mantra for fear.

("Fear is the mind killer that will lead to the death of body and soul, I will not fear. Instead I will feel peace; then as the danger and fear passes by, only I will remain.")

The two acolytes and two high priests begin a séance like chant they were all taught at the school on Mire.

"Oooommmsssaaaaad daaasssssaaaammmmm seyoooooo"

They begin, and they have to continue through a series of these chants until the ceremony is over.

Adam watches his cousin Lucas take a big bite of the sacred fruit and chew it well before swallowing, then take another. Lucas pauses and holds his hand with the fruit in front of him. Adam keeps up with the chant as he watches his cousin's eyes go from eyes with a bright green cornea to nothing but black and white as his pupils expand to encompass all. As he watches; Lucas's hand goes transparent and the fruit falls though it to land on the ground. He raises both his hands close to his face in complete amazement as they begin to vanish. His whole body suddenly begins to glow at the same time as going transparent; looking up into the tree, Lucas says two words. "Oh my…"

He then vanishes completely from sight.

Twenty four hours later

"CHECK CHECK… Just making sure this camera is working."

Adam says as he stands on a grassy knoll looking at Eve who is dressed in a skin tight suit with a helmet on. Adam is wearing a suit just like hers and the two of them are with three other people (2 men, 1 woman) unknown to them; they are the providers and business owners of 'Extreem Ehdon'. A facilitator of extreme sports on Ehdon. Adam takes the camera off his helmet and holds it in front of him to watch the replay of him saying exactly that…

"Ok, the cameras are working… We are going at the same time right Eve?" Asks Adam as he puts the camera back into its slot on his helmet and hits play.

Eve slowly walks over to the edge of the grassy knoll and looks over to see the whole scope of Ehdon; a paradise, island colony where nature meets urbanization and advanced society in a harmonious balance. Yet she sees the rest beyond it as well…

(DJ Tiesto – "Wasted")

Past the city center is the suburbs; past that is the orchards and farmlands. Where Adam and Eve stand, they can see the shore line and the ocean a hundred something kilometers away. Adam looks back to the three facilitators who get right to it. Nathan is the lead instructor.

"Ok… We all have to get a running start and just leap like a bullet off the edge! Count to two and spread your arms after you jump…" Nathan says and spreads his arms to show the wing like flaps that stretch from his wrists and follow the curves of his body down to his midsection.

"Ok, let's do this." Says Adam and retreats from the edge along with Eve.

The five of the stop and line up side by side looking at their target; the edge of a mountain.

"Three, two, ONE!" Shouts Nathan and all five of them run hard for the cliff edge…

Next thing Adam knows, they are all gliding like eagles towards the suburbs of Ehdon's south west end.

"Woo Hooo!" He shouts in a state of total excitement; Eve shouts "woo hooo" too as they glide through the air together.

After base jumping a mountain side Adam and Eve spend some time lounging with Lynn at the resorts pool. That night they meet up with Lucas who is freshly back from the nether-world and un-killed by the experience. They go to a club together in the heart of Ehdon City and dance the night away…

The next day they sign up for snorkeling and see some amazing fish and crustaceans in the shallow waters of Hornbi Cove. During the night Adam, Lucas, Eve and Lynn attend the harvest festival. People are everywhere, there's: fire breathers/jugglers, musicians of all kinds and vendors selling all kinds of exotic foods. They reach the centre of the town where they witness the last minute of a fighting match between two trained fighters and then fireworks go off way in the distance at the edge of town yet close enough to captivate all at the festival. They all return to the Cobalt Hotel late that night to turn in, rest up and prepare for their flight back to Mire tomorrow.

Darius Siscerelle leaves the company of High Priest Gary Ulrich and Will Duncan the acolyte to wander the streets of Ehdon and take in the festival on the last night of his stay. He wanders down a street to a park with several trails; he doesn't know what way to go so he just picks at random. Right down this trail, left here followed by another left down a narrow path and suddenly before him is a beautiful waterfall slightly lit up by the sheer amount of visible stars in the sky. He is amazed by the beauty of it and stands to stare at it for a while and take it all in… The sound of branches rustling alerts him to the right of the falls. A beautifully colored bird hops up from out of hiding in a bush and perches on the branch of a bush close by him… "I know that kind of bird… It's a Parakeet. A rare bird to see on Ehdon… Someone must have lost a pet from Mire." He thinks to himself.

"Oh yeah, my smart com. has an animal translator on it. This thing is cool."

Darius pulls the device out of his pocket and after navigating his way to the app for "Animal Talker" he holds the slim, advanced piece of technology to his mouth and quietly speaks into it.

"Greetings sky dweller…"

Darius speaks into the device and a second later it makes a series of chirping sounds out of its speaker. The Parakeet is taken by surprise and stays silent for a moment like a thief getting caught… After a minute or so it speaks.

("Swee sa sa sweept.")

The smart com. translates "Who are you and how do you know my language?"

Darius is excited. "My name is Darius. I know your language because… Because I am an enlightened one." Answers Darius.

"Are you now?" Asks the Parakeet and quickly flies over to a branch of a tree closer by Darius's head. "Tell me then enlightened one. Where are you right now?"

Darius looks around and then is about to answer with a plain answer of. "In a park on this planet with a million other life forms." Then he re-thinks his answer. "In the Garden of the Creator." Answers Darius.

"You are an enlightened one… You're part of a feeble minded race, but you are not among them."

"Thank you kind sky dweller… Please tell me why it is you think my race is feeble minded?"

"Most of your kind living here have no idea the amount of power that lies within this planet. That power comes from the creator… It's in the heart of the universe which is the heart of God. You seem to be the only one not blind to that…"

Darius has no response to what this little bird is saying to him. This little Parakeet seems to know more than most high priests of the holy order know.

"What else do you know about my species young sky lord?" Darius asks.

"Sky Lord!? Now you flatter me Shinue copy. Thank you but the truth is that we have songs of the past and your kind is…"

Darius zones out on the translation on the holographic screen in front of him. "Shinue Copy? What the heck is that supposed to mean?" He asks himself then speaks into his smart com. device and asks. "What do you mean by Shinue Copy?"

The Parakeet is silent for a moment, then asks rhetorically. "So you don't know? …You are not truly enlightened then as you say you are."

"I only live one life and a short one at that, full of obstacles and learning curves… I'm open minded is what I really meant to say. Where many other humans are closed minded." Answers Darius; the smart com. translates. "I don't know anything about these Shinue…"

"Then telling you about them isn't going to matter and I may as well leave you to your ignorance." Says the bird.

"Wait!" Darius says without any thought of how to keep the bird there, other than a question… A question brought on by what he heard a dejected homeless man say while at the train station in Onydath.

"Did you hear that the dark lord lives as one of us?"

"Sweet wee tweet twee." The translator sounds his last question and the little Parakeet stops and is silent for a moment before responding.

"You know this for a fact?" The bird asks.

Darius stays silent as he reads the question on the screen. Darius stays silent.

"If he is among you Earth bound, then we are all in danger."

Darius can't believe what he is reading on his screen. This little bird really does know more than any high priest.

"What is it I can do to stop him?" Asks Darius.

"Us Sky Lords know of a secret weapon… Wielded by the right Earth bound, you may have a chance." Answers the Parakeet.

"Earth bound you call us? Because we walk on our feet connected to earth matter. I get it… What is this secret weapon? How do you know about it?" Asks Darius.

"It seems we were meant to cross paths to enlighten one another… Did you know that your kind tried long ago to start a colony in the middle of the Jungle?" Asks the Parakeet.

"I heard of it, it's a story meant for children. A fable that's not taken seriously by my kind. The lost city of Odaan."

"That would be the one… The weapon is real… I saw it myself but…"

"But what?" Asks Darius.

"The Earth moved and many creatures moved about it trying to eat me so I had to leave. It may have been moved by them down there… There was so many."

"What kind of weapon are we talking about here?" Asks Darius.

"I don't know what you earth bound would call it but I know where it would be. The area is very dangerous… True strength comes from within earth walker… The desire to overcome all odds. The courage to act and win."

A young couple approaches the waterfall from the path, probably looking to skinny dip and have some adult fun. Both Darius and the Parakeet hear them and that means it's time for the Parakeet to leave.

"Seek out Odaan enlightened one. Find the weapon and we may stand a chance… All life is at risk here if you're right and only your kind can stop your kind."

Darius quietly dykes into some underbrush close by. The young couple stumble upon the falls and pool seemingly alone and laugh light heartedly as they enjoy each other's company and jump into the water. Darius quietly makes his way back onto the path and finds his way back to his hotel where his companions are asleep. He creeps into his bed and falls asleep with heavy thoughts on his mind.

A shuttle lifts up to the sky inside a launch balloon and as it reaches the upper atmosphere it's fired up with a CO_2 can, and as it clears the balloon it fires its engines up and clears the planet to dock with a speed launcher in orbit around Pangaea. Moments later the shuttle is speeding through space towards Mire. The trip from planet to planet depends largely on the proximity of planets during their orbital path around the sun and at this time the two planets are close together. The trip will take the ship twelve hours to complete. Aboard the ship is a small lounge that has nine tables for six people and five tables for two with a bar counter that seats another six. A metal door opens and Adam walks into the lounge; he goes right for the bar counter.

"Give me a double Ehdon Sunrise." Adam tells the barkeep.

Moments later the square faced, black hair, cookie cutter barkeep hands Adam the drink he asked for. A pale orange on the top of the glass, hot orange in the middle and a fiery red orange on the bottom.

28% alcohol from start to finish.

(Deadmou5 – "Errors in my Bread")

Sitting there at the bar sipping on his drink, Adam looks around the lounge. He spots Darius sitting at the table located at the far right corner of the establishment and wonders. "What is a high priest doing in a lounge?" Adam asks himself and gets up from the bar and walks over to the table.

"Hey there Darius." Adam says as he sits at the table in a chair right across from him.

"Amad… I mean Adam… I'm sorry but you caught me off guard."

Darius stares at him with a smile. "No worries Darius… I can't believe we brought Lucas back in like nine hours.

That must be close to some sort of record by my understanding."

"You might be right, I'll have to get a consensus from the council of Elders but you're probably right." Darius replies.

Adam sips on his drink and looks at Darius as he holds his Smart com. device towards his face. "What is it you're searching there?" Asks Adam as he head nods to Darius's device…

Darius pauses for a moment then makes a choice to tell him. "Adam; I doubt you'd believe me if I told you… But lucky for you I'm a bit of a gambling man… Don't tell the other High Priests… That I Gamble." Darius says jokingly in an attempt to lighten the mood.

"There's been a disturbance… Or like an imbalance… Us I mean… Humans have been messing with the natural order of growth on three different planets; just look at how bad Mire has gotten in the last ten years. I was once told in school that for every yin there is a yang… An opposite to correct an imbalance." Darius explains. "We have become the imbalance, the correction is coming and stopping it depends on me… Me finding a sacred weapon made by the first colonist of Pangaea; the builders of Odaan."

Chills run up Adam's spine as he hears those words and wants to help right away. "I can help you find these ruins of Odaan... My father works for the Empire and I can get any records or documents you may need straight from the archive itself."

"Hmmm... Can you call him right now with my smart com. and ask him to send all available files of Odaan to this number?" Asks Darius as he holds the device out in front him for Adam to take.

"I sure can! Wow, you don't play around huh? Just get at it..." Adam says as he takes the smart com. and starts dialing but pauses as he thinks to ask Darius how he knows about all this...

"He's a high priest and knows almost everything. That will be his answer." Adam thinks out his own answer to the question and continues dialing his dad's number.

"Doot doot doot" Adam hears over and over from the ear-piece of the smart com.

"He must be out on a patrol... Voice message just kicked in... [Umm, hi Dad. Just wanted to see how things are going for you over on Gorgon. We're on our way home to Olyra Valley and, I need your help with something very important. Please call me back at this number as soon as you can.] Sorry Darius but that's all I can do at the moment." Adam says and hands him back the device.

"Were you having any luck with the net-search on there?" He asks.

"No Adam; no luck at all... Just a once upon a time in a jungle far away story stuff. Meant to scare children and nothing more. It's all been taken by those writers and directors in Gul'Danar on Gorgon and ruined for ever with horrible movies. No one would believe it to be a true story." Darius responds in frustration.

"That drink of yours looks good, I'm going to get one." Darius randomly says.

Adam watches him go to the bar and thinks to himself. "Something's off with him."

Darius returns to the table with that fancy orange drink and sips on it as he takes his seat. "So the holy order doesn't know about this then..." Says Adam and that freezes Darius in his place for a few seconds with a straw in his mouth.

"You are a clever one Adam… We are High Priests trained to read signs and clues and make sense of things that wouldn't to ordinary people… Did you see the homeless man in Onydath station just before we met with you at the café?"

Adam simply nods his head and allows Darius to continue.

"These people are afflicted with visions… It's why they lose their jobs, their credibility and their dignity. Because they can't control it, they just see and have to tell others what they see but 98 percent of us would only hear crazy talk… Weather systems on Mire and Gorgon have recently been going crazy; drought in one country while another is washed away in floods. Volcanoes have become more active on all worlds and deep crust quakes have devastated the north east provinces on Mire. All the while the economy is collapsing; unemployment rates are at all-time highs because robots have replaced millions of people as workers. Riots have broken out in several provinces on Gorgon and there's been over a dozen Imperial delegates that have gone missing on Mire in the past two months alone. These are all signs of an impending disaster and/or war." Darius finishes explaining.

"All that and a little bird told me that the ruins exist and the weapon there may hold the key to our salvation."

Adam stares at Darius for a second and asks him. "A little bird told you!? You should be talking to the guy at the train station, I'm sure you two would get along." Adam Teases.

"Haha, very funny. You've heard of the Smart com. app 'Animal Talker' haven't you?" Asks Darius; Adam nods his head. "Well I was using it the other night to speak with a Parakeet."

"That's a Mirosian bird; what's it doing on Pangaea?" Asks Adam.

"A smuggled and long lost pet of someone from Mire, who knows, but more importantly it flies… It's been in the jungle and knows."

"Ok, let's say it's all true. You're not going to find it without some idea of where to search; which means waiting for my Father to call us back."

Just as Adam says that, Darius's Smart com. rings. He hands it over to Adam again who puts it to his ear.

"Adam; I got your message. Is everything alright?" Asks Corso, Adam's Dad.

"Yes Dad, everything is fine but I need you to help me with a project. I need to find any kind of factual information about Odaan. There's an artifact there we need to find…" Adam tells his old man.

"How did you find out about that? Did Lucas learn about it during his ascension ceremony?" Corso asks his son.

"That's right Dad, but we can't get the coordinates out of him and now he's in the trance. Can you access the archive for anything relevant?"

"I can do one better; my computer at home has a hidden and encrypted file on it. Within the file is everything the Empire has covered up about Odaan… We should end this call Adam; this is some dangerous information. I'll message Eve's Smart com. with the passcode. Be careful Adam."

"Well, that's awesome news. I'll be fine Dad; take care and I'll say hi to mom for you."

"Thanks Adam; bye." Says Corso and ends the call.

"It's all on my father's computer at home… We have to find Eve right now." Adam says handing back Darius his Smart com.

Eve is in her assigned quarters of their spaceship that's returning them all to Mire. She is listening to music through her Smart com. and doing push ups when her song is interrupted by an incoming message. She stops to pick it up and read it.

"Passcode is Vkl172hC5"

"This makes no sense…" She thinks to herself.

"I'm just going to erase it."

She thumbs the tab on the screen for "erase" just as Adam and Darius reach Eve's room and open the door.

"Don't erase that!" Shouts Adam, stopping Eve just in time. "We need that passcode."

"Why do you need this code? Whose computer and what's on it?"

She asks, more like demands to know.

Eve gets up and shelters the com device in her hand. "You can tell me or I can just hit this delete button."

"Ok Eve." Adam gives in with a calm voice. "We are investigating; searching for an artifact that lays within some ruins called Odaan and that code there unlocks the file on my dad's computer where we can find the exact coordinates of the lost colony." He says walking right up to her with his hand out gesturing for her to give over the device.

"Cool… I want in." Eve says.

"Wait, no… I don't think so Eve…"

"Oh come on! Why Adam? You don't think I could keep up in a hike?"

"No, I know you can. I just couldn't live with myself if something bad was to happen to you is all."

"That's sweet Adam. I know the two of you will protect me and I can manage myself quite well. I may wind up protecting you… So I'm in."

"Ok Eve, you're in." He gives up fighting her resolve on this.

She hands over the Smart com. and fist pumps the air with a supressed "YESS!" shout.

The space shuttle soon lands at Onydath space launch station on Mire and comes to a stop at the reception hallway suspended at the height of the shuttle's main doors. An extension of the hall unfolds and connects to the shuttle. Passengers all leave and among them is Lucas, Darius, Adam, Lynn, and Eve. Lucas parts ways with them at the train station and then a couple hours later the four of them get off the train in Olyra Valley and take a hover-cab back to their home. Night falls over Mire as they watch the landscape go by on their short ride home.

CHAPTER 3

THE FIRST BLOW
Mire - Road to Okladore - Lucifer's Base

A convoy of five hover cars are heading down a dirt road in the desert landscape of rocks, dust and cacti. The middle car is of a limo style and has two flags mounted to the hood; all five are painted black. They approach a steel fenced compound and are forced to show I.D at a heavily guarded gate. The gate opens and the convoy is allowed to go through; dust kicks up as they speed towards the bases parking lot.

Lucifer orders the guards to open the main steel doors of the base. The doors slide open and Lucifer steps out into the heat to greet his guests. About two dozen men exit the vehicles and approach the doors and Lucifer who's standing there at the doors; all are wearing similar black suits.

"Mister President; welcome back to Okladore. Please come in." Lucifer suggests and turns to head inside; a host of men follow.

President Steve Kephness is a tall and fit looking ginger who is in his early fifties; he approaches Lucifer through the group of body-guards.

"So Lucifer, you're done all of your experiments and our deal is finally over. I finally get to have my wife and daughter back... Can't say I believe you; a part of me feels like this is some kind of a trick."

Says the President.

"Think what you will... They await you inside the base. If you would just follow me." Lucifer says and begins to head back inside the base.

The doors close and they find themselves surrounded by jeeps, tanks and crates full of weapons as they walk into the heart of it; it's an assembly area for an army. They come upon a large rock wall with four sets of elevators.

"Mr. President..." Lucifer begins. "Look at me... I am un-armed and these elevators only go to the right floor with this one key I hold in my hand. Chose five of your best men to come along because two dozen will not fit into a single one of these elevators." Lucifer states the fact dryly.

Steve looks around to his men and then to Lucifer and sees the one silver key Lucifer is holding in his right hand.

"Ok Lucifer..." Steve says.

He turns to his crew of guards to pick. "You, you, you and you." He says as he points to the men he wants to join him.

They all enter the one elevator and all watch as Lucifer puts the key in the elevators computer panel and turn it. The doors close and the group inside watches the group outside disappear as the solid steel doors close.

"So Mr. President; are you excited to be seeing your family again after so long a time?"

Steve gets very angry to hear the mockery and amount of control Lucifer has over him; especially when he is five inches taller and at least thirty pounds bigger than him. Steve turns and quickly pins Lucifer to the elevator wall with a right elbow against the neck...

"I should kill you right here for all the grief you've caused me." The President says right in Lucifer's face.

"I have guards posted... Grraa..." Lucifer struggles to speak against the pressure on his neck.

"They die if I'm not there in exactly three and... Arrg, a half minutes." Lucifer manages to spit out.

The president loosens his pressure and then let's go of Lucifer completely. "You always have all the angles covered don't you?" Steve asks rhetorically.

"That's what separates great leaders from nobody's... You could learn a lot from me Mr. Kephness." Lucifer says; Steve lets go of him as the elevator doors open.

"This way gentlemen." Lucifer suggest with his hand for all of them to proceed to the left as they exit the elevator.

The six of them exit the elevator and proceed down the steel walled hall way.

"You may be glad to know that the Empire is about to fall Mr. President. Think about what that will mean for the people of Mire." Lucifer chats it up as they walk.

"Why is it then, that all I think it means is more suffering for our people? Oh yeah, because I think you're a poser. Someone who thinks they can do the impossible and all it'll bring is pain for everyone." Steve replies.

"Oh ye of little faith... I have seen the final fight in a dream of the future and guess what? ... I win Mr. President... I'm leaving this base and this planet in about six hours to put an end to the Empire... You'll see Mr. Kephness; it's not even going to be a challenge."

A couple of minutes go by, the six of them are walking down the bases corridors in silence when Lucifer stops at a large steel door with two guards posted there.

"Well here we are." Lucifer says and gestures to the door in front of them.

"Well open it then..." Demands Steve.

Lucifer is about to hit the open button on the wall panel.

"They better be in there Lucifer, or my men here will end your life on the spot..."

"Oh they are in there; just open the door on the other side of the room." Lucifer says and hits the button on the wall panel to open it. The President and his four bodyguards walk into the room first, followed closely by Lucifer. They see computers sitting on tables against the flanking walls. Wires and cables from all the computers run along the floor and into the thing sitting with its back turned to them all in a great big chair.

"What is this Lucifer?"

"That's just my brother Gabriel; don't worry he's sleeping. Look there; you see the other door on the far wall just past him?" Lucifer asks making the President walk farther into the room.

"Yes I see it." He answers and walks past Gabriel, eyeballing the giant man the whole way and then stops three feet shy of the door.

Lucifer stands back right next to Gabriel. "You promise me they are in there Lucifer?" Asks Steve.

"I promise you, they are in there. Just hit the open button on the panel there (he points to it while standing right beside Gabriel) and go on in.

It was my brother's bedroom but as you see, he doesn't need it anymore." Lucifer answers and then mutters under his breath. "Gabriel; activate program omega one."

Gabriel's eyes open as the President reaches his hand to the electrical wall-panel that opens the door to the bedroom. Half of his face is metal with implants and he is bald on the skin side of his head. He is very big and muscular where his body hasn't been replaced with implants. Seeing through his cyborg eye, it looks as though you are seeing the world through a computer. Numbers and letters pop up at the top left corner of his sight.

[Op – al23-59 omeg-17666]

[Discon – 1101100 – 1001011]

[Power up sequence active…]

[Elim – targets – 5… calculating…]

At the speed of thought the signals travel from his brain to the input nodes on his arms, chest and head; the electrical cords that send signals to computers to monitor his vitals suddenly disconnect from his body and fall to the side; not one of them notices.

The President of Mire hits the button to open the door and the steel plated door slides open to a small dimly lit room with a big bed on the opposite wall and not much else. Steve sees that there are two human figures under the blankets of the bed and slowly enters the room; he feels scared and excited at the same time. He hasn't seen his wife and son for a long time and feared that they were dead at the hands of this madman that somehow became the governments lead military science officer some two – three years before his election last year.

"Myriam… Dallas… It's me, Steve… Dad is here to bring you home; Dallas… Wake up you two I'm here…" He walks to the side of the bed and throws the blanket back to see his wife and son's dead faces.

"NOOooo!!!" Steve screams in utter shock and horror; he really believed that they were still alive, wanted to believe it so badly.

He turns to see Lucifer standing in the lab just about twenty feet away from the bed he is now kneeling beside; his four body guards look at him with pity and shame and then suddenly pull out hand guns from concealed parts of their coats and point them at Lucifer waiting for the order to fire.

Gabriel suddenly stands up out of his chair and takes a step towards the five men he sees before him, none of them with an inhibitor chip implanted in their hands. Their guns flash red in his sights and the readings of their make, model, bullet velocity and more flashes up in his screen sight. The kinetic array on his back quickly unfolds to look like he has wings of wired steel. An electric crackle sound follows as the array gathers ambient energy out of the zero point flux and charges his weapon. His right arm is almost all made up of metallic implanted components that make up a two part weapon/shield device. At the speed of thought Gabriel can switch his gun arm from an electro-magnetic shield to an electro-magnetic force cannon capable of firing a compression ball of energy that rates at about 2000psi and losses momentum after ten feet by a decay rate of 100psi per foot after that.

"You Liar! Scumbag piece of shit!" Shouts the President as he finds the strength to return to his feet, pull a gun out from within his own inner coat pocket and step towards Lucifer will bad intentions.

"I'm going to blow you brains all over the wall you stupid ass mother fu…" He stops and sees Gabriel step in the way of all their shots on Lucifer.

"Did you really think I would be so dumb as to let you in here and see their dead bodies without a backup plan? Gabriel here has not killed yet since he has only been fully functional as of yesterday. Before then he was a retard in a mental home and before then he was a normal boy… The brother that would have ended my life had I not altered his… Try your worst on him, because to get me you will have to go through him." Lucifer says.

"Fine then; men, shoot the freak down."

As the President and his guards open fire with high powered hand guns, Gabriel holds his right gun arm in front of him and activates the invisible shield. The bullets hit the shield five inches away from the furthest point of the implant which looks like a cannon with tubes and wires jumping in and out of the metallic casing. His gun arm also has three metallic fingers that can extend out to grab as well as retract into the casing to allow the gun to fire or shield to repel. When each bullet hits the shield, it looks like a small ripple in the space/time continuum. Gabriel keeps the shield going until all four guards have emptied their clips. Gabriel drops his shield and moves to his left with a spin, moving his massive body with the ease of a slim athlete. Steve fires his gun at Gabriel and misses. In slow motion Lucifer watches as the bullet speeds towards him now; just as Gabriel is moving to attack and this leaves him open to harm. With lightning quick reflexes, Lucifer leans to his right and back, just out of the way of being struck by about two millimeters.

The four body guards are pulling extra clips out of their pockets and in the process of re-loading, just as Gabriel comes full circle from his spin and (at the speed of thought has switched his arm mode from shield to cannon) fires an energy blast at the two closest body guards. The shot looks like a high speed blast of pure energy making a transparent wave though space/time. It hits the two guards and sends them flying backwards with crushing force as they strike the labs steel paneled walls and collapse in Gabriel's old bedroom. One is dead and the other dying of internal injuries. (Gabriel switches back instantly to shield) Steve aims at Gabriel after watching two of his men vanish behind him and takes another shot which hits the shield. The other two body guards have their clips in and are cocking the chambers of their guns as Gabriel jumps sideways to his right (avoiding another bullet from the President who continues to fire his gun at him) and fires a compression blast at the other two guards who make the same mistake as the last two guards of standing to close to each other… Right before they can take aim, Gabriel fires in mid dive; the last two body guards are hit with a force blast and sent flying back into the useless bedroom to be crushed against the wall and die.

A loud "THUD!" fills the room as Gabriel lands on his steel shoulder, meeting hard with the steel floor. His kinetic array had folded up in mid jump to his back to avoid breaking; he rolls over quickly and is back on his feet with the shield active in front of him and his wing like array spread out behind him. President Kephness continues to fire his gun at Gabriel in vain as every bullet just bounces away; after several more shots the gun goes "click, click, click." As the clip is empty of bullets. Gabriel closes the short distance on the president with a couple of steps and grabs him by the neck with his big human, un-tampered with, left hand and then picks him up off the ground and slowly chokes the life out of him.

"Gabriel! Release the man!" Lucifer orders and Gabriel does just that.

Steve falls to his knees gasping for air. Gabriel steps back and allows Lucifer to walk up to a now unarmed President. Steve gets to his feet and feels like crapping his pants he's so scared.

"You see Mr. President, your life is so useless to me." Lucifer tells him and then delivers a vicious double fisted punch to Steve's chest, sending him flying back into the bedroom to crash on top of the bodies of his wife and son.

"But your death… Now that's so much more valuable… Good

bye Mr. President." Lucifer says and turns to Gabriel to order the execution.

"Finish him."

Gabriel walks up to Steve with his gun arm pointed to his head. There's a loud electric crackle sound just before Gabriel's cannon goes "BOOM!" and the President is no more.

Satisfied with the outcome, Lucifer returns to his private quarters and gets on his Smart com. device.

"Call Chief Doberlin." He says to the device and it does just that.

Ten seconds later Chief Doberlin picks up, Lucifer sees his face on the screen and starts the conversation.

"We were attacked Doberlin! Agents of the Empire snuck into my base as I was reuniting the President with his family. There was a big gun fight and… People are dead… Both sides suffered losses but at the end of it all… We lost the President… and his wife and son were caught in the cross fire too… I'm sorry but they are all dead." Lucifer lies so convincingly.

"Oh my God! This is horrible news Lucifer. What are we to do? Our leader is dead…" Says Max Doberlin as the shock of it kicks in.

"The President would want us to find justice at any cost… Some of the assassins we killed were wearing the Pendants of the Holy Order and a couple others were wearing Military sashes of the Empire… It's a collaborative effort and so we must enact the order as I had earlier foreseen… God has given me the gift of foresight and now it's come to pass. Execute order twenty six right now Doberlin. I'm going to get the Mir'Denack up in space and assemble the fleet to take guard over Mire." Lucifer says to Doberlin who simply says "Yes sire" and hangs up on his end to do what he's told, which is tell all the Generals of Mire to execute order twenty six and detain all Gorgon loyalists and their families currently on Mire. A big operation like this takes the combined effort of Mire's police and military.

Lucifer makes another call with his Smart com. to his second in command at the base; a general named Liam Xavier. His face pops up on Lucifer's Smart com. screen.

"Master Lucifer; is it time to order the evacuation?" Asks the General who has narrow facial features and jet black hair; his look could be compared to that of a crow.

"Yes Liam; sound the evacuation notice. Have my brother moved to the Sayberus and make sure the Thumpers are loaded in their launch bays. I'll gather the remaining crew for the Mir'Denack and activate the take-off sequence; once I clear the inner atmosphere, you take off with the Sayberus and go right to pre-programmed position by Gorgon's second moon and launch the Thumpers... You call me after the launch and give me an update. Got it?"

"Yes Master Lucifer, it will be done." Liam responds and hangs up on his end of the call.

Lucifer walks over to the corner of his room with the crystal skull sitting on its shrine and covered by a black curtain just loosely draped over top of it. He whips the curtain off of it.

"I'm going now and I thank you for the help on designing those Thumpers as well as helping with my brother. You won't be coming with me because I no longer have any use for you and something tells me that any further advice from you is going to be counterproductive to my plan. Good bye Dai'Alzan." Lucifer says out loud to the skull and then collects a few books and papers from his desk before leaving for the bases armory where his weapons and armor are stored.

Walking down the halls of the base, Lucifer stops at a steel panelled door and then stops a base soldier on his way to where ever, Lucifer doesn't care; he is walking towards him at the present time and that's why he's going to help.

"You there soldier!"

The soldier knows who Lucifer is and snaps to a salute holding his right hand as a fist that's pressed against his left hand, palm open and fingers up, bowing slightly as he does this.

"Yes Master Lucifer."

"Come in here and help me with my armor. The moments of war is close at hand and I will be ready when it comes."

"Yes Master Lucifer."

The two of them enter the armory. It's basically a big square room full of display cases; most of them mounted to walls but some are in the midst of the room and are shaped like pyramids but as small shelves... Shelves full of guns, knives and explosives. One display pyramid is different though; on it is a bunch of small, carefully fashioned pieces of black steel that make up a full suit of armor. On the wall rack directly behind this display case there's a unique sword mounted on it using a few hooks. It's made almost entirely of titanium steel with the exception of two small black orbs; one cast close to the hilt, the other cast into the upper area of the blade.

"Um, I'm not familiar with this armor." He says.

"I'll direct you through it... let's get to work." Lucifer commands the soldier.

Mire – Olyra Valley – Adam's Home

"Home sweet home." Lynn says as she unlocks the door and allows Eve, Adam and Darius to enter with all their luggage.

Lynn retrieves her luggage and follows the three of them inside shutting the door behind her. Adam turns on the foyer light so they can all see as they take off their shoes and place their luggage against the walls and out of the way for walking.

"So Adam..." Darius begins. "Where's your father's computer?"

"What is it that you two want with Corso's computer?" Asks Lynn who is not yet clued in to their plan.

"Dad has some information about Odaan on his computer mom. We hope it will help Darius here find its exact location so we can be the first to discover it and find a treasure that lays within it."

"That old myth!?" Lynn asks. "Really!? Corso is in on this and helping you? I'm going to have to have a talk with him..." Lynn says clearly upset by the news and walks off to the kitchen turning to add one last thing... "I hope you aren't thinking of going with Darius to search for it."

Adam looks back at his mom not knowing what to say.

"All three of us are going to look for it." Adam answers.

"Eve? You too!? No, no, no… Neither of you are going to step one foot into that jungle." Lynn says with conviction and turns about to continue to the kitchen.

Darius, Adam and Eve all look at each other in a state of loss for words; Darius speaks first.

"Well, looks like you two have an awkward conversation ahead of you. In the meantime, can we get to this computer and find this file?" He asks looking at both Adam and Eve.

"Yeah, of course Darius. Follow me." Adam says and leads the way down the hall, to the left past the kitchen and into his dad's little office.

"Here we are. Give me a minute to get this thing booted up." Adam says as he takes a seat in the office chair and hits the on button on the computer tower below the desk by his feet.

"Old technology takes so long to get going." Adam adds while they wait for the computer to load all the programs to the monitor.

"Ok Eve, give me your Smart com. again." Says Adam; Eve hands it over to him.

Adam uses the mouse to click on the file that says "encrypted files". The screen changes to show a window with like a hundred encrypted files starting with file "01001".

"Crap!" Says Adam. "We're going to have to try this passcode on each of these files until we hit the right one; this may take some time."

Inside a Military Hover-Jeep

Captain Bart Krezler is sitting in the passenger seat of a black hover-jeep; military issued, covered with a top, tinted windows. The driver is his Lieutenant Lyndel Whatts. In the back seat is two new recruits of Mires military initiate program. Neither Krezler nor Whatts cares who they are; they are just there to back them up on an arrest warrant for a Corso Belckhiam and his family. Another hover-jeep with two men inside follows closely behind Krezler's jeep and will be the one they will use to transport the prisoners. A third hover-jeep (all three painted jet black) follows that one with five more soldiers inside who are extra backup in case of some sort of violent altercation. All they know is that they are to arrest the loyalists and are allowed to use deadly force if encountered with extreme resistance. Krezler holds a Smart com. in his hand. Watching the screen that currently is showing a satellite layout of Olyra Valley; the device speaks to him with a pleasant but robotic like female voice.

"In five hundred meters, turn right. Destination is twenty meters after turning."

He thumbs a few buttons on the screen of his Smart com. and exits the application pathways for the GPS and thumbs into a rare military application to shut off the power grid to any place on Mire that runs on grid power.

Inside Adam's House

ADAM IS TRYING the passcode for the thirty-second time when it accepts and launches the screen into a window with multiple folders and pictures.

"Whoa. Well here we are at last." Says Adam and clicks on a picture of some mossy, vine covered stone pillar in the midst of a jungle.

"Wait…" Darius says noticing a file off to the side and behind the picture. "That file there!" He points to it on the screen.

Adam down-sizes the picture and selects the folder named "Mathusila Journal".

"Adam, could I take the chair for a moment?" Darius asks.

"Of course Darius." Adam gets up and allows Darius to sit in the office chair to take control of the search. Darius enlarges the folder to full screen and quickly assimilates entry after entry of the journal log of a scientist. Martin Mathusila was an expert in botany, genetics and chemistry making one of the most useful people in the tale of a long mission to Pangaea almost five hundred years before this very moment.

As Darius reads on at close to the speed of a computer, he finally gets to it. The man reports the exact longitude and latitude on Pangaea to where they are building the colony...

"Quickly Adam write this down... 20.638728 latitude - 78.661446 longitude."

"Ok. I got it."

Darius looks over to see that Adam has written the coordinates on his right forearm with a permanent ink pen.

"Hmmph; way to make yourself indispensable Adam." Eve says jokingly.

"Ha, ha... Ok you got me. What? I want to make sure I'm in the search team alright? This could be the biggest adventure ever." Answers Adam.

Eve looks at him with a "I give up" look and has a thought.

"Hey Darius? Now that we have its location, how about looking farther ahead in that folder to see how it ends?"

"Ooh, yeah! I like that idea." Adam seconds the motion.

Darius does as is suggested and scrolls down on the side bar until he gets close to the bottom of the file; like the last ten pages. Darius begins to read the journal out loud to them...

["After Commander Gillihad killed the first Tyranos-X with a grenade launcher; it seemed to signal more of the creatures to our location. I'm guessing it was the smell of its dead carcass that attracted them. Raptors, Tyridactlin, and those annoying little Ladricose that are like Raptors but like one third their size and come in droves. All of them came for the dead Tyranos-X but found us instead because we were trying to build our colony right there where it died. Last night, three fully grown Tyranos-X's came busting though our barely built walls and were followed by a pack of Raptors. Once they got into the main camp, it was a slaughter. Soldiers tried their best to fight them off but failed and now we have taken the only Skylark drop ship in an attempt to get off this wretched Planet but the thing doesn't have enough power to make it out of the atmosphere... We are just flying aimlessly right now. We had to leave the Commander behind; he's most likely dead right now. I'm going to suggest to the pilot to land on that island we found last month with that strange tree we found with the glowing fruit... I saw the commander slice one of them fruits open and coat the razor sharp bone fragments he collected from the dead Tyranos-X's spine; the tail section of it. The bone shards began to shine with the same light that caused the fruit to glow. I don't know how the Commander knew to do that he just was curious I guess and the result was astonishing. He found a way to fashion the links of bone into a masterpiece of a..."]

The power to their entire house suddenly shuts off; the computer screen dies out and all of them are now in the dark.

"Hey, What the Heck!?" Adam shouts.

"Mom; did we pay our power bill for last month!?" Adam shouts out the office door to Lynn who is in the kitchen.

"Of course! Automatic withdraw from Royal Mire Bank!" Lynn shouts back to Adam from the kitchen.

"Then what the heck is going on?" Adam asks himself and anyone else.

The three of them leave the small office. Eve has her Smart com back in her hand and is using the devices flashlight app to see through the dark. Darius walks past them as Adam and Eve pause to link up with Lynn. He goes down the hallway towards the front door; his eyes have adjusted to the dark and his gut is telling him that something is really wrong here. Adam looks back and doesn't see Darius.

"Hey Darius!?" He shouts. "Where'd you go?"

"Down the hallway; over here." Darius announces. "Eve, please shine that light on my luggage here."

He requests of her right as she catches up to him along with Adam and Lynn. Eve does as she is asked and Darius gets to work unzipping several compartments of his travel bag. He retrieves from within it seven separate oddly shaped pieces of metal mixed with plastic, and other electronic components that are built in on each odd piece.

Darius gets to linking each of the seven pieces together.

"What in the world do you have there Darius?" Eve asks first as Adam and Lynn were about to ask the same thing.

"It's a plasma pistol." Darius answers dryly and pauses to look up at each of their confused faces.

"This sudden power outage doesn't happen on Mire anymore unless it's meant to." Darius says and continues to put his gun together. "I got it through all the scanners because as seven separate pieces, it can't tell what it is… I always carry it with me because I'm a High Priest and know that lesser people would see me dead for who I am… Right now is not that moment, but something close." He says with utter certainty in his voice.

Adam, Eve and Lynn are still confused as hell; Darius sees it as he looks back up at them after connecting the last piece (not quite). He holds in his hand a cannon of a pistol with inter-connecting, ribbed little tubes that wind in, out, and around the muzzle.

"They'll be here soon so I don't have a lot of time to explain… The Empire has long feared another Mirosian rebellion and called upon the council of the High Priests for advice, that was six years ago and I was there at the gathering… After a long debate we came to the conclusion that we could have peace through the puppet government they had installed and through media and false information. But we also all agreed that if the puppet government was ever infiltrated by one of these rebels, like the old Mara'Kree clan (which were devious and ruthless) the first thing they would have to do to ensure victory is to gain full control over Mire. The only way to do that would be to arrest or kill all men and women who are in the service of the Empire and currently living here on Mire. To arrest them all they would have to catch them all by surprise or some may escape and warn the Emperor… Or some of us would even stay and carry out covert missions against them… A sudden power outage like this is quite the surprise, maybe if there was a storm but the night sky is clear."

Darius finishes explaining and then takes off a small wrist bracelet that no one noticed before; he slides the bracelet over the gun's hilt to snap into a certain spot and suddenly the gun is filled with an eerie, green glowing light that pulses from the hilt and lights up the pathways of plastic tubes that snake around it.

As they stand at the front door inside the house, they all stop talking as they hear the humming engines of several hover-vehicles come to a stop just outside the door in their driveway.

"Holy Shit Darius, you're right." Lynn says as she looks closer out one of the small side windows that flanks the doorway.

"I see three black, military like hover-jeeps out there." She adds.

"I knew it." Darius mutters under his breath.

"We're going to need an escape plan as of right now." He adds.

"We can go out through the back patio." Eve says. "It's just past the dining room; we'll have to make our way out through the greenhouse and then it's a quick run over to the neighbor's yard and wherever after that."

"Shit, they've spotted us." Krezler says as he holds his Smart com in front of him.

He is using a military application called "Infra-finder" which allows the devices camera to see through walls and other materials, to see the heat signature of living beings. He sees the heat signatures of all four of them in the house and figures that one of the two adult males is the man of the house, Corso. The others are Lynn, Adam and Eve. He sees a strange green glow on the screen as well. Something that (supposed) Corso is holding. As he steps out of his jeep and is joined by the remaining soldiers in his party, he realizes what the green glowing thing is.

"Shit, it's a gun." Krezler says to his crew.

All of them instantly draw their fully automatic machine pistols to eye level and turn on their laser sights, all pointed at the front door of the house. Krezler has an idea.

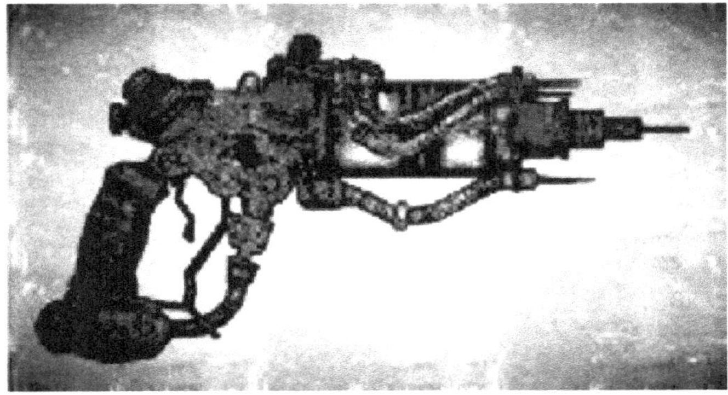

"General of the Empire, Corso!" Shouts Krezler. "You and your family are under arrest under Mirosian order twenty six. Drop your weapon and surrender. Do it now and your family will be treated fairly and brought to Ozorack Detention Center until the war is over! Do this now or I will be forced to use…"

Krezler's speech is cut short as Darius opens the front door a crack, points his gun at the one speaking and takes a couple of shots with his plasma gun. "Pew, Pew!" Two bright green balls of super-heated plasma whiz by just inches away from his right shoulder and slam home into the chest of one of the soldiers sent to help him with arrests. In slow motion Krezler watches the plasma bullets just miss him and send a man beside him flying back through the air to hit hard against the door of one of the hover-jeeps and hit the ground dead. The remaining soldiers open fire at the front door sending streams of hot lead in Darius's direction.

Darius instantly slams the door shut after firing twice and runs as fast as he can up the stairs to the second floor knowing that he wouldn't have time to make it down the hallway to the dining room before the enemy's bullets tore him to shreds. Adam, Eve and Lynn had left down the hall just five seconds into Krezler's speech and are in no danger of being hit in the assault.

"Hold your fire!" Krezler orders his men and holds the Smart com back up to see where his targets are. "They're escaping through the back." Ten men including himself remain.

"You three head around the left of the house." Krezler points to the men he's talking to. "And you three head around the right side and the rest of us are going in the front door! Move, Move, move!" Krezler orders and sends his men into motion.

Inside the house, Darius opens the upstairs hallway window at the very end of the hall. He climbs out onto a narrow and steep section of the homes roof that runs the full length of the side, from front yard to back yard. He quickly makes his way to the back yard and leaps down from the roofs edge to ground level with a hard "Thud". Rolling once and getting to his feet, Darius runs the short distance over to the greenhouse. He enters it and sees the three of them hiding by a planting table.

"Why are you three still here? You should be half way to the neighbor's yard by now." Says Darius as he crouches down beside Eve and looks at Adam.

"We thought we should wait for you seeing as you're the only one with a gun among us." Answers Adam.

They all hear the heavy footsteps of soldiers coming from each side of the house, entering the area of the back yard. Directly across from the houses porch is the greenhouse, made up of all glass panels with an aluminum support frame. The soldiers on each side take aim at it suspecting the targets to be in there but it's too dark to see anything. Darius knows that he has to take the pre-emptive strike or the soldiers will find them inside this greenhouse while too close for Darius to successfully hold them back.

Inside the greenhouse, Darius runs through a handful of scenarios in his mind and realizes the best defence is a strong offence.

"If we run now and they will gun us down. Use the tables here for cover. At the count of three you and Eve knock that table over and I with Lynn here, will knock this table over giving us cover from their bullets both directions. Then I'll have to shoot all of them before we can make a break for it." Darius says and begins to count quietly.

"One... Two... Three."

The soldiers outside the greenhouse and inside the home with

Krezler all put their night vision goggles on. The soldiers in the back yard take a few more steps towards the glass hut and then see the tables inside get knocked over so the tops are facing them (as well as hear the pots on top crashing to the ground). They all instantly begin to open fire at the greenhouse. The initial volleys shatter the glass panels of the greenhouse before slamming into the steel topped tables. Adam, Darius, Eve and Lynn all duck as bullets rip through everything around them except for the tables they now cower behind. Eve and Lynn are scared to death but not Darius or Adam; the training from the holy order has taught them both to channel fear into a means of survival at any cost. A kind of heightened awareness of things. Adam sees a three pronged weed pulling tool with a four foot long wooden handle, it is basically a small spear laying on the greenhouse floor seven feet away by the door they all came through. There's also a pitch fork and short handled garden axe laying close by the weed puller, and close to those is a small steel frame & top table with seeds and stuff on it.

"A small arsenal lays right there, just need to time this right." He thinks to himself as does his best to ignore the bullets slamming into the tables opposite side just inches away from him.

Darius closes his eyes and imagines the back yard as he knows it from his short intro with it moments ago. He has the gift of photographic memory and so he can recall it with clarity. Now he uses the distance of the sound of each soldier's gun as it fires to locate their exact position in the yard as he sees it in his mind. Two of the soldiers on his east flank run out of ammo and stop to reload. Darius takes the moment to attack; he pops his gun over the table to fire two shots blindly towards the group to his west flank causing them to break their fire and dive for cover. One of those shots comes close to hitting a soldier, but more importantly the flash of the gun as it fires sends out a super charged beam of U.V light and has blinded the men watching through their night vision. Darius turns to the three soldiers on the east flank and pops up from behind the table to take a good aim at his targets. The two are just popping in fresh clips while the third has just ran dry and goes to reload as well. He fires two good shots at the one in the middle of the group hitting him once in the chest and once in the face. The impacts send him flying back six feet to land in some bushes. The other two soldiers there make to take cover; one diving to the right as the other dives to the left. Darius takes aim quickly and fires three shots at the soldier diving to the right of the first one he just shot dead. (Pew, pew, pew) He hits the soldier with the last shot right in hip and tweaks him sideways as he lands in the slightly overgrown lawn. Bullets begin to whip past him from the other direction so he ducks back down under the shelter of the galvanized-steel top planting tables.

Adam watched as Darius fired his gun one way and then as he turned to fire the other way; there was the moment he needed to make his move. Eve watches him scramble up to run in a ducking position over to the deadly garden tools. Adam grabs the short handled axe first in his right hand. Looking back out through the shot up glass doorway of the greenhouse, Adam sees four soldiers with guns drawn coming out of the house and down the small staircase of the porch. They don't yet see him but will soon so Adam reaches back with the axe and tosses it perfectly at the first soldier to step foot on the lawn. The axe spins flawlessly through the air and hits the soldier in the chest blade first, knocking him on his back to lay motionless and quite dead. Krezler, Whatts and another recruit open fire in Adam's direction. Adam ducks under the planting table closest to him and tips it over, knocking all the items off. He quickly shifts the top towards the greenhouse doorway and towards his attackers. The three of them slowly down and carefully advance, firing constantly at the table hoping to hit Adam with at least one bullet. Adam grabs the weed-puller and then notices several cans of aerosol pesticides laying on the concrete floor. They must have been on the table with all the other clutter before he knocked it down. On the can is a symbol of warning, "danger, highly explosive!" it says. A roll of red packing tape lays just inches from the cans; Adam gets an idea.

Darius looks over to Adam after taking out two soldiers on the east flank and watches as he basically tomahawks a soldier out with a small axe and then topples a table to take cover from incoming bullets. Now he's taping three cans of pesticides together with one thing in mind. Adam looks over and sees Darius looking back at him; looking at him with an odd expression. Adam makes the motion of tossing the taped up cans over the table and then motions for Darius to shoot it with his index finger and thumb shaped like a gun. Darius nods his head as bullets continue to whiz by them all. ("Holy shit, this kid's scary." Is the look on Darius' face.)

Krezler has a high powered semi-automatic hand gun and is firing at Adam when he sees in the background, several other figures are taking cover from his soldiers shooting from the sides of the yard, but he has a clear view of them.

"Forget the kid hiding behind the table, I'm gonna get the ones I have a clear shot on." Krezler thinks to himself and takes aim firing once, twice and "Boom!" the third shot hits Lynn from the side and a bullet drives deep into her chest. It happens just as Adam tosses the taped together cans of explosive gas towards Krezler. Darius takes extra careful aim and lets a shot go. Krezler gasps as he sees his death about to occur and instinctually grabs his Lieutenant Whatts and pulls him in the way just as the plasma bullet hits the trio of exploding cans and engulfs Whatts and the other soldier in a ball of fire with shards of hot metal. The explosion sends them all flying backwards. The two instantly die, but Krezler remains alive, covered by the smoking body of Whatts.

Adam grips the pitchfork and makes to get one of the dead soldier's guns when the only remaining soldier on the east flank shoots at him. A bullet grazes Adams upper right thigh in mid run and makes him stumble and roll on the lawn as bullets continue to seek him but just miss and hit close by into the lawn. Darius notices Adam's distress and fires at the one soldier there hitting him with the first shot right in the side of the head. From the west flank, the soldiers have regained most of their sight and are tired of holding their ground so they advance on Darius, Eve and Lynn just as Darius takes the shot to save Adam. A bullet tears through Darius's left shoulder and sends him barrelling over the edge of the tipped planting table. The soldiers continue to advance on them and are about five feet away from the tables, still firing down at them incessantly when Adam busts back into the scene with one of his fallen enemies machine pistols and flanks the three soldiers firing it at them. Adam hits them all multiple times with a flurry of bullets thus ending their lives. Adam stops shooting as the last soldier falls down dead. He feels sick as the gravity of killing people sinks in and buckles over to fall to his hands and knees.

Krezler's vision is fuzzy and his body feels weak, like he's just getting out of bed; he takes a deep breath and smells burned clothing mixed with burned flesh and it almost makes him puke. He pushes the body of Whatts off of him and crawls in the darkness underneath the porch steps and through them to the side of the house where he stops to look back. Looking just in time to see the young lad Adam gun down the last three of his recruits. He quietly growls with frustration and turns to go back up the side of the house to the driveway in the front yard.

(D.J Tiesto – Kyau & Albert remix "6AM")

"Oh Shit! Adam!" Eve shouts which gets him back to his feet. Adam walks over through the now open side of the greenhouse and steps around the table to see his mom Lynn laying there with her head resting against Eve as she cradles her arms to support her. He sees the trail of blood oozing down from her side and is struck with a flood of emotions. Anger, fear, grief, and despair are gripping at his throat making it impossible for him to make a sound. He drops to his knees beside her and lifts her arm up slowly to see the full extent of it. He cringes with an overwhelming urge to cry.

"Mother." Is all he finds the strength to say.

Lynn breathes slowly and looks at Adam. "Son… You tell your father for me… that I love him… And I love the both of you so much…" She looks from Adam over to Eve and back again. "I see it now… You two are…”

Her last words are cut short as her heart beats its last beat. Adam is distraught and starts to cry without any sobbing though; just tears flowing down his eyes. Eve is also crying and sobbing slightly too. Darius can't help but be moved by this but he knows that the chance to escape Mire gets slimmer with every moment they waste.

"I feel your guys' loss right now, I really do. But we have to leave this planet and not an hour from now or two, or three, but right now." Darius says to the two of them.

Adam and Eve look up at him with tear covered faces unable to speak still.

"Look, Do the two of you want to die along with her!? Because if you stay here like this, they'll come back with more soldiers and kill the both of you! Then what will her sacrifice have accomplished!? NOTHING!" Darius shouts at the two of them to snap them out of their grief.

Adam rises to his feet quickly and just shouts "Rrraaa!!" in his face as he's overcome with a wave of rage.

"Good Adam, use that anger if it's all you have right now and get your sister to her feet." Darius says.

Adam looks down to see Eve still sobbing there and reaches down to grab her by the shoulder and look her in the eye.

"We're going to find the one responsible for this and make 'em pay Eve, but right now we gotta go. We have to run away to fight another day, so come on and get to your feet Eve. We're getting off this stupid ass planet to regroup and come up with a plan to avenge mom's death."

Adam says and it works; Eve gets to her feet and instantly walks over to where Darius gunned down the first couple soldiers.

"Eve, where are you going? We should go through the house and patch ourselves up a bit first." Adam says as he hobbles along after Eve, blood still oozing from the grazing shot.

Eve stops and bends down to recover the soldier's weapon. Adam catches up to her as she gets a hold of the second soldier's gun.

She checks the clip; it's the full one. She pops it in and tosses the one to Adam then checks the clip of the one she's keeping, it's a full clip too.

"Darius, how good of an idea is it to go back inside? Would they booby-trap the place?" Asks Eve.

Darius is just catching up to them and thinks about the question for a second.

"Hmm; it's a possibility that I don't wish to find out first hand… Right Adam?"

Adam figures they are both making a good point and will grab his luggage from the front door and find some shirts to cover the leg wound and a clean pair of pants.

With guns drawn, all three of them go around the side of the house to the front door and get the luggage they left behind there and run over to the first empty hover-jeep of the two parked in the driveway and toss their belongings inside.

"Darius? You know how to drive one of these right?" Asks Adam.

"Yeah of course, just like riding a Daxaur on Ehdon." Darius responds randomly as he jumps into the driver's seat.

Adam and Eve hop into the back seats, close the doors and buckle up right away. Darius doesn't buckle up but instead tries hitting buttons on the dash panel to start the friggin thing up. He soon finds the on button close to the steering wheel and starts it up, the occupants are slightly jerked around as Darius gets use to the controls. Adam & Eve buckle up.

"OK, I think I got it." States Darius as he begins to turn the hover jeep around to face the exit of the driveway.

Suddenly they are all violently jolted about as Krezler has rammed into them with the third hover-jeep head on. Darius's head hits the dashboard hard and he then falls over between the drivers and passengers seats. The craft comes to a crashing halt and in the back seat Adam tries to help unbuckle Eve. He fumbles a bit in his state of shock and then manages to free her from the restraint, and then frees himself right after.

(Godsmack – "Awake")

Eve is first to get out of the vehicle and as she steps out the door she is greeted with a body slam by Krezler who then turns her over to her belly and tries to slap a handcuff on her wrist.

"Eve! Nooo! You bastard, you fight me!" Adam shouts as he sees Eve go down on the opposite side of the jeep.

He makes his way around the front of it and hobbles over to face and tackle Krezler. He gets two feet when Krezler quickly gets up and swings the loose driver side door open right on Adam's face. As Krezler stands at the open door watching Adam tumble backwards, he's greeted with a swift kick to the face by Darius who is still inside the hover-jeep. Krezler flounders away to his left as the kick has him seeing stars and feeling light headed. Darius steps out of the jeep with blood oozing down the side of his head and is breathing really hard. Darius seems to be in some sort of amped up state of adrenalin. As Krezler recovers his balance and shakes the stars out of his sight, he sees who he thinks is Corso but suddenly realizes that he's not.

"Hey, you're not Corso." Krezler says.

"That's right, I'm Darius and I'm going to kick your ass."

Darius dashes at Krezler and starts swinging, throwing left jabs and hard right hooks with furious speed. Darius's attacks are all met by blocks or thin air as Krezler finds the speed to block & dodge out of the way. Darius sweeps a leg out to trip and Krezler hops it with a perfectly timed thrust kick that catches Darius in the face as he rotates about from the sweep. "BAM!" Darius is knocked backwards, his feet fumbling for solid footing. He finds the open driver's seat of the jeep and leans against it to try steady his vision from the blow he just took and all he sees is three blurry Krezler's coming right for him. He tries to throw a weak punch but Krezler blocks it easily and elbows Darius right on the jaw and then starts to choke him out with his hands around his neck.

Adam has since got up from being knocked down by Krezler and now sees him choking the life out of Darius who's leaning against the driver's seat just inside the jeep.

The open door of the jeep stands in his way from getting a clean shot and as he looks at the open door of the hover-jeep he realizes that if he tackles it… Adam does just that, using the vehicles door as a weapon and slamming it as hard as he can on Krezler's back.

"Ahhg, you little shit!"

Krezler is hurt by the move a little bit, but is more annoyed to be interrupted while he's trying to kill someone and now he's squished into Darius in some weird, gay struggle snuggle. Krezler uses the top frame-work of the jeep, and with both hands pushes back with all his might as Adam tries to keep the door pressed on him. After a short struggle he gets as much distance as he needs to roll away from the door just as Darius tries to give Krezler a head butt to the jaw. Both Darius and Adam don't expect it and Adam winds up slamming the jeep door accidentally on Darius' face.

"Oh no; sorry Dar."

Krezler catches Adam off guard with a spin kick to the side of the head which sends him reeling over, stumbling like a drunk, he falls to his hands and knees seeing stars.

"I told the bunch of you that you're under arrest and by the GODS I will arrest you all!"

Krezler shouts in frustration before grabbing Darius at the neck and throwing him to the ground in order to arrest him.

"Hey Douche Bag! Arrest this!" Eve says from inside the jeep as she aims the gun out of the open door.

She has the gun she had lost in the crash and has now recovered because the men kept Krezler occupied long enough for her to find it. She fires three bursts. "Brradtt, brradtt, brradtt!" Eve's aim is true and as she exhales from holding her breath. She watches as the last Mirosian soldier in black takes about six of the nine bullets right in the chest from the side where the body armor he wears has a gap. Slowly he falls to his knees; blood squirts out from the bullet holes in his chest. He wobbles a bit there on his knees and then collapses on his face and lays there dead. Adam and Darius stagger over to Eve. She gets out of the jeep to stand in front of Krezler's body still holding the gun and pointing it at him, suddenly in a state of shock.

"I… I just killed a man… He's dead because I shot him… I could have just told him to stop…"

Eve starts going on in a sudden state of remorse. Adam carefully removes the gun from Eve's hand, thumbs the safety over and tosses it on the seat of the jeep.

"Look Eve… It's not your fault ok. He was going to kill us… Both Darius and I would have done the same thing; actually we were just about to… You just happened to kill him first so… Thank you."

Adam tries to comfort her, but Darius has no patience for that at the moment.

"The three of us have now killed like ten or eleven of these soldiers, and the fact we're alive is a miracle alone. Truly sorry about your guys' mother but we have to move." Darius watches the sanity return in her eyes.

"First we have to patch you boys up. You can't go on a train let alone a spaceship looking like that." Eve says.

"There she is, Eve's back in da house yo!" Adam gets her to smile.

"Shut up Adam; you do a horrible gangster voice." Eve teases.

"Oh do I now?"

Adam and Darius are first to grab their bags and from the now destroyed hover-jeep and transfer them to the one farther to the shoulder of the driveway; the only one not smashed up. They open their luggage and take out a change of clothes before going back inside. They go to the upstairs bathroom. Darius helps Adam up the stairs while Eve trails slightly behind and goes to her room to change. In the washroom, Adam gets the meddie-bot out from a drawer under the main counter-top (with the tap and sink) and turns it on, holding it about two inches away from the gash on his leg caused by the grazing of a bullet. The device is about the size of an electric shaver but this emits a ULF healing light to use the body's own repair processes to fix wounds but at an exponential rate. By the time Darius has washed most of the blood off his face and out of his hair, Adam's leg wound is closed and fully healed; all that remains is a thin layer of dry, crusted blood. Sitting on the closed lid of the toilet he wipes the dry blood off with a wet towel quickly and holds the meddie-bot up towards Darius. Standing up, Adam gets Darius to remove the towel he has pressed against his head and quickly waves the glowing blue light of the device over his wound there. Next to heal is the bullet hole in the shoulder.

They exit the washroom as Eve exits her bedroom. All cleaned up, Adam is wearing a white dress shirt (top two buttons undone) with a black and teal colored t-shirt underneath. With loose fit navy-blue jeans and black dress shoes. Darius is wearing a tight white muscle shirt with a green, red and white checker patterned long-sleeve dress shirt over top. With black dress pants and black dress shoes on; topped with a black and white bowler hat. Eve is wearing her typical skin tight, black jogging shoes and pants with a checker patterned mini-skirt over her waste-line. She shows off her tight abs and sexy figure by wearing a half-top black workout shirt and a small sized, pure white long sleeve, button up shirt but only does up two of the buttons right below her breasts. Adam loves that outfit and is hard pressed to stay focused on the tasks at hand, like walking back to the hover-jeep without stumbling over his own feet and remembering to breath. "Just look at the wall behind or ahead of her and get moving you idiot." Adam thinks to himself as he makes his way down the hall and follows Eve down the stairs and out the door.

The three of them pile into the undamaged hover-jeep and shut the doors. Darius is at the wheel and this time he gets the vehicle turned around and moments later is speeding away down the road.

"Ok now, what's the plan here?" Adam asks Darius who takes a moment to think it over.

"We drive this jeep over to Olyra's magnarail station and take a train to Onydath space launch station. Then we get off of this planet." Answers Darius.

"And go to Gorgon to find my Dad." Adam throws out there.

"Gorgon is a two day trip at this time in the solar calendar where Pangaea is like twenty hours away right now… I think we should go to Ehdon and find a way to get in the jungle, discover something amazing." Darius suggests.

"No, we need to find my Dad. He can protect us and find us a safe place on Gorgon to stay while we figure out what the hell is going on here." Counters Adam.

Darius understands his position but doesn't agree… "No Adam…"

"What?" Adam asks slightly shocked.

"Relics and ruins are pointless right now… We need to get to Gorgon and…"

"I know what you're thinking and it seems like a smart plan but I highly doubt Gorgon will be any safer than living on Mire. If it is war like I think and pretty well know it is, then Gorgon is about to become a battle ground. And after many cities on Gorgon are destroyed, they will respond and destroy twice as much here on Mire. Both worlds will be full of danger and destruction but Ehdon is small and of no threat to anyone. They will be left alone there and while the rest of the solar system goes to shit, we can distract ourselves with an adventure." Darius pleads his case with Adam. Eve doesn't seem to care where they go as long as it's off this cursed rock.

Darius parks the hover-jeep in the almost abandoned parking lot of the train station. All three of them get their bags from the back seat and walk up the three steps to enter the stations automated ticket booth/room. Two guards stand at the security scanning gate. As Adam walks up to a booth to purchase the tickets, Darius kneels over his travel bag and unzips the compartment with his gun in it. His back is turned to the guards as he disconnects all the seven links that make up his plasma gun, starting with the wrist band power source back on his wrist. Just as Adam finishes buying the tickets, Darius zips his bag back up and stands up to grab the ticket out of Adam's hand. Adam hands a ticket to Eve too and they make their way to the security gate. The two guards are men and both are staring at Eve's cleavage as she walks through the scanner with a big smile. Adam walks through next and the guards gloat at him thinking him to be the lucky boyfriend; little do they know… Darius walks through last and no alarms go off but one of the guards looks curiously at several pieces of something in the man's travel bag.

"Hey you there! Stop!" Shouts the guard from behind him.

Darius freezes and tries to think of a way to play this out so he doesn't have to injure or kill either guard.

"Your travel bag sir. I'm going to have to ask you to put it on the ground and step away from it."

Darius turns around to confirm the guard is talking to him. He drops his bag and steps away as he's told.

"I'm sorry officer but is there something in my luggage that concerns you?" He asks the guard who looks at him and gets to un-zipping the compartment that he saw the strange object in.

Seconds later he pulls one of the gun pieces out of the bag. "You want to tell me the hell this thing is?" Asks the guard, the other one simply looks on at them silently; clearly just a backup for this guy.

"Yes sir. That is one of those new personal hair removal devices." Darius answer as the guard digs further into his bag and pulls out the trigger piece.

"And what about this piece here?" The guard asks him.

Adam and Eve just watch in an almost nervous breakdown. Both are thinking that Darius is about to be busted on having a deadly plasma pistol.

"That piece there is… Hmm… You know it cradles the balls as the light removes hair…"

"Oh shit!" Says the guard quite shocked and disgusted as he drops the two pieces back into the bag.

"What!? I like to be fully manscaped down there. You never know when a hottie will want to jump you in a public restroom you know."

"What the f**k are you? Some sort of gigolo?" Asks the guard.

"I get around… What the hell do you care? You gonna arrest me for it?"

The guard gets to his feet shaking his head. "Unfortunately there's no law against being a tramp… Get the hell out of my face." Says the guard and then turns about and walks away.

"That was close." Eve says quietly to Adam as they watch Darius zips up his travel bag and walks over to join them using a jaunty strut.

"Bravo Darius." Adam says as he gets close enough to hear him.

"I know hey… Took some quick thinking but he's off my case." He looks back to make sure.

The train arrives shortly after that incident and the three of them board the train and take up a section of seats.

"Deja'vu." Adam thinks as he takes his seat.

Going back to Ehdon the same way he went last time. Technically he has only spent about three hours on Mire and already he is making his way back to the space center to leave again. The only difference is that his mom isn't sitting in the empty seat across from him as the train's doors close and they get moving. The feeling of loss threatens to take over him again.

"Why did she have to die?" He asks himself.

Eve sees Adam staring at the empty seat and feels the same thing. She reaches over and rubs his shoulder. Darius watches them share a moment and then stares out the window of the train as the landscape goes whizzing by.

After a couple hours on the train, they hear the automated female voice of the trains computer say that they are about to stop at Onydath central station. They get ready to leave, grabbing their travel bags. The train stops, doors open and the tree of them exit the train among a crowd of other travelers. Eve takes the lead, making her way through the crowds from the train station to the space launch centre. Down a flight of stairs, past a row of food vendors and down an alley they come out to the street. Right across from them is the staircase to the reception area of the space launch centre. They cross the street and climb the stairs to the top, walk through the doors and approach the ticket booth line-up. Adam buys the tickets to Pangaea for all of them and they repeat the process of going through scanners past some guards and into a line up to board the shuttle. As they make their way down the line up, they hear a station wide announcement over the P.A.

"All expected flights to Gorgon have been suspended at the moment due to severe weather on Gorgon. All passengers of flights to Gorgon are advised to check in with their launch centres security personnel right away."

"That's strange." Says Adam. "Severe weather, go to the security guards for answers?"

"It's not strange; they are using quick and easy ways to detain anyone potentially from Gorgon." Darius Says to them quietly as they are approaching the boarding gate.

"Good thing you talked me out of getting tickets for Gorgon." Adam whispers in Darius' ear.

They each take turns presenting their tickets to the female gate-keeper and proceed down the hall without any more interruptions. The three of them take their seats on the shuttle and buckle in; moments later tow cables attach and the shuttle begins to slowly lift off the ground to enter into the cradle of the giant, floating launch balloon. Adam looks out the window of the shuttle as it rises. He usually feels scared at this part of the takeoff sequence, but at the moment he feels nothing at all. The shuttle could blow up right now and he would just continue to stare out the window as it falls back to Mire in a ball of flames, but no such thing happens. The shuttle launches from the platform as it has done at least a thousand times before. Every time a shuttle comes back to a launch center it gets re-vamped for another journey into space and back; re-using it over and over again. Things could go wrong but usually don't.

Adam gets up from his seat after the launch sequence ends and the long flight sequence begins. Eighteen hours and seventeen minutes until landing on Pangaea. Passengers are allowed to wander around and go visit the arcade or the lounge for some drinks. Adam doesn't realize he's being followed until he is sitting at the lounges bar and ordering a drink. Darius sits at the chair beside him and orders.

"A Winstons double on the rocks." Darius says to the gentleman behind the bar counter.

His drink is served seconds later.

"What did you get?" He asks Adam.

"A Pangaean Sunrise…" Adam answers.

"Moms favorite drink."

"I remember when my mom died…" Darius tries to recon with Adam. "She was still young; in her early fifties she was when the Lungvarras hit her. Remember the stories of that horrible disease in the Beneska province on Gorgon five years ago? Well she was one of its victims. Two years ago I found out that Gorgon spies tried to instigate a war using a false flag, viral weapon attack. The Lungvarras disease… The local authorities covered it up as just some random outbreak but it was an actual plan of attack… The School of the Order, Mire's government, even the inner circle of the Empire was all in on it together and after only one thing." Darius pauses.

Adam is impatient and has to ask. "After what Darius?"

"Ultimate control…" Answers Darius and the two of them stay silent for a few seconds.

Suddenly Eve enters the lounge and sits beside Darius at the bar.

"I'll have what he's having." She says and points to Adam's fruity drink when the bartender approaches her.

"So here's the plan." Darius says after a short moment of silence and the bar tender has walked away.

"Once we get to Ehdon, we rent the same rooms at the same hotel you two stayed at just a day ago… From there, I will take a Daxaur cart or hover-cab to the Cerbey'Rus building and convince the E.D.F commander there that Ehdon is about to be attacked. I'll tell them something… Wouldn't be hard to believe after all the chaos that's just gone down on Mire… I'll get them to fly us out to the ruins… You'll see… Commander Enders is an old friend. He'll help us out."

Adam stares at him with a skeptical look.

"He will. Trust me." Darius says hoping Adam will.

Adam almost polishes off his drink and stands up. "I guess we'll find out soon enough Darius; till then…" Adam slams the last sip. "I think I need to be alone for a bit." He says and leaves Eve behind with Darius in the lounge.

CHAPTER 4

WHAT IT TAKES

Sub Chapter 1: "The Empire Responds"
Lucifer's base – "Okladore" – Mire

(FFDP – "Cradle to the Grave")

Lucifer is walking towards the launch bay of the base now fully dressed in his dark-armor that's made of a special metal blend of different alloys. Super light in weight but super strong in resisting damage. The design is his own and makes him look formidable and evil with spikes on the forearms, knees, shoulders and elbows. His sword is sheathed and strapped to his back in a case specially made for it. As he reaches the bay doors from the lower hall of the east wing; the steel door slides open and Lucifer enters the gigantic underground ship hanger. Captain Vraad Massar and General Ulric Urmack are standing at the lowered launch bay doors of the Mir'Denack. Captain Massar is dark skinned and short meaning he's from the Ozgolath region of Mire where the intense sun and gravity of the planets pole, shrunk these people and tanned their skin. Not making them any less dangerous than the Brua'Ada race of Gorgon, which Urmack is. Six feet nine inches tall and two hundred sixty pounds strong. Skin white as a ghost from living on the extreme edge of the Brua'Ada Province where gravity is weak and the sun shines for only five hours out of a twenty nine hour day cycle. Men who survive this harsh world can survive anything. Scars cover half of his blocky, muscular frame. He's wearing the black and red uniform of a Mirosian officer and salutes Lucifer as he approaches.

"Ahh Urmack… And Massar! So good to see you both up and ready to make history on this fine day. Tell me Massar… How have the engine output test gone on the last few tries?" Lucifer asks as he walks between the two men and motions for them to join him up the drop doors acting as ramps, and into the belly of the ship.

Massar and Urmack turn and walk along with him.

"Engine tests have got as good as ninety five percent efficiency, meaning they will get us off the ground and into space but once we break Mire's gravity we'll be at about fifty five percent until the cells can recharge." Massar reports.

"How long for a re-charge from fifty back to go back to ninety?" Lucifer asks.

"About eleven to twelve hours…"

"That's fine… the closest squadron of Imperial war ships are over fifteen hours away at best… Urmack how are the weapons systems coming along?"

"All cannons have test fired with a hundred percent success rate and shields have shown to withstand the enemy's weapons time and time again. We are all set to rule." Urmack says with his accent.

"Good! Then let's get all the last of our people aboard and leave this Rock! Sound the countdown; T-Minus thirty minutes and we hit the launch button!" Lucifer orders the men as he finds his way to the command bridge of the ship.

Lucifer enters the command bridge and looks around impressed by the neatness and cleanliness on the whole area. Computer terminals are spread about the entire room; most of them are holographic displays of engine power levels, space trajectory paths, coolant levels, live support systems… Everything to do with the ship is in his control as he takes a seat on the big gold framed, red silk upholstered, commanders chair. Captain Massar heads over to the hanger bay aboard the ship and relinquishes his over-all command to

Lucifer. On the command deck, the countdown begins. Outside of the base, the ground shakes as giant underground rollers are powered up by motors inside the base, dividing the huge launch-bay doors. It takes a few minutes for the concrete slabs to fully retract and reveal the Mir'Denack space-craft underneath. The ships engines roar to life with a loud wind and electric crackle. The anti-gravity, super-charged magnetic thrusters lift the ship out of the hanger and steadily up into the sky.

Planet Gorgon – Emperor's Council Room

IT'S A LARGE ROOM inside the Royal Palace with a mostly black carpet that has magnificent patterns running through it in white and gold. There's a big, solid marble topped, oval table in the middle of the room surrounded by chrome framed chairs with an upholstery almost identical to the carpet. Perfectly painted pictures adorn the walls and several desks and smaller tables sit in random spots pressed up against a wall or in a corner and out of the way. The center table can seat twenty-four people but only ten people sit at it now. Emperor Kattan is a big man in his late forties and is wearing a fine gold colored, silk, long sleeve shirt and bright silver colored dress pants; both items are made with a weave of something that makes them glimmer in the light. Sauldur Kattan is white skinned like most Gorgon born people. He has a comely brown goatee and short cut, wavy, brown hair with handsome facial features.

"So let's get this council meeting started!" He says loudly with a low baritone voice.

"Your excellency..." A council-man named Gregwar stands up.

"We are receiving reports from our spies on Mire that the police force and military groups there have begun to detain everyone on Mire who serves us or is in any way connected to our great empire. There have been altercations and casualties are mounting on both sides." He reports to Kattan.

"This is the craziest slap of news to the face I've ever had..." Sauldur replies and continues.

"What of President Kephness? Why hasn't he contacted us?"

"We fear that he's dead sire... A news report was just released on Mire about fifteen minutes ago." Gregwar says and pulls a Smart com out of his pocket and puts it on a built in small notch on the table top. It clicks into place and they all wait a moment as Gregwar presses a few buttons on his device to get the video feed going. In the middle of the marble table is a small glass ball which now lights up and begins playing a holographic, pre-recorded telecast of the events on Mire. All members of the meeting are silent as they watch.

"Horrific news comes to us tonight as our beloved President Steve Kephness has been assassinated."

A young female reporter announces and then cuts to a picture of the President with his family for a second then back to the reporter. "The official investigation is still underway but it's believed that the president was just making a routine stop at a military outpost to speak with some of his key advisors when a large group of terrorists attacked the base by surprise. There was a massive gun fight that resulted in the death of all the terrorist attackers and the President with his personal guard were gunned down too…" The reporter pauses and shakes her head in disbelief before carrying on.

"Several of the Terrorist have been identified as High Priests of the Holy Order of the Tree, a religious group we all know to be heavily involved with the Empire of Gorgon. Tensions are high in almost every city on Mire as the remaining presidential body; a group made up of councillors and judges has decreed that swift action must be taken to discourage any future acts of aggression. Military personnel have begun to round up and detain residents of Mire who have connections with the Empire. Probably for our good and their own good too as citizens of Mire look for answers and some form of revenge… From channel eight news, this is…" Gregwar cuts the end short by disconnecting his Smart com from the table top port.

"Suddenly the Plate-shift in the Varuna Province isn't that important anymore." Says Council-man Raymon two seats away from Gregwar.

"Gentlemen! All issues are important that concern the lives of Gorgon citizens. Did the plate-shift in Varuna province have any casualty's councillor?" Asks the Emperor.

"Only seven, your grace. And the tremors have already stopped, cleanup has begun. This Mire issue is a much bigger problem." Says the short and fat councilman Raymon.

"Indeed… And why do you think that is Councillor."

"The needs of the many out-weigh the needs of the few your Excellency. We currently have, or had just over fifteen thousand people roughly living on Mire. People who serve this Empire and work to make us prosper here on Gorgon. Ores are, or should I say were still trickling through to our markets… Not anymore if I understand things correctly."

"I believe you do understand Councillor… We must move quickly to put down this new threat. Who here has any idea of the enemy we face?" Asks Emperor Kattan.

Councillor Gregwar speaks up once again. "Again my Lord; my spies have reported back just hours ago but what they have gathered is that the Mirosian Military has been infiltrated by a terrorist known as Lucifer… He has been with the military there for a while as a science officer and has recently brainwashed the whole lot of them… Crazy right? I mean; who can brainwash thousands at a time right? …My spies also say that he ambushed the President, killing all of his guards too and then fabricated the story we just saw on the Mire news network."

"This Lucifer… A former science officer. What do we know of him?" Asks Kattan.

"Not much your grace. He's from Gorgon somewhere judging by his color and stature but Lucifer is not his real name so we have no records of his past. We do know that as of right now he has Mire on lockdown and any incursion of Imperial troops will most likely be met with extreme prejudice." Councillor Gregwar finishes saying and sits back down in his chair.

"Thank you Councillor Greg…" The Emperor is interrupted by a dignitary who was just outside the room. The man walks briskly towards him and whispers something in the Emperors ear, then turns about to leave. The others look on with curiosity.

"Wait! Are you sure?" Asks Kattan.

The dignitary nods and holds a Smart com in his hand which he now holds out for Kattan to take.

"Well gentlemen… It looks like our enemy wants to be found." The Emperor says and takes the Smart com then dismisses the man. "Satellites just picked up this ship now in high orbit over Mire…" Emperor Kattan places the Smart com in a port on the table and again the image flows to the central holo-projector ball so all can see. "It's not of any registered design, make or model so it's got to be him… Let's find out if he wants to talk…" Kattan presses some buttons on the device and speaks to it. "Smart com access Sat-Com. Core-Dex grid one…" He leans back and watches as the device navigates itself into a program that shows all the available satellites operating in the solar system. Sauldur Kattan now presses on an icon on the device that represents a satellite close to Mire and then thumbs the option for all open channels and speaks into the device.

"This is Emperor Sauldur Kattan of the Gorgonian Empire. I wish to speak to the one named Lucifer… Will you speak with me?" Kattan asks and the room goes silent for a spell. He tries again. "Lucifer… I know you're there in that strange ship over Mire… I can see you there… You're probably calling around, gathering a small army to prevent any of my ships from reaching Mire… I can predict you like all my enemies. Enemies that have fallen before me…" Static begins to fill the light of the hollo-globe, image emitter in the center of the table.

Lucifer is aboard his ship the Mir'Denack and sitting in his Commanders chair when an officer at the Communications station shouts his name.

"Commander Lucifer! I'm getting a message from the Emperor… It says he wants to talk with you." Announces the officer.

"Ah! It's about time…" He gets up from the chair. "Put it through to the ready room and place us on a secure channel." Orders Lucifer. And walks over to the farthest wall from his chair where a door blends in; it automatically slides open as Lucifer gets real close. He walks through to enter a room with a rectangular wooden table and a bunch of office chairs surrounding it. The door closes and Lucifer takes a seat at the table. He swipes his thumb across the surface and a small panel slides open in front of him as well as one in the center of the table. Just under the surface of the table is a small computer console (touch screen) at almost every available seat around it. In the middle is one of those Holo-globes of glass and crystals that display a holographic image just above it. Lucifer touches a few icons on the port in front of him and presto, Sauldur Kattan's face and upper body appears in an image of light above the device.

"So you are the one called Lucifer, yes?" The Emperor asks from his seat inside his Palace's Council-room on Gorgon.

Lucifer decides to hold nothing back and begins talking in a deep, raspy, demonic like voice. *"Yes, I'm Lucifer… Emperor Sauldur Kattan; have you called to barter for the lives of your people we have taken prisoner?"*

"Those people did nothing wrong and should be freed… What are your terms? What is you want in exchange for their lives? Money, Gold, Power? What is it? I can give it to you." Kattan says calmly and with all seriousness hoping to strike a bargain with this man dressed in black armor and speaking to him like growling wolf or something.

"Wrong? They served you and your Empire. That's wrong to me… But I will free them… If you meet my space fleet in battle at this location…" Lucifer pauses to press a bunch of icons on the table computer and transmit a set of coordinates in space. The Emperor gets the message on his table computer and ignores it for the moment.

"So you just want to fight me?" Asks Sauldur.

"No. I want to obliterate you… It's time for Mire and the human race to be free… Free from being raped by Empire scum… Just take, take, take… It all ends now." Lucifer replies.

"Obliterate me you said? Ha, you have but one ship! I can see you with a satellite… I have over two hundred ships. Destroyer class war-ships! And you're challenging me!? I'll be at these coordinates soon so don't back out on me you animal because I'm coming for you."

"I'll be waiting for you there." Lucifer finishes the call and hits the end button on the screen in front of him. He swipes his thumb over the table the opposite way he did to activate the computer systems. The Holo-globe retracts into the surface and both the panels close to make it look like a table with nothing else on top once again.

Lucifer exits the room and is back on the command bridge of his deadly new ship. He returns to his chair and thinks for a moment… "Telemetry!" He shouts to the officer at the station to his right. "Plot a course, pre-program Lima-Alpha! Engines station, engage when ready! Full power!"

"Yes sir!" They all shout back in turn and the space ship is quickly on its way.

Lucifer gets out of his chair after a few minutes and walks over to his special ops station in the near left corner of the room from his chair. The officer there is slim and built woman named Rennea Zinara. She wears the black and red uniform like everyone else there. Her hair is black, cut short and spiked up.

"What's the status of the Sayberus Zinara?" Lucifer ask from behind her catching her off guard.

She stands too and salutes him."Commander Lucifer! The Sayberus is…" She pauses and turns back to her hollo-com console and quickly enters a series of commands and the device suddenly lights up and displays an image of the solar system with the sun in the middle and all the planets in their orbits. "The Sayberus launched right after us and is now seventy-one sectors from rally point one." She answers after reading the space chart on the screen below the holographic image. "Placing it right here." She says and points her finger into the holo-image of the solar system; where she pauses, a red light appears to mark the spot.

"Good… Take a walk with me lieutenant Zinara." Says Lucifer.

"You know how long our trip is right?" Lucifer asks her as they both leave the bridge and walk down a hall towards the elevator system.

"Like fifteen hours; give or take ten, fifteen minutes. Why?" She asks.

Lucifer stays silent for a spell. They reach the elevator and Lucifer presses the button to summon it. "Do you believe in me Rennea?" He asks as he takes off his helmet and holds it at his side.

The Elevator door opens and they step inside. The door closes behind them and Lucifer presses the button marked "LQ" for Living Quarters. Rennea clues in to what Lucifer wants.

"Of course I believe in you. You are strong and only a strong man can free Mire from the Empire…" She says and looks at him. "Can't wait to get the rest of that armor off you M'Lord." She says.

Lucifer smiles at her with thoughts oh so sinful.

BACK ON GORGON in the Emperors Palace, Sauldur Kattan is furious at Lucifer for taking him so lightly. He stands up at the head of the table in his Council room still looking at the now lifeless holo-com.

"I want my fleet ready in one hour!" He says loudly. "We will destroy him and his pathetic little ship, then free our people from prison and liberate Mire! This Lucifer is a poser and nothing more..." He says and looks around the room. "You all have your posts... Take care of Gorgon in my absence. I'm heading for my ship to assemble the fleet. A hundred ships, which is over half the armada, will come with me. Should be enough to turn this lunatic into space dust." Boasts Sauldur Kattan and with nothing left to say, he leaves the Council-room.

CH. 4 – Sub Chapter 2: Prepare for Panjacca Jungle

ADAM FINDS HIMSELF stepping out from the launch centers shuttle-hall and into the space center itself. Eve and Darius are with him but he also keeps half expecting to see his mom walking along with them. Pangs of despair hit him again as he knows she isn't going to be there but this time he is able to conceal it well enough and just keeps walking onward through a sea of people who are all trying to go here or there; it matters not to him. They make their way out of the launch center and at the street side they all pile into a Daxaur-Cart. The driver opens the window to the inner cab and ask them. "Where to my friends?"

"The Cobalt Palace Hotel. Do you know where it is?" Asks Eve from inside the cart.

"Yes I know it. It'll be one and a quarter credits and because of thieves, I take payment up-front." Says the driver of the Dino-taxi. "There's a computer console right below this window; see it? Place your card over that and if it glows gorgen, we go." Says the driver. Adam shakes his head in disbelief and gets his card out of his wallet to do what the driver just told him to do.

Almost a half hour later, the three of them are walking through the door of their hotel room at the "Cobalt Palace" on Pangaea – Ehdon Colony. The suite is luxurious with a tear-drop shaped, white couch and a state of the art Virtual reality game console and Holo-com emitter in the mid left portion of the main room. The kitchen and dining room are one in the same and raised by a foot above the main room in the far right as you walk in the door. A hallway veers off to the left of the door and leads to the bedrooms and one washroom. A nice chandelier hangs on the ceiling and tasteful paintings adorn the walls which are painted a nice tan color.

"I'm calling firsts on the washroom." Eve says and walks off down the hallway.

Adam looks at Darius who is closing the suite's main door behind him. "My head is pounding. So much has happened that I just couldn't fall asleep on the shuttle. Even though my body was screaming for it… I'm feeling it now so I'm heading right for bed." Adam says.

Darius looks at him with exhausted eyes. "Me too Adam…" Darius looks at the suites clock mounted on the wall by the kitchen. "Six hours till sunrise here. Let's get some sleep and in the morning, we'll figure all the rest out." Adam nods his head once and disappears down the hall to pass out in his bed.

Crawling under his beds blankets he quickly gets to seeing color patterns which quickly become faces of people and also swirls of color turn into landscapes of potential elaborate dreams. Adam suddenly feels someone crawl under the blankets with him. He doesn't startle or even move. Adam just breathes in through his nose and right away he knows its Eve…

"She never did anything to deserve dying like that…" She says to him without really knowing if he is awake. She suspected that he wasn't sleeping.

"No she didn't Adam… All this brings back feelings of when my mom and dad died… I remember watching through the crowd as the riot-squad opened fire… They were shot down in front of me and all

I felt was like falling… Falling into a pit… And then you with your parents came and pulled me out… You can't fall into that pit now Adam." Eve says softly inches from his ear and hugs him from behind.

"Is this genuine Eve love that penetrates my soul right now or the love of a sister?" He asks himself. He can't be sure and is so very afraid to ask as a misunderstanding at this level can be disastrous. Adam decides to keep it mellow. He grabs Eve's arm and curls it over his waste so her elbow is at his belly and he holds her hand in his at chest level.

"I love you so much Eve, you have no idea." He says and squeezes her hand gently.

Within moments he falls into a deep sleep and so does Eve… Sleeping there in a bed together without it being naughty…

The light of the sun shines through the cracks of the bedroom window curtains and catches Adam's Eyes. Even though they are closed it disrupts his REM sleep and knocks him back into reality. Eve is still sleeping next to him and low and behold, another part of him is awake too and at attention. "Damn it." He thinks to himself as he lays still trying not to wake Eve. "Umm, stinky Daxaur poop… Aaah, fat old men in skin tight trunks… getting kicked in the head last night… Oh, that did it." His little man is settling down and he reaches his hand to the side of his head to press on the bruise there from being kicked by Krezler. It hurts him a lot. As he attempts getting up and out of bed; his brain feels like it could explode inside his skull so he kneels over and sort of crawl-walks over to the washroom where he turns the shower on to fairly hot and climbs inside.

Eve wakes up at the same time Darius wakes up in the other room and they both step out into the hall at the same time and make for the washroom. Just as they get to the door washroom door, Adam opens it and steps out looking at the two of them. "Well I'm glad I woke up when I did. You two can share right?" He asks jokingly with a smirk and walks past Darius and into the kitchen.

"You first Darius… I'm most likely going to take a while." Eve says and watches Darius nod and step inside then close the door behind him.

"Is there any fruit juices in that fridge!?" Eve asks and follows Adam to the kitchen.

The morning turns closer to noon and the three of them are finished breakfast and are watching a news cast on the rooms Holo-com about the onset of a war between the freedom fighters of Mire and the oppressive Empire of Gorgon. This time it's a man reporting.

"Tensions are high between Mire and Gorgon as forces are gathering in space and it's most likely that the Royal armada will be leaving space above Gorgon within the hour. The meeting place is unknown but analysts say that wherever they meet, there will be a battle. We've seen this once before about twenty years ago with the militant group who called themselves the Mara'Kree. A small army of soldiers with cybernetic implants and made up of defectors from both the Mirosian and Gorgonian army's. The result was that the Empire won, wiping them all out. The feeling here on Gorgon is that the same thing is about to occur and then peace will once again stand firm between our two worlds..."

Darius shuts the Holo-com emitter off and stands up to think. "This isn't going to be like last time..." Darius says distractedly.

"What do you know? You <u>think</u> the Empire is going to lose this time? After winning every battle they ever had?" Adam asks.

Darius paces and thinks harder. "I don't know Adam. You don't just start a war with the Empire and not have a strategy... I don't know why but I just feel like finding the lost colony Odaan is going to shed so much light on everything else going on between Gorgon and Mire... Like everything is connected somehow."

"It is rather strange that my dad had detailed files about it on his computer..." Says Adam.

"That's right, he did and the coordinates that you wrote down on your arm."

"Oh crap! I took a shower this morning and forgot about them." Adam checks his arm. "No, it's all washed off. I can't read it anymore." Adam shakes his head disappointed in himself. "And my dad's computer is back on Mire, there's nothing we can do."

"It's a good thing I trained my mind to have photographic memory." Announces Darius. "The coordinates are…" He closes his eyes to better remember. "20.638728 latitude - 78.661446 longitude."

"Umm, yeah… That sounds right. Wow, you have to teach me that Darius." Adam says.

"It's more of an acquired thing; right now we need to get to the Ehdon Defence Force (EDF) and talk to Commander Enders. Armond Enders is an old friend of mine or should I say opponent… I was his trials combat opponent long ago and failed him… But I think I have a way to convince him to help us. Both of you will have to play along, and we're going to have to bend the truth a little, just enough to get Enders to fly us into the jungle… You both ok with that?" Darius asks them. Both Adam and Eve agree. "Ok here's what we do…"

Darius, Adam and Eve step out of a bright green hover-cab with white trim panels and walk up to the building; going through the doors they walk into a building full of people. Once you walk in the doors it opens up to a reception counter with walkways in between five separate steel topped counters; three clerks per counter and behind those is a sea of desks in a big open office area that rises up two tiers as you make your way to the back of it. Darius leads them up to one of the counters and face to face with a female clerk.

"Welcome to EDF Command, what brings you here today?" She asks.

"I need to… Sorry, my name is Darius Siscerelle and I've been sent on behalf of the Holy Order and the Empire of Gorgon. I need to speak with Commander Enders right away."

"I see." Says the clerk.

Darius sees her name tag read "Sonya".

"Do you have some sort of I.D card?" She asks.

"Look Sonya; I'm an old friend of Armond and must see him right now… The solar system is at war and I have Intel for him…

He'll I.D me the second he sees my face and that will be good enough for now. Do you understand the severity of the situation?" He asks. "Call him on your headset and tell him my name. Darius Siscerelle."

He steps away from the counter and watches the clerk get on her headset communicator and tell the commander who's here to see him. Moments Later, Commander Enders steps out of his office at the top, far back tier of the large room. He stops at the stairs and looks right at Darius; the clerk sees him too. Enders waves them up and off the three of them go; past the counters, through the sea of desks and people to reach the top tier of the room. Enders ushers them into his office and then takes his seat behind his desk. Six chairs sit in procession in front of his desk.

"Please Darius, friends; have a seat and let's talk…" Enders says and watches as his company does as he asks. "You know Darius, there was a time not long ago where I hoped to never see your face again…

But now I'm actually glad to see you.

You're the only official High Priest to get a hold of us since all this madness began on Mire the other day… What the hell is going on Darius? None of my communiqué's are getting through to Officers on Mire and Gorgon. What can you tell me about the situation?" Enders Asks.

He is a tall and lean man; not overly built with muscle but still a deadly fighter. He wears the green, brown and white camouflage uniform of the EDF.

"We have been gathering Intel lately and just recently, several spies have confirmed a hostile take-over of Mire has occurred. They plan to beat the Empire using a technology long thought to be lost, we aren't sure what the weapon is just yet but we know that they are heading here to Pangaea to get it." Darius says to him.

Armond scrunches his left eye and looks curiously at Darius. "What technology? What weapon? We have nothing that both Mire and Gorgon don't already have." Counters Enders.

"It's not here on Ehdon; it's somewhere in the ruins of Odaan… The story of the first colony is true; a general in the service of the

Empire confirmed it. That general is this young man and woman's father…" Darius says and looks to Adam to join in.

"It's true; the files were on his computer the whole time. The only problem is that our home was on Mire and they attacked us before we could even think to copy the files once we found them." Adam adds.

"So why would they go to war with Gorgon without this weapon?"

"Our only guess is that they must have already found it long ago and made a copy of it… Now they can come here in full force and recover the original without fear of the Empire. You see? No fear because they know that with this weapon they will be unstoppable."

Enders shakes his head at him. "I don't know how you know what you know, but the enemies ships are heading our way… And the Emperor himself is leading a space fleet to cut him off. This can't just be a coincidence." He scratches his chin and looks deeply into Darius's eyes. "You have the coordinates of Odaan don't you?" He asks and cracks a sly smile at him. Darius nods his head, and smiles back.

"Gunship?" Darius asks with a bigger grin on his face. Enders thinks for a moment and then slowly nods his head. "Gunship it is… You're all going tomorrow morning though… The Mirosian ships are still some fifteen hours away…Today you will gear up and I'll assign the crew that will be escorting you. Get familiar with your weapons and armor Darius; friends… The Jungle is a ruthless bitch and will chew up the weak like puppy chow… Go to the front counter and find Karla; she will show you three over to the armory."

Darius, Adam and Eve make to leave his office when he adds one last thing.

"And Darius, I want updates. The moment anything happens in that jungle; you got it?" Darius nods his head and leaves the office door open behind him.

Adam, Darius and Eve make their way back to the front counters and finds Karla staring at them as they approach. "Right this way guys and gal." Karla says and leads the way. She is tall, like six foot three inches tall and slim yet muscular. Her hair sort of dances behind her when she walks with a dark brown pony-tail, and she is quite good looking. Darius is quite taken by her and catches up to walk by her side.

"I'm Darius… So Karla, how long have you been working with the EDF?"

"Since I was a young recruit from Gorgon eight years ago."

"Really… I was in here just two years ago and several times before that and I never saw you at the counters."

She opens a door to the buildings stairwell and walks down the stairs as she talks. "That's because I started here as a grunt and worked my way through basic training and over the years I've been in the scenes behind all the P.R. crap… Commander Enders just transferred me to the counters three months ago." She says then looks into an eye scanner on the wall beside the door at the bottom of the stairs. Karla opens the door to the lower level of the base and allows her guest to walk in first.

"Well I'm glad he did…" Darius says while walking past and looks into her eyes for a moment. Karla turns her gaze away somewhat bashful and smiles; then when Darius is past her, she glances at his backside and eye's him up.

Karla retakes the lead in the group and stops them after a short twenty foot walk down a wide, steel panelled hallway. At the end are three doors. There's a large door in the center of the hall with two smaller steel doors there; one on each side of the big door. Karla leads them into the room to the left of the big one. This room is a long rectangle shaped warehouse of weaponry. Shelving and racks against the walls here hold all sorts of guns, while crates are neatly organized on the floor. Each crate holds weapons or armor of some kind or another. Karla leads them farther to the back of the room…

"So all those guns and armor at the front are for battling people, so we won't use any of them; instead we will be using these here." She says and stops at the back wall and gestures to what looks like a medieval times museum display. "You will be wearing those pieces of armor overtop of these." She says and pulls a onesie suit made of some special fabric, out from a nearby crate. "This is something we call fabri-tech. Clothing that responds to the environment and the body. In the cold and rain, it closes up an outer membrane to prevent the person wearing it from getting wet and cold; cycling your own body heat to keep you warm. It can also sense toxins in the body; the sensors are compatible with any Smart com. All you have to do is hold your Smart com. up to this node on the collar here while holding your sync button and presto; your vitals will appear on the screen. There's even a nifty little pocket for your Smart com devices right here." Karla points to a spot on the suit. "Another interesting feature is the glide tech. If you ever find that you have to leap from a cliff, spaceship, or other types of airships there's a strong magnetic cable that slides down on these thin lines here under the arms and down the length of your rib cage which deploys a super strong polymer cloth automatically as it senses the velocity of a free fall which activates it. This is also built into the crotch area and shoots the fabric down between your legs for an optimal glide. Of course a parachute is recommended when falling long distances." She smirks at them and carries on. "We fight with guns so fighting humans with guns makes sense but the creatures of Panjacca jungle don't know guns; don't care about guns either. They have claws, sharp teeth and big mouths and many have scales, or plates of armor and tails that can kill. We have found that shooting them isn't as effective as a clean slash with a very sharp sword or chop of an axe. The metal armor is made of a titanium and dual carbon steel alloy; it's really light to wear and super strong against the slashing claws or biting jaws of meat eating dyno's... Thing is, dyno's aren't all you have to worry about; the bugs in the jungle are just as big as us and can kill us just as easily as dyno's... Well, I'll let the bunch of ya get changed and pick your weapons. If you have trouble with any of the pieces of armor, just... See that wall panel there?" Karla asks while pointing to the rear wall of the room; a section between two display cases has a small computer console built into it. "It's a laser-light scanner, so just scan the piece of armor three inches in front of it and it will tell you where to place the piece and how it connects… Come find me in the training room when you're done; that would be the through the big doors you were all wondering about a minute ago." Karla says and leaves them; they all watch her leave.

"Well she sure is an interesting woman huh Darius? She's beautiful and super smart. Bit of a sense of humor… You like her don't you?" Adam asks after the door closes and Karla's no longer there. Eve gives him a light shot in the back of the ribs as they all still stare at the door as if she'll walk back in at any moment. He looks at her and she shakes her head at him and shrugs her shoulders to ask "Why?" without saying a word. Adam winces and presses his hand against the spot she hits as he looks over at her and shakes his head while shrugging his shoulder as if saying "What? No harm in asking right?" Darius turns around and both of them look onward as if nothing was said between them. "I'm not surprised that you've picked up on that Adam… Friggin school of the order teaches us all kinds of stuff huh?" Darius says half joking and half serious. "Doesn't matter right now; we have a mission… So let's get on this and do some training. God knows you two brats are gonna need it."

Fifteen minutes after; Darius, Adam and Eve step out of the armory and back into the hallway all dressed in armor. Darius walks over to the far edge of the door where the frame-work has a computer panel with a small screen. He swipes the green glowing icon to open the door. The three of them walk into the large underground room that looks like a big jungle gym for adults. Four hundred and fifty feet long and two hundred and eighty feet wide, with twenty foot ceilings. There's climbing walls to the right as they walk in, with ropes you can grab as you reach the top of the walls and swing over to the makeshift wooden fort in the middle to land on a balcony where if you miss you fall down six feet onto some puffy blue matts. The fort is a fairly big one with two sides and rope woven Gang-planks in between for soldiers to cross; if they fall, there's more blue matt's below. To the far left is an elaborate obstacle course with large sand bags that swing on poles and are timed randomly to strike you down if you don't react quickly enough.

"This is the best training facility I've seen so far." Says Adam.

Karla sees them gazing around at all the training room has to offer and makes herself known. "Hey there Darius, Eve, Adam… Welcome to the training room… I have arranged a couple of special alterations to the course. We do these for everyone going into the jungle; the bad news is that they are hard moves to perfect, the good news is that here, you don't die for screwing them up and get to try again… You also get to know what those alterations are."

"Sweet." Adam says and gets looks from both Eve and Darius.

"You're either really good or a sucker for punishment young man… Any-how, while you three climb the walls; one of my recruits will be at the top throwing water balloons with died water at you. If you get hit it means a falling boulder has struck you and you are dead. Repel down and start again; after you make it up to ten feet they will stop tossing the balloons so you can get to the top easier. At the top you will swing to the bases balcony over the gap but my recruits up there…" Karla points to a rafter beam on the ceiling where three recruits are sitting with a sand bag tied to a rope in each one of their hands. "Those swords you have holstered to your backs… As you hold the rope with one hand and swing across, you will wield your swords in your free hand as you defend against these oncoming sand bags. Two for each of you but one at a time to be fair… Then in the base are three round, arm shields; with these you will cross the rope bridges while being fired upon by these bean bag cannons on the opposite side." She points to the cannons on the bases parapets. "Don't worry, the psi will be set on a low rate but still, getting hit with one isn't going to feel good so use your shields and dodge everything else. Again, once you get close they will stop firing to allow you to cross the bridge but once you get to the other side. You will be faced with two of my recruits in a wrestling or combat match; the shields and swords are forbidden. It's a straight up handicap match because in the jungle, you are always at a handicap and will know how it feels.

Good thing is that win or lose the match; you don't have to do the course over again."

(Bassnectar – "Underwater")

Adam, Eve and Darius stand side by side by side as they get ready to climb the wall and battle the course; they wait for Karla to begin the countdown. "Everyone in place!?" She shouts across the room.

"Hoo Raa!" Is all that Karla's recruits say back to her.

"Ok… Three… Two… One! Go, go, go!"

Eve, Adam and Darius dash towards the climbing wall and start to climb. Two feet up and Darius has to hug the wall like a worm to avoid an ink balloon coming down at him. Three feet up and Adam has to let go of his left hands grip on the wall and lean out to avoid an ink balloon to the face. The recruits at the top are making a game of it and trying their hardest to hit them. Eve is level with Adam and looks up too see an ink ball coming for her; she hugs the wall like Darius just did and feels the ball graze her back and then hears it go "Spatt!" on the matting below. They continue to climb. Another ink ball comes down for Adam who lets go of his right hand grip; holding firm with his left hand, he leans out of the way. Darius pulls the same maneuver to avoid one and looks over to see Eve get hit on the left shoulder. He recovers his grip and continues to climb has Eve has to start again.

Adam and Darius avoid three more ink balloons on the way up and make it to the safe zone. Eve makes short work of the first six feet knowing where the grips are now; she leans away twice and hugs the wall once to avoid hits and finds herself in the safe zone watching Adam and Darius above get ready to leap the gap… With their ropes firmly gripped at the top of the walls, they unsheathe their swords at the same time and share a glance of pure exhilaration. They look down at the knot in the rope where they need to place their feet once they leap and take a deep breath. "Weeyaaa!!" The both of them shout as they leap off the edge of the top of a twelve foot tall wall holding a rope in one hand, sword in the other. As they swing across the gap, the sand bags get tossed at them by the recruits in the rafters. Darius re-adjust his body on the rope as he swings to avoid one sand bag by a couple inches. The second sand bag he takes a heavy swing at with his sword in a controlled spin and cleaves it in half. Adam sees the first bag come for him and points his sword right at it, impaling it as it connects with his proximity. A bad move as the momentum of the bag carries on past him, pulling him sideways and into a spin. His sword pulls free and as he spins, Adam instinctively thrust it out to his left following in the spin. He slashes the second sand bag in half just before it would have hit him. Now at the end of the gap, Darius is first to let go of his rope and land perfectly on the balcony of the fort. Adam comes in spinning and lets go at the edge and off balance; teetering there and about to fall. Darius reaches over and grabs Adam by the shoulder cuff of his armor; hauling him onto the balcony. They both stand there and look back at Eve who is just making her way to the top platform of the climbing walls. She pulls herself up and grips the rope tied at the top and pulls the draw-string to untie it. She then unsheathes her sword, gripping it firmly in her free hand; she looks over the edge and shakes her head.

"You can do this Eve; trust yourself!" Darius shouts back.

Eve leaps off the top of the climbing wall with the rope firmly in her right hand; she finds the knot with her feet quickly and begins to swing the gap. Not even half way across and the first sandbag is coming her way. She pulls herself up on the rope with the hand that grips it and lifts her whole body weight up on the rope to straddle the upper length of it with her muscular thighs. Making a loop with the rope around her ankles, she reaches out with the sword as she is totally upside-down in the swing. She strikes the first sandbag with a strong slash and is spun by the momentum to swing to her left where she strikes out at the second sandbag cleaving it in half with just as much ease as the first. As Eve comes to the end of her swing to the fort, she releases the grip on the rope with her legs and swings from upside-down to right-side up and pushes off flawlessly to land on the balcony in a crouch. Adam and Darius' jaws drop as they can't believe what they just saw.

"Holy Smokes Eve! How about we just let you loose on some enemies and pray for their souls! How'd you do that!?" Darius asks.

"I don't know… Just been practicing in gymnastics lately; it all came naturally to me… Come on; let's keep going." Says Eve.

They sheathe their swords and make their way into the inner rooms of the fort. Just before the exit of the rooms to the inner sanctum of the fort, they see the round shields that they are to use sitting on the floor in the corners of the rooms. They each grab a shield and fit it onto their right arm; surprisingly the shield doesn't interfere with their armor. They peek out the opening to the forts inner sanctum and see the gang-planks they have to cross to the other side.

"If we each take separate bridges, it'll be harder for them to target us with those bean-bag cannons." Darius says; Adam and Eve agree and they each pick the bridge they will cross.

"Ok; on the count of three…" Adam says and begins to count. "One… Two… Three!"

They dash out from the forts hiding rooms and make for their own gang-planks to cross. Not even five feet down the hanging, rope bridges and they hear the "Poof" sounds of the cannons firing bean bags at them. Eve grabs the rope handrails and leans back to avoid a beanbag coming for her head then springs herself forward and blocks a beanbag with her arm shield; she keeps going. Adam and Darius are forced to block and dodge beanbags as well, but their balance on the teetering suspended bridges isn't as good as Eve's; she makes it across first. On this side of the fort, the balcony is several feet wider to allow for hand to hand combat. She sees the doorway in front of her that leads to the ramp down to ground level and victory, but two female recruits are blocking the way.

"Remember the rules." Says one of the recruits. "Lose the shield and sword… Just place them off to the side there." She points to Eve's right.

Adam and Darius make it across the rope bridges and see Eve already placing her sword and shield down. They look across to their doorways they need to get through to victory and see four big guys; recruits of the EDF, and all are wearing jungle camouflage clothing. Darius and Adam lay their weapon and shield down and slowly step towards the door. Adam plans his next moves carefully; Darius has no real plan other than to counter anything the two men have to throw at him.

"You two little runts couldn't hurt a fly without wings. Come get some, time to take you boys to school!" Adam taunts his two opponents. They take the bait; getting angry with Adam's lack of respect, the two of them charge out the doorway at Adam who is about eight paces away from the edge of the forts balcony behind him. Adam turns to run away from his attackers and takes three good sized steps to the edge; he hears them following close behind probably intent on just pushing him off the edge and calling him a coward. But Adam ducks down low as he stops at the edge to corkscrew, springboard himself backwards and low to the ground. The resulting move catches both his recruits by surprise; Adam's elbow clips one on the knee while the rest of Adam's head and neck, slams into the other recruits upper thigh. Both collisions happen as the recruits are still in forward momentum and so they both trip, stumble and roll of the edge of the bases balcony to fall six feet down and land on some mats. Adam looks over and smiles as he doesn't see his attackers anymore. He's on his rump about to get up when."Hmmm; I wonder how Eve and Darius are doing. Maybe I'll just sit here and watch for a bit." He thinks to himself.

Adam watches on… Eve is having a hard time with the ladies that Karla chose to fight her. One has her in a head lock while the other punches her in the gut twice and then in the face once. The woman attacking Eve is short while the one holding her head is tall. Eve sees the short one is about to give her a sweep kick to the head and as she comes up with her foot in full swing Eve pulls her body weight down and inward slightly causing the short recruit to miss her head and strike the tall recruit hard on the elbow of the arm around Eve's neck.

The tall woman's arm goes limp as she shrieks in pain and much discomfort to say the least. The short woman also shouts out in pain having connected her foot to a hard elbow bone. Leaping in place on one foot, she holds her other foot in her hands trying to relieve the pain of connecting full force to an elbow. Eve takes advantage and leaps up with the tall one right behind her; Eve wraps her right arm around the woman's head so her jaw is resting on Eve's shoulder bone. Her feet are in the air and now she heaves herself back down with the help of gravity to deliver two moves. As Eve's rump connects with the floorboards, the tall woman's jaw smashes hard against Eve's shoulder bone sending a shock through her nerves there which causes her brain to temporarily shut down; K.O. Her second move as she lands on the floor boards is a straight kick with her left leg to the ankle area of the short recruit who is hopping on that one leg of hers. As the tall woman bounces off Eve's shoulder and goes out-cold, the short woman is sent forward face first from standing to smash her head on the floorboards. Eve rolls over and gets to her feet; she looks over to see Darius beside her and then beyond him to see Adam sitting comfortably there just watching.

Darius blocks a punch from one of his attackers and then leaps back to avoid a spin kick from the other while the first jumps at him with a superman punch at the same time. Darius backs up close to the edge of the forts balcony and watches the two almost identical men switch places and close in on him. Darius fakes a right hook to the guy on his right who flinches slightly and then leaps towards him with a right spin kick that Darius steps into and catches with his left arm. At the same time he grabs the man's leg, Darius grabs him by the neck with his right hand to spin him around and then release him. The result is the recruit goes sailing in a spin, off the edge of the balcony, but now Darius's back is turned to his second opponent who lunges at him to tackle him off the edge. Darius hears this man start to dash at him, he bends his knees and leaps into the air performing a back-flip. Just as the recruit dashes in Darius is in mid-air, the recruit reaches out to grasp thin air and goes flying off the edge of the balcony. But the recruit is saved as grabs the rope hand rail of a close by bridge. After he lands, Darius sees the recruit grab the rope and dangle for a moment then pull himself up and look back at him; he simply waves goodbye to the man as there is no one there at the doorway to stop him from walking out. No one to stop all three of them and so they walk out of the doorways and down the ramp on the side to step foot in the winners box (Lines painted on the floor). They watch a bunch of other recruits head up the ramp and then come back down with the ladies Eve knocked out.

"Very impressive!" Karla says as she approaches the group. "That was one of our harder difficulty settings and you three did great. Eve! I loved that acrobatics you showed up there on the rope swing. Adam!" She smiles and shakes her head at him. "I've never seen taunting and misdirection used so well; both your opponents out of the way in about ten seconds from the first encounter. And Darius… You never got hit with anything; you did the whole course flawlessly and… Nice backflip at the end there." A couple of recruits have gathered each of their swords and interrupt them to give them back. "Now that we know you can survive, let's go check out the Gunship. She's on the roof nestled in a walled up landing and takeoff pad… There's an elevator just outside this room, it's the one door out there you haven't opened." Karla tells them and turns about to lead the way there. Darius is first to follow, then Adam and Eve. They walk out the training room door and wait in the hall as the elevator makes its way down to get them. The door finally opens and the four of them pile in.

"So Karla, what kind of things do you do when not on this base?" Darius asks making things kind of awkward.

"I'm dedicated to a twenty year term. I don't get off this base."

Darius doesn't know how to proceed after that so he keeps quiet.

The elevator doors open and the four of them step out on the roof top which has a wall going all the way around it. Straight across from them as they walk out the door is a large, sleek looking, black painted quad-chopper. Four arms extend up and away from the large hull in an arching shape and at the end of each there's a powerful oxigel fueled thruster. The main hull is made up of three sections; the rear (loading) section of the craft has one big drop down door.

"Off to each side of the drop down door are these glass spheres big enough for a person to fit inside and operate the Gatling gun within; the muzzle has a series of sliding tracks cut into the glass that it can follow as well as the ball or sphere itself can swivel a bit in its housing. A limited defence but those guns can shred a target to bits if it comes into the crosshairs. The middle of the ship bulbs out a bit from the front and back to allow for more space for things like the fuel tanks, ammunition, on board computers and passengers among more things. And at the front of course we have the cockpit and a small privy just behind that, but more thrilling is the Stinger missile packs that sit in the housing just to the sides of the cockpit. Just below the cockpit is an auto tracking Gatling gun that's similar to the ones on the back side. That there in the middle is an emergency hatch for if passengers ever have to bail out. This thing can make some crazy moves if it has to." She watches as the three of them walk around the ship and marvel at it.

"So I've decided that because a lot of the recruits want to harm you for schooling them so badly, you three will have to stay in the mechanics shacks up here on the roof just for the one night."

"But we have all of our things back at the hotel." Adam points out.

"Don't worry; we will arrange for everything to stay the same for the next day. When you three return from your mission, all your things will still be there. We just can't afford to have any of you be late on the departure. The trip there and back will be between four and five hours; depending on how far in you have to go. There's a shack with two beds over there." Karla changes the topic and leads them to the edge of the wall that hold the elevator and points to the shack another fifty feet down an open section of the roof. "Two of you can stay in there and the third will have to stay in the smaller shack over by Gunship back there." She says and walks them back to the ship to point out the shack off to the corner of the far left wall. Karla then hits the button at the elevator wall to call it. "Let's take you three to the kitchens. You're all probably hungry." She says and steps into the now open elevator; they all follow her.

"So if we're in the mechanics shacks, where's the mechanics going to stay?" Eve asks concerned she's pushing someone out.

"Don't worry Eve we gave them a vacation to Emerald Bay Resort. After all the hard work they've done to maintain this craft and the buildings infrastructure; they deserve it."

The door opens and they step out to a large food court. Tables and chairs all over the place along with a lot of people sitting at them. Along the right wall is an enclosed area with several easy swing doorways; that would be the kitchen and just in front of that long enclosure is a countertop full of trays with many different types of foods in them. Eve takes a deep breath in and can't believe the blend of so many awesome smells. Suddenly they are all hungry and rush to the food line to grab a plate. Karla leaves them there and attends to other duties.

They turn in for the night and at the rooftop, the three of them decide on sleeping arrangement. "You two should take the far shack with the two beds and I'll take this one here; I hope they changed the sheets and blankets for us." Darius says. Adam and Eve agree on the far shack. "Well, Good night Darius. Guess we'll see you bright and early in the morning huh?" Adam says.

"Yeah I guess so… Good night you two." Darius says and walks away from them. He walks the distance over to the shack and steps inside. A ceiling light is on and illuminates the room; a coat/uniform closet stands against the wall as he walks in, its doors are 2/3rds closed. To his right the room opens up and is split in half by a cheap plywood wall.

The front half has a ton of tool cabinets full of tools and a full-on work bench between them. On the other side of the wall is a sink, small table and a bed against the back end wall. "Oh good; clean bedding." He says as pulls the blanket up to his nose and smells it. He begins to strip off his armor and then unzips his fabri-tech onesie and hears something behind him as picks it up to place it on the table.

Now in just his underwear, Darius turns around to see Karla standing there wearing a tight black sports bra and black spandex shorts.

"You find me attractive don't you Darius?" She asks and steps towards him.

He swallows hard and answers "Yes".

"I noticed you… being so nervous and shy. It gets me going Darius…" She stops in front of him and closes the distance so that she is just inches from his mouth, arms, and hip.

"You're strong… But most men who venture into the jungle are dead men, they just don't know it until it hits them out there."

"We're all dead… Those of us who sit in our homes and take no risks… Seek no adventures and find contentment in doing nothing with our lives… Me; I feel most alive when close to death… I also feel most alive with you, here, right now." He says starting to get aroused and kisses her passionately.

"Take me like it's your last night alive on this planet…"

She kisses him back passionately and gets to taking his clothes off; he works to get her out of hers.

"Last night alive in the solar system." She says and takes him down to the bed and…

Adam and Eve walk into their shack and see a place much like the one Darius is in but slightly bigger to accommodate two people. They strip their armor, settle into their beds and fall asleep soon after…

CHAPTER 5

DISCOVERY & DESTRUCTION
Pangaea - Ehdon Colony - EDF base

A dam and Eve wake at the crack of dawn and re-dress themselves in their fabri-tech and pieces of armor, then step outside and walk around the corner of the wall that makes up the elevator and ventilation rooms.

Darius is already outside by the open dropdown door of the gunship; Karla is not around but Darius is smiling at the memory of last night with her.

Adam looks at him. "You're looking real chipper this morning." He says as he approaches him.

"Well we're about to make an amazing discovery so I'm super happy..."

Adam waits for more but that's all he says. "Ok Darius, let's go make a great discovery... Still got that plasma pistol on you?" Adam asks.

"Tucked away in this holster at my left rib-cage." Answers Darius.

"Good, I brought a couple other things in this backpack, courtesy of the mechanics." Adam says.

Darius remembers back on Mire, the taped up cans of explosive pesticide he shot after Adam tossed it and killed two men with the resulting explosion. "You worry me Adam." Darius says with

144

an insincere grin. Truth be told, Darius likes Adam's pyro-technic abilities and thoughtfulness; comes in handy in a pinch.

The Elevator doors open on the rooftop cradle for Gunship and five men walk out and head towards the ship and the trio hanging out there. One man splits from the group and goes right for the ships cockpit; obviously the pilot because he's wearing no armor while the other four walking towards them are.

"Enders tells us you three have an important mission into the jungle to retrieve an artifact that's a weapon. A weapon being used by this new Mirosian upstart they call Lucifer… So how come I don't believe a single drop of this horse shit!" Says Lieutenant Commander Edvin Markov; leader of the squad.

Darius knows just what to say. "Look, you can go back and tell Enders that we don't need to be babysitting a bunch of…"

"Excuse Me!?" Markov shouts and gets in Darius's face. "Not a single one of us needs to be babysat OK! If anything; Enders sent us to babysit you three… I'm Lieutenant Commander Edvin Markov. This here is Private Kirk Mullen." Markov introduces himself and his combat mates. "Next to his ugly mug is Private Jordan Cutter, and then we have Frank Jenkins here; demolitions expert." He pauses and steps closer towards them. "Look, I'm going to follow my orders not because I like those orders, but because I'm a good soldier… Panjacca jungle is a deathtrap and if it comes down to my men and you three; I'm saving my men's lives and leaving you three for chow…"

Darius, Adam and Eve glare back at him and pretend to have no problem with what he just said. Secretly they are worried about that; being abandoned in the jungle means your days are numbered (usually down to the first hours of the first day).

The first of the day's sunlight comes shining through the small windows in the hull of Gunship. They are all in the holding area; the belly of the craft and where the seats are that passengers can buckle into so they don't get messed up during extreme maneuvers even though the need for them has never occurred; better to be safe than sorry. The ship is rising into the sky above Ehdon and quickly maneuvers to fly up and away. The thrusters aren't so loud from inside but they can still be heard; sounds a lot like a big waterfall. They are on their way to the Panjacca Jungle. Markov pops out of the cockpit and into the holding compartment where they all sit.

"Hey Darius; the pilot wants those coordinates right now!" Darius gives him the coordinates and he disappears back into the cockpit… After a little while Markov pops back out from the cockpit and takes an empty seat in the holding area beside Darius.

"Those coordinates you gave us will take just under a sixty minutes to reach. Gives us some time to talk… So let's say you're right and there's a weapon down there and we find it without dying. Then what?" Markov asks Darius.

"We figure out how it works and use it against the enemy."

"That simple huh?"

"No, it's probably going to be quite complicated, but it has to be done."

"Right. Because the Empire is about to be defeated… For the first time in recorded history; the Empire is gonna lose. Ha!" Markov mocks Darius's prediction and then they sit there for a spell in silence.

Private Jordan Cutter gets up and makes to leave the holding room where all the passengers are sitting.

"Where are you going Private?" Asks Markov.

"To the loading bay to check on all the equipment; bored just sitting here sir." Cutter replies and looks to Markov who gives Jordan a little nod of the head and out the doorway he goes.

"So if the area has a decent L.Z then we can land and walk out. If not, we'll have to repel down from the back door from just above the tree's canopy line." Markov tells them.

"Sounds like fun; are we there yet?" Adam asks.

Markov straightens up in his chair and looks at him with an angered face. "Boy, I can tell you're gonna piss me off already… Keep asking that question, see what happens."

Adam doesn't like Markov much and decides to leave the room and go check out the loading bay.

Adam walks out of the room and into the short hallway that divides the loading bay from the holding room; he sees Private Cutter at the far end of the bay. Private Cutter is leaning against the wall and on his Smart com. with his back turned to him… He hears Adam approaching and quickly hits send on a message and then tucks the device away in a pocket and turns to face Adam.

"Oh, it's you… What do you want?" Asks Jordan.

"So if we have to repel out that door, how would that work? I mean, I don't see any ropes around."

"See those two steel loops woven into the waste buckle of your fabri-tech suit? That's so you can hook up to these ropes here." Jordan bends down and places two fingers inside a small notch on the steel paneled floor and pulls up on a tab that blends into the particular panel. A thin steel door opens up for a cubby hole; Jordan reaches down into it and pulls up a length of rope just far enough for Adam to see. "If you have to repel, this is where you get the rope.

Toss the length of it in front of you feed the end with the metal loop in those rings on your suit and then reach the end down into the cubby and you'll find a spring loaded latch to hook the loop into; that's your anchor to the ship.

Got it?"

Outer Space – Aboard the Mir'Denack

Lucifer is putting his armor back on with the help of Rennea who is just in her underwear. A "doot, doot, doot" sounds out of the rooms intercom speakers. Lucifer walks to the computer panel beside the door and thumbs the button to answer the call from someone on the ship. "What is it?" Lucifer asks dryly.

"We've just received a message from one of our spies among the EDF. You're going to want to read this one yourself." Says a man's voice.

"Store it on the ready-room's computer; I'm on my way there now. Lucifer out." He looks back to Rennea. "Take your time; see you back on the bridge." Lucifer says and leaves the room.

Stepping through the doorway onto the command bridge, Lucifer walks straight over to the small ready-room off to the side; the door opens. He walks on in and sits down at the computerized table. Swiping his thumb over the sensor pad, he activates the concealed panels which slide open to reveal the hollo-com device. After pressing a series of icons on his computer port, the message pops up in an image above the table; he reads it.

"Some High Priest named Darius says there's some sort of secret weapon inside the ruins of Odaan. On rout to the location now. Track my Smart com signal. GTG..."

"How the hell did Darius find out about that? He must be after the abandoned weapons that lay in those ruins." He thinks to himself. "Whatever he's up to, Darius Siscerelle is a threat." He concludes his thoughts and orders the computer console with the press of a few icons to find Liam Xavier. The computer generates a hollo-image of the ship's schematics and 3-D zooms to a part of the ship where a red dot begins to glow. The room he's in, is the flight simulator room where twenty pilots can train to fly a strike craft called a "Zeek". The crafts are shaped like regular jet fighters but have been retrofit with space flight technology. CO_2 blasters placed all around the hull allow the pilot superior maneuverability. The main weapon on a Zeek is a 30 mm calibre mini-gun with over two million rounds of ammo packed neatly inside the gun compartment and one plasma bomb on a spring fire mechanism just behind the gun compartment. The Mir'Denack has fourty two Zeeks aboard it packed tightly in a small launch bay in a section of the underbelly of the ship. Also in the launch bay is a specially designed attack craft that can withstand entering a planet with a strong atmosphere like Pangaea's; it's called the "Dark Arrow" (mostly because it's painted black and shaped like a giant arrow head).

Liam Xavier is flying like an ace through a mountain range and has a target locked on ahead of him. He thumbs down on the fire button and instead of shooting a missile, the simulator goes dark. Words appear in red against the blacked out screen of his simulator. "Get to the bridge now! See the Boss!" It says in the screen. He opens the simulators door and hops out; quickly he makes his way to the ships elevator and is gunning for the bridge…As he gets just ten feet or so from the door of the command bridge, it suddenly opens and Lucifer steps out and walks towards him. "Come with me and listen…" Lucifer says and continues to walk, forcing Xavier to go back from the way he came. "There's a team of scientist being escorted into the jungle to find an old device. They won't be able to recover it but they will learn of its existence, maybe even figure out how it works. They can't be allowed to leave the jungle; do you understand me?"

"Yes my lord. They are to die in the jungle or in the skies above it."

"Good; take Dark Arrow… Do not mess this up… I'll try to save some of the Empire for you to hunt down after you finish this crew off."

"That would be most generous of you my lord."

Twenty minutes later and Liam Xavier is buckled into the pilot's seat aboard the Dark Arrow ship. The ship is strapped to a harness mounted to the rooms ceiling. The floor panels below and in front of him split open; air can be seen getting sucked out as the room is de-pressurized by space. A light on the wall to his right changes from red to green; a light on his computerized dashboard does the same thing and "BOOM!" the ship is shot out of the launch bay super-fast. His mission is to kill Darius and all who are with him.

Pangaea – Skies above the Jungle

MARKOV DISAPPEARS into the cockpit of the craft called Gunship for a moment and reappears with news. "There's no good L.Z for over five hundred meters in any direction. We're going to repel out in two minutes, then the pilot will fly over to a nearby volcano; it's currently asleep and there's a few places to park Gunship around it. He'll come get us once we call for extraction but we need to give him a five minute advanced warning. Now come on; we have a window of time to work with here! Let's strap up." Jenkins, Cutter and Mullen fall in line behind Markov. Adam, Darius and Eve fall in line after them and all group together again when they walk out the short hall and into the cargo bay. Some steel crates or lock-boxes sit on the floor here and there against the walls; fire suppression equipment is mounted on the walls here and there along with instructional signs and some wall mounted computer terminals.

Edvin Markov quickly goes through the hook up procedure for Adam, Eve and Darius; making them link up as they go along.

"Now in that crate there are gloves to protect you against possible rope burn." Markov points to a crate and Jenkins is helpful enough to open it and hand a pair out to everyone. There's a light flashing red against the wall by the drop-down bay door that suddenly turns to green. "Alright, we're hovering above the jungle about one hundred fifty feet and ready to repel down. Once we touch down I will place a beacon on the ground. This is where the pilot will pick us up… We do a quick sweep of the area; report everything on the open channel." Markov says and presses in a small blue button mounted just below the signal light that's now green. Locks at the top of the door disengage and the steel door/ramp slowly lowers itself with cables, obviously tied into motors inside the walls of the craft in order to lower and raise it. Fresh jungle air rushes into the loading bay; they all take a few deep breaths of it as it smells lightly sweet with the aroma of many types of flowers. The door/ramp comes to a stop now level with the floor they all stand on; Markov walks over to the edge first with his length of rope in hand and tosses it over the edge as he and all the others there are anchored into the floor of Gunship with the other end as Markov instructed. The six other people in the bay walk over to the edge of the ramp and do the same thing, tossing the two hundred foot length of rope down to disappear under the canopy of the tree's that shroud their view of the bottom. Adam and Eve share a nervous look as Markov holds his rope tightly and leans back over the ramps edge; they look over to him just as he drops out of view.

One by one they all drop off the back door of Gunship and repel down; disappearing under the canopy after twenty feet or so. Markov is first to touch the ground and quickly unbuckles the rope from his waste area. He looks up and sees the rest of the group coming down. He unsheathes his sword and holds it out in front of his as he looks around as the others make landfall and unbuckle their ropes. Satisfied that there's no current threats; Markov pulls a small round device out from a pouch of his uniform and places it in a small nook at the base of a nearby tree. That done, he re-sheathes his sword and joins back up with the group. The undergrowth there isn't so thick but the plants that are around look strange. Gigantic ferns and Hosta's grow in the midst of giant tree trunks that belong to giant trees if you followed them all the way up; every here and there they see some big thorny plants they all instinctively avoid. The ground is scrunchy with years of decayed matter under a topping of freshly dead, drying stuff.

"Ground leader to Gunship; all spiders have jumped the web you are free to roam." Markov says into a small, wrist band communicator that's locked on to the Gunship's radio frequency. They all step back from the ropes ends; about ten feet out of two hundred lay coiled on the ground until Markov gives the ok to go. Now they stand back and watch as the ropes and their armored, flying taxi leaves them in the thick of it.

"Ok Darius; my Smart com places us smack in the middle of the coordinates you gave; so where to now?" Markov asks glaring at him…

"Just before repelling down I saw a slight gap in the tree's canopy to the north of here, we should check that out." Answers Darius.

"North huh? You sure?"

"Yeah I'm sure." Darius says and starts to walk in that direction even though no one else is moving.

"Ok; north it is then for twenty minutes… Then someone else gets to pick a new direction for twenty minutes and then twice more until we end up back here. After eighty minutes of exploring we should find something right? And if not we call for extraction and that's the end of it." Markov sets the rules as the commander in charge of the expedition.

Corporal Mullen is at point (head of the line) with Darius behind him and the rest of them following closely along. On a narrow pathway that seems to be used by other jungle creatures, they march onward for a full twenty minutes and come across nothing but more jungle.

"As much fun as it is looking at all the weird insects around here, we have yet to see anything that looks like ruins of buildings… We pick a new direction; look up ahead." He points up the north path. "A trail veers off to the east there, and five feet ahead of that is a trail to the west. Who's turn to decide?" Asks Markov.

Clearly he doesn't want to be responsible for failing to find something important should the fact come to pass that they could have and didn't.

"Well since this is our three's little theory based on many solid facts and I picked first. I think Adam should pick the next direction." Darius says in an attempt to make some kind of order out of a somewhat crazy situation.

"Oh really? Because I was thinking that Eve should pick." Says Markov; Mullen, Jenkins and Cutter just stand by and quietly watch.

"Sure; fine by me. Adam or Eve; because after this pick, there's only really one direction left to go and that's south twenty minutes. And then it's back whichever way, to the beacon at the extraction point."

"You High Priest were always the clever bunch. So what? These are the terms of my protection and access to my Gunship… I don't care if we don't find a thing, because personally I don't think there's a damn thing TO FIND! …Eve; pick a direction."

Eve steps past Markov, looks ahead and sees both the paths that she has to choose from. "I don't know… What is it they say in the Holy Order again?" Eve basically asks herself as no one answers her.

"The path harder traveled reaps the greater reward? Something like that... The close one here to the left or East I guess you'd call it; looks denser and tougher by a bit. I choose that one."

"Ok then, East it is... Want to take point too Eve? Lead the way?" Markov says standing in front of her and eyeing her slim body up. Adam sees it and starts to get pissed off at him.

"You'd have a lady like me take point?" She says bashfully yet joking.

"Well; it was only a suggestion. I could have..." Markov gets cut off.

"I'm only joking around; of course I'll take point. I don't give a shit, but you don't get to follow behind me. Adam and Darius will be right behind me to rescue me from any potential danger. Won't you boys?" Eve says with a smirk and pushes Markov aside as she walks past him to take the lead. Adam and Darius step to and fall in line behind her.

"You heard the lady." Darius says as he passes Markov. Eve pulls her sword out of its sheath at the mouth of the trail and takes a hack at a large fern leaf in her way.

Farther down the trail Eve chose and nothing seems to be changing; its jungle after jungle followed by more jungle.

Her twenty minutes is almost up and Markov is about to stop the group when she hears the sound of trickling water up ahead and knows exactly what it is having heard the sound before a hundred times.

"There's a creek coming up just ahead of us another twenty, thirty feet or so." She says as she pauses and looks back to see the rest of the group catch up and cluster together. "It's a creek just up ahead; let's at least get to it and check it out before we look for a new way south, back to the Drop Zone." Eve says. Everyone there agrees and they carry on.

The creek is shallow as they get to the edge of it and spread about, moving away from one another from just being sick of the cramped space in the trails.

"It's nice and cool here..." Jenkins says and kneels down to splash some of the cold creek water on his head and neck to cool down. "Damn jungle is so hot and stifling; needs air movement." He adds.

"That's for sure..." Cutter says and hears something move in the bushes close by him. Following down the bank of the creek, Cutter goes to investigate the disturbance. Suddenly he sees a large bush ruffle like a strong wind has hit it; Cutter grabs his sword, pulls it free from the sheath on his back and gets in a defensive stance.

"Cutter? What is it Cutter?" Markov asks as he sees him get into a fighting mode with his sword out. They stand there for a spell; everyone is watching Cutter about fifteen feet down the creeks bank. Nothing happens for more than a minute and they start to wonder; Cutter lets his guard down and turns back to face the group. He shrugs his shoulders. "Sorry everyone, I'm probably just hearing thi..." Cutter says and is cut short of finishing because a Raptor leaps out of the bush beside him and tackles him down into the creek bed. Everyone flinches in shock and total surprise, watching as the scene quickly unfolds. Cutter lands hard in the shallow water and one of the beasts talons slips by his body armor at the waste and digs into his groin area. He screams a gurgling scream as water rushes into his mouth from being pinned down sideways. They watch as Cutter tries to rally his strength and use his sword to stab the Raptor in the neck but it reacts quickly and jumps backwards off of him.

Markov, Darius, Jenkins and Mullen all pull out their swords and make to challenge the one lonely Raptor for Cutter's life. Suddenly Three more Raptors leap out of the same bush as the first one and eye up the group of humans... "REEaaahhh! Wrrhhoop, Rrhhop... Arrah, Arrah!" Shouts the Alpha Raptor who was the first to pounce on Cutter. Cutter is now cut off with three Raptors behind him and one scary Alpha Raptor in front of him. The three lesser Raptors are ordered to hold the six humans back. Suddenly the Alpha leaps up into the air and crashes on top of Cutter with a calculated move. His left leg and claws come down on Cutters sword arm first, only a fraction of a second before his entire head is inside the Raptors mouth and then being ripped free from his body… The raptor drops the man's severed head to talk again in raptor language.

"We need to get the hell away from them; slowly back away down the creek. With any luck they'll stick to eating Cutter and leave us alone." Markov whispers to the group. Adam and Eve are furthest in the back of the group and are already making their way farther back down the bank of the creek.

"Aaarrak! Aaarrak!" Shouts the Alpha Raptor; the other three raptors look back to the leader then back to the humans and then continue to hold their ground. The human trespassers back away down the side of the creek.

Ten feet away, fifteen feet… Twenty feet… "Maybe the Raptors won't care to follow." Adam thinks to himself and pauses to look up ahead where Cutter's body lay and suddenly sees three more Raptors that leap out from the same bush as the others; obviously they have a hunting trail there.

"This isn't good at all." Markov says and shakes his head.

Adam looks behind him as he backs away from the Raptors and sees something odd. Another twenty five feet down there is a corridor or cave, or even call it a hallway. It's carved out of pure stone and obviously man made.

"Darius! Markov!" Adam kind of whisper yells to the men ahead of him. They look back at him. "Quickly; down here! Escape is this way!" Adam whisper shouts and nods his head towards the moss covered, weed infested tunnel that the creek so happens to follow. They can't see it until they get to the bend in the creek right by Adam; Eve is already a few feet ahead of them to getting in there.

"What the hell is that?" Markov asks as he looks back and sees the stone structure there; the creek flows and disappears inside of it.

"I don't know but it's a chance to get away from them." Adam replies and nods towards the Raptors.

"Good point." Markov says and turns to run the short distance to the subterranean hallway; unsure of where it leads but also uncaring at the moment as anywhere is better than here where seven blood thirsty Raptors stand or were standing. The moment Markov turns to run, five of the six Raptors break from the leader and dash towards them with one thing in mind; to kill and nothing else. Jenkins and Mullen catch up with Adam and Eve in the scramble to the cavern; they breech the barrier of it and are now blanketed in darkness. Darius is last to enter the cavern as he turns in mid run to push Markov beside him, into the cavern's darkness with his left hand while drawing his plasma pistol in his right hand. No one but Eve & Adam knew he had smuggled it with him the whole way from Mire before the whole ceremony and vacation. Darius leaps backwards with a half spin and fires five quick shots of green glowing plasma balls at the Raptors pursuing him.

Darius watches in slow motion while diving backwards, as the first two plasma shots hit the lead Raptor square in its mid-section from five feet away, while in mid-air which knocks it back to the side of the caverns entrance to lay still being quite dead. Darius's third and fourth ("Pew, Pewt") miss the following Raptors. Then, as the one at the rear of the attack party dives to the side to avoid a shot, the fifth shot hits the middle of the three attacking Raptors right on its snout; sending it reeling once around and then crashing to the mucky bank screeching in pain. Darius lands on his butt and reverse summersaults to his feet in a crouching position with his pistol aimed for the caverns entrance; just three feet ahead from where he now kneels. His heart is pounding as beads of water drip off his hair and off his body. He's waiting for another Raptor to enter the darkness of the cavern, poised to blow it away if it enters. The remaining Raptors squawk a bunch at each other and then call off their attack and leave the humans to their fate inside the caverns of Odaan.

"I doubt they will come in here now that the rest of them know we can kill them as quickly as they can us; we have the advantage now… It's dark in here and their eyes have to adjust making them temporarily blind; like five to ten seconds long. And in that short time we could kill them all… Especially now that I know you're packing a plasma gun." Says Markov as he relaxes a bit and looks around. "Great, water is soaking into my boots… Looks like this tunnel goes back quite a ways." He adds and takes a few steps further in. Looking down into the darkness; they all strain their senses to see or hear anything else that may lie down there.

"This was obviously made by people; look at the straight edges. Almost a perfect 90 degrees in the stone, and I bet at one time they were perfect 90's but time degraded them." Darius says as he stands with his face inches away from the smooth stone wall and looking up; he presses his hand upon the surface to feel it. "I think we just found a piece of Odaan colony." Adds Darius and looks at Adam and the group with a big smile. "Our spies in the Order may have been right after all hey Markov."

"Whatever, so we found a piece of an old ruin. Doesn't mean there's a secret lost weapon here or anything, but I do hope you're right from now on. Cutter just died and his death better not have been for nothing." Markov says looking right at Darius.

Adam sees Eve standing close to the caves entrance with her sword held close to her body, looking like she's praying.

The shaded light glinting off her armor; Adam is spell-bound by her radiance.

"Look; we all have our Smart coms with us right?" Eve buds in to ask; they all say yes. "And on them is a strong light; you all have the flashlight application on it, so let's use them and find out where this goes." Eve says as she feels for the fold in her fabri-tech suit by her right hip. She finds the Smart com and activates its light, shining it down the passage way where the creek flows ever onward into darkness. All the others but Darius have their devices out and are shining the lights into the darkness ahead as they make their way down the corridor. After carefully walking through the shallow water and down the cavern for about three minutes, they come to a split in the tunnel.

"This must have been like an aqueduct of some sort to serve as sanitation for the colony being built above." Darius says as they pause at the junction. It's a four way split that continues onward in the same direction and splits to the left and the right.

"Great, a fork in the road." Says Jenkins.

"We should let Adam pick the way to go seeing as he was next on the list to choose from an already chosen route." Says Darius.

"Ok Darius, that's fair… What's it going to be Adam?" Asks Markov.

"Well the water runs ahead straight and also to the left, but not to the right. I personally want out of this water; my feet may not be wet but damn are they ever cold." Adam says.

"I know right? That's some cold friggin water." Markov agrees. "To the right it is."

After about fifty feet down the corridor, Adam at the lead of the group starts to see natural light. "We may be coming up to an exit, look up ahead." Adam alerts the others behind him. They all pick up the pace and walk out of the corridor and into a large oval shaped room; maybe fifty feet at its widest and a hundred feet in length. The ceiling of the room touches with the forest floor twenty feet up, and over time has decayed to make small holes for sunlight to come through. In the middle of the room is a whole bunch of steel rods placed in some sort of pattern. The steel itself is rusted badly and moss is growing on almost everything there. The steel rods start out fat, like a foot in diameter at the bottoms; getting ever thinner as they reach upward towards the ceiling and have a spiralling pattern in them. The thinnest points on some are in the one – two millimeter range but were much finer in their conception for sure.

"What is this place?" Asks Mullen. "There's like sixty of these rods placed around the middle of this room, and they are shaped rather strangely… Kind of like the Voltrax Coils the Empire uses."

"I don't know Private Mullen but aside from those few holes in the ceiling, I don't see another way out of this room. Do you?" Darius asks and points out. Everyone looks around and finds that Darius is right.

"Ok, it looks like we have to go back but first…" Markov looks around at them. "Can anyone even take a guess as to what this is? I mean, is it the secret weapon or not?" He asks.

There's a spell of silence as they look at the series of rusted steel rods; Darius has a thought. "It's some sort of old communications array… A way for those on the ground here to talk to those in space up there."

"Hmm, works for me…" Markov says and turns around to add; "Let's get back to that fork in the road." They all hike back down to the junction and stop. "Now do we keep going straight down there to what would have been left from the entrance, or do we go right once were down there? Or do we go see if the Raptors have left the area from where we came?" Markov asks the group.

"I think we should see what's in the opposite direction of here." Answers Corporal Jenkins. Darius, Eve, Adam and Private Mullen agree. "Well alright… Let's go check out the other side of these strange tunnels. Maybe we'll find something that can make some sense of this." Markov waves behind him as he makes his way back down the corridor. "Well here we are at the junction. Is everyone sure about going straight on that way?" Asks Markov. Everyone pretty much agrees and Eve goes on and walks past him to lead the way. "Fine, let's all follow Eve." Markov shakes his head and pauses there for a moment wondering. "What's so wrong with following the creek down that way?" As he asks himself that question, Markov suddenly sees two evenly spaced orbs of light being reflected back at him from the glow of his Smart com quite few feet down there. He hears a creature some twenty or thirty feet down that passage way take a deep breath and growl in a long low toned rumbling sound that stops all of them dead in their tracks.

"Tell me that was your stomach Markov." Darius says as he and all the others are now looking back at him.

Markov shakes his head and looks over to them with a genuinely worried, almost panicky look on his face. "We just woke up some big Friggin creature down there didn't we? I'm willing to bet it's not a vegetarian… Run! Just friggin Run!" Markov shouts as he hears the thing begin to shuffle towards them and then takes his own advice and start to run down the corridor to which they have never been down. Water plashes about his boots and some of the stones they travel on are slippery and hard to keep balance on but this is do or die for them. The corridor could end abruptly and doom them all to die in the jaw of some freaky creature or it could lead them to safety and a way to escape these ruins. They are about to find out…

Outer Space – Above the Planet Gorgon
Aboard Sayberus Ship

Urmack is standing on the bridge of his ship the Sayberus; given to him by Lucifer for one sole mission.

He's looking out at space through the thick glass window that has all kinds of technology built into it; his armor is a shiny, polished black like Lucifer's but Urmack has no helmet or fancy sword.

He grows tired of looking at the planet on the viewing screen ahead of him; the planet is Gorgon.

"Optic station! Prepare to drop cloak!"

Urmack shouts as he turns to face the crew aboard his command deck. This command deck is similar to all others; there's computer stations all around and officers of all kinds to operate the many functions of the ship. "But don't do it until my mark! Coms station; put me through to officer Choldar in the launch bay." (Bleep Bleep – computer makes a noise to symbolise a patch is made)

"Duke Choldar here." His voice comes up on the room's inter-com system.

"Count thirty seconds and then launch the thumper drills."

Urmack orders the man and then signals the com station to cut out the call with a wave of his hand. He waits a few seconds. "Optics; un-cloak now! Special ops! Do we have a sync on the thumper drills onboard ECU's?"

"Yes Captain! We have a sync; data and telemetry is coming through nice and clear!" Reports the officer.

"Then all we have left to do is watch… Optics! I want that cloak back up as soon as the last thumper has launched! Oh, and look at that." Urmack says looking at the view screen as the first thumper comes into view on its way to the planet's surface. "There they go now."

Following one of the six thumpers just launched from the Sayberus; an on board high tech computer inside the giant steel (egg looking) device uses small booster jets to keep its flight path steady towards its destination. The six of them spread out as they enter the atmosphere; following the one down as the smooth tip of its design allows it to cut easily into the atmosphere with minimal resistance burn. The metal does begin to glow a light red but then quickly cools as the device reaches clouds among the inner atmosphere. Down it goes, dropping towards the surface like a bullet. This one is poised to hit the ocean like most of the others, but before it does it quickly activates a program. The program is the landing sequence which involves the front tip of the thumper to break open. Six identically curved panels that make the tip break apart to reveal a spiked up, scary looking drill bit. Diamond crusted, titanium combination alloy of steel; the drill is made to boar through almost anything and push the matter it drills through, aside and then back on top on its way down. It's a one way trip for all six of them but all they have to do is get down to the spot where upper mantle and lower mantle meet. Once they get there they perform their last function…

A parachute suddenly deploys from a panel on the back of the thumper to slow it down just before splashing into the waters of Gorgon; then down it goes into the darkness of deep water. A sensor detects that hard matter is coming up soon sending power to the drill; it begins to rotate faster and faster. A cloud of sediments kicks up around it as it hits the ocean floor and instantly, as it hits is drilling its way into the sandy bed.

Back aboard the Sayberus; once again in a state of cloak as Imperial ships are all over the sector. Urmack Orders the helm to plot a course to the rendezvous point and then orders the engines station to punch it. Urmack walks to a free Hollo-com console close to the door of the ship and makes a call to the boss. Within a few seconds he has Lucifer on the line; his helmet covered face appears in the glow of Hollo-light.

"Lord Lucifer, the devices are all deployed. We have about ten more minutes before they execute their final program."

Urmack reports.

"Good; and you are on your way to the rally point?" Asks Lucifer.

"Yes my lord, on the way there now."

"The Emperor's fleet is close Urmack... If I should fall in battle you are to take Gabriel to the Tree of Life and Death;

follow through with the plan. You got that?" Urmack nods his head and Lucifer just cuts the signal making the Hollo-com go dark. He sits there and turns to face the crew and the rest of the bridge.

"This is going to be a long flight." He says to himself.

Pangaea – Panjacca Jungle – Inside the ruins of Odaan

"THE WATER'S GETTING DEEPER NOW; not good!" Adam shouts back to the rest of the group as he's in the lead of their mad dash to escape something large behind them. Quickly the water level rises as they make their way down; from ankle deep to knee deep and then to waste deep. Yet as the water level rises, the corridor also gets wider and the ceiling of it gets higher. As they get a little further in, their lights shine upon a large cavern with slightly raised stone shelves on either side that level off and provide a walk way for them.

All of them choose the left side shelf to climb up and get out of the water. Shining their lights around they see about a dozen, human carved stone pillars holding up the ceiling. The shelf they all stand on extends back a ways and they instantly take notice of the many small holes all over every wall and along the ceiling of the cavern.

"Gggggrrraaaawwwww!!" The creature chasing them grows out to let them know it's still coming for them.

"Come on guys, let's keep going." Markov says and heads farther down into the corridor. Moments later they hear loud splashing behind them and look back to see the beast for the first time.

Its head has an elongated mouth with lots of razor sharp teeth and a slight over-bite. A narrow forehead where its eyes sit and look at them with their lights flashing out at it.

The creature is about the size of a city Hover-Bus with a long body that has four somewhat stubby legs with sharp and deadly looking claws on its feet; then there's the green scaly plates of armor that covers it from snout to tail-tip.

"It's a friggin Dyacromallus." Says Jenkins who shines his light at its eye from about thirty feet away which pisses it off and makes it roar again.

"It gets tighter the farther back we go! Maybe we can find a nook where it can't reach us back there… Come on!" Shouts Markov.

They all start to dash down the shelf towards the rear of the cavern, two things happen; the Dyacro splashes in the water as it begins to pursue them and a funny sound begins to be audible by them. They hear the Dyacro grunt behind them, then suddenly stop splashing and moving about. They all stop moving as well… The sound in the cavern gets louder and louder every second.

"What the hell is that?" Asks Mullen.

"Friggin Dyacro seems to know what that is; look it's playing dead…And I'm thinking we're about to find out." Answers Jenkins.

Eve takes a few steps back and trips over something on the ground behind her. Everyone shines their light on her as she yelps slightly in the fall to her behind. They see what it is she tripped on; the skeletal remains of a person. They shine their lights over the floor of the shelf up ahead of them and notice about another dozen skeletons laying there. Eve sees a strange looking dagger attached to a belt around one of the skeletons and grabs it out of curiosity; she pulls the whole belt free from the skeleton and gets up to her feet. The sound of a million tiny legs clinging to stone is what fills the entire cavern as the look around in nervous anticipation.

Markov pulls his sword free from the sheath on his back and everyone else there follows his lead; Smart com light in one hand, sword in the other. Eve buckles the dead man's belt around her waist and pulls her sword free; all of them continue to back away to the far end of the cavern. Tentacles are the first thing they see, or feelers of giant centipedes; their bodies quickly follow as thousands of them begin to pop out of the holes in the walls and ceiling to slowly fill the entire cavern. One pops out of a hole by Markov who quickly stabs it in the face and shines his light on it to see that they have two large and deadly pincers in front of their mouths to rip apart larger prey, making them easier to eat. They also have six very sensitive eyes (three per side of the head) as their entire lives are spent in the darkness of caves or under the cloak of night when they breech the surface for food. Darius looks down in the water and sees the Dyacro playing dead in order to avoid being noticed by these Centipedes. He aims his plasma pistol at the Dyacro and takes two shots at it. One of his shots smashes the surface of the water and hits the Dyacro right on the snout causing to thrash about in pain. The Centipedes take notice of the new creature and potential prey.

As Darius turns to flee with the others, two of these Centipedes drop from the ceiling and land in front of him. With his free hand he reaches to his back and whips his sword out and down in one fluid motion to cleave one's head in half while he quickly points his plasma pistol at the other and shoots its head clean of with one shot at point blank range. Orangey red bug guts and blood spray out and the bodies of the two fall limp on the dusty stone floor.

The Dyacromallus roars and thrashes about in the water as more than fifty giant Centipedes crash down on top of it and begin to assault it, chomping away with their large pincers and trying to break through the beast's thick armor plating. It kills many of them with its claws as it spins in the water and also crushes some against the rocky walls of the cavern; it catches some of them in its mouth and chomps them to a bloody paste. As it does one of its spinning thrashes, a Centipede catches the Dyacro on the underside of its throat where its armor is weakest and bites a big gash into it. The beast roars in pain and agony as more and more Centipede's fall upon it and make to finish it off.

"There's nowhere left to go!" Eve shouts as she reaches a wall at the end of the shelf and end of the cavern; there's nothing but stone in front of her and to her left. To her right is a three foot drop off the stone shelf into water. Centipedes drop out of holes and land right in front of them; Jenkins slashes one in half as Markov skewers another. One lands on Adam and takes a chomp at him but bites down on his metal shoulder plate. Adam thrusts his sword into the face of that Centipede killing it and then using the sword he tosses it off of him to land with a splash into the water below.

"We can't take them all! Once they finish with that Dyacro they will swarm us and overwhelm us!" Markov shouts at them in an amped up state.

Suddenly a Centipede lands on top of Mullen who panics and drops his Smart com into the water so that he can grab the critter at the neck and stop it from chomping at him. "Snap! Snap!" sounds out as it takes a couple chomps of thin air close to Mullen's face. Out of nowhere Darius fires a shot and blasts the critters head clean off; they all get hit with a splatter of blood and entrails. Darius spins about and fires three more shots at advancing Centipede's just feet away on the stone shelf. Each shot kills a bug.

"What do we do? We can't fight our way through that crowd of them!" Eve shouts back at Markov.

Just then time slows for Darius as he looks over the shelf and into the water where Mullen dropped his Smart com with its light still on. Down in the pool of water, a glimmer of light catches his eye…

"What is that?" He asks himself and looks deeper through the water.

Several feet away from the submerged Smart com Darius sees a tunnel and above the tunnel on the surface, a swirling eddy. The eddy indicates that the water is being drawn out somewhere; somewhere through that tunnel.

"Look Everyone!" Darius shouts. "There's a tunnel in the water there!"

Everyone takes a quick glance and then back to hacking down Centipedes. Adam impales one as it comes out of a hole in the wall right beside him and Jenkins slashes one in half as another bites on to his leg right where his piece of steel leg armor is. He flips his sword around in his hand and drives the blade down hard through the critters head and looks back to the group.

"Anywhere is better than here!" Jenkins says.

"We'll have to lose most of our armor or we'll sink like rocks." Darius announces and tucks his gun away in its holster at his side and begins to undo the straps to his chest plate. They take turns quickly undoing their armor and hacking down Centipedes until they are all ready. One by one they leap off the stone shelf and into the cold, deep water of the cavern.

Mullen jumps in after Adam who is following Eve; the first to dive in. He recovers his Smart com. from the sandy bottom and swims hard to follow Adam into the underwater tunnel. Darius has a Centipede land on his arm causing him to drop his sword as he shakes it off; killing another one makes no difference and so he dives into the water after Jenkins leaving Markov as the last to jump in a split second after him. Markov falls in more than jumps as he wrestles with two Centipedes on his way into the water. Darius pushes down and feels about on the sandy bottom for a quick second where he thinks he saw something, the light of the Smart com. is gone…He feels something solid and gets a grip on it; it feels like a thick animal bone of some sort. As he pulls the item free from the sand he realizes that it's not a bone but some sort of a sword. Then he sees the face of a human skull in the sand beside him and decides it's time to swim as hard as he can for that tunnel as the light of Mullen's Smart com. is beginning to disappear up the tunnel with him. He tucks the sword into the waist band of his fabri-tech suit and pumps his legs and arms, swimming hard to catch up. As he gets several feet into the tunnel he looks back and sees Markov come up behind him with his Smart com. light, kicking at one remaining Centipede determined to get him. His lungs begin to burn with spent air; he needs to surface soon.

Eve is at the lead inside the submerged tunnel and just as the air in her lungs is burning with the lack of oxygen, she surfaces in a small pool. Shining her light ahead, she sees a stone shelf three feet in front of her and quickly makes her way to it and hoists herself up. Adam surfaces with a gasp for air and Eve shouts to him ("Hey! Over here") and grips his hand to help him out of the water. Mullen surfaces as Adam is climbing out; he reaches back and grabs his hand pulling him to the rocky shelf beside him. They climb up and turn around to face the pool of water; waiting for the other three to surface. Still, the only source of light is from their water-proof Smart com. devices. The space here is tight so Adam backs up away from the pool and shines his light up the tunnel they are now in. He hears the break of water as another member of the group emerges and shines his light back to see Eve and Mullen pulling Jenkins out of the water. As they hoist him up onto the ledge, Darius breaks the surface and paddles over to receive their help up out of the pool… Darius and Jenkins push Eve and Mullen back away from the edge of the pool and look back in anticipation… Markov sees Darius's feet disappear upward ahead of him and thinks to himself. "Thank God there's a way out." As he pumps his legs to swim he feels a sting and a burn on the back of his right calf. He Curls his legs in and turns about in the tunnel to see the Centipede that has braved the water to chase him down. It lurches at him to bite his stomach open and he instinctively grabs its two pincers with both his hands and holds it back. It pushes him backwards up the tunnel in a death match. Markov notices the tunnel begin to widen enough for him to make a move. Holding the Centipedes pincers, Markov bends his body up so his feet meet the wall of the tunnel and bounce him over and onto the Centipede's back where he grapples his legs around its body breaking a few of its legs and with the help of adrenalin he rips the bug's pincers apart, splitting its skin and tissues causing severe trauma and death of the creature. They see some bubbles surface and pop with the help of their lights. Not knowing if it's Markov or more of those wretched Centipedes about to break the surface; the four at the pools edge lean back. Jenkins draws his sword, Darius pulls his pistol free and aims it at the surface of the water… Markov suddenly breaks the surface and draws a deep breath in. Everyone lets out a sigh of relief. Darius reaches his hand out and helps Markov up onto the stone ledge of the pool; Mullen and Eve are forced to take another step back. They look up the tunnel and see Adam ahead of them all by ten feet or so.

"Can you see a way out?" Jenkins asks him.

"No, but it keeps going up a ways and then it looks like it turns to the right… Come on guys, what other choice do we have?" Adam asks and leads the way up the tunnel.

Markov gets to his feet and falls over with a slight yelp and shines his light on his left leg to reveal a gash.

"Markov, you're hurt!" Eve points out the obvious.

"It's nothing Eve. We have a medibot aboard Gunship, it'll fix me up but for now I'm going to need that belt of yours to wrap this gash and slow the bleeding." Markov says pointing to it around her waist. She unbuckles it and hands it over then watches him wrap it around the wound and tuck the end into a fold. Darius helps him up and wraps Markov's arm around his neck. Markov gives him a look. "I'm not paralyzed Darius, I can still walk."

"We have a long way to go and it'll be easier this way so shut up and accept my help." Darius replies and pushes on up the tunnel with the others.

They take a turn to the right after about thirty feet up and come to a stony wall at the top another twenty feet up.

"So what now?" Eve asks Adam from behind.

"I don't know." Adam says as he looks back and shrugs his shoulders.

Darius is trained in noticing subtle things and now is his turn to notice a thin breeze of air coming through one particular section of their dead end wall. He steps up to it looking closely at the wall and sees the chink in its structure; one stone stands out to him. At this moment the rest of the group takes notice of what Darius has clinched in his waist band.

"What in the world is that thing?" Markov asks shining his light on it and pointing at it.

"I'm not entirely sure but it's a sword of some kind." He says and pulls it free from his waist band for all of them to see. "I pulled it free from the bottom of that cavern right before the tunnels entrance… There was a skeleton there too; must have been the owner of this." He says looking at it in the artificial light of the devices his companions hold… (The sword is made entirely of bones that are linked together with some intricate, inner mechanical workings. The hilt has a strange little claw or fang on the side of it that looks like some kind of switch. The blade is made up of twelve links of bone with the sharpest looking edges and connect perfectly into each other going from three inches wide at the base to a fine one millimeter point at the tip. He breaks the spell of it, realizing what it is he must do to this wall so that they can escape.

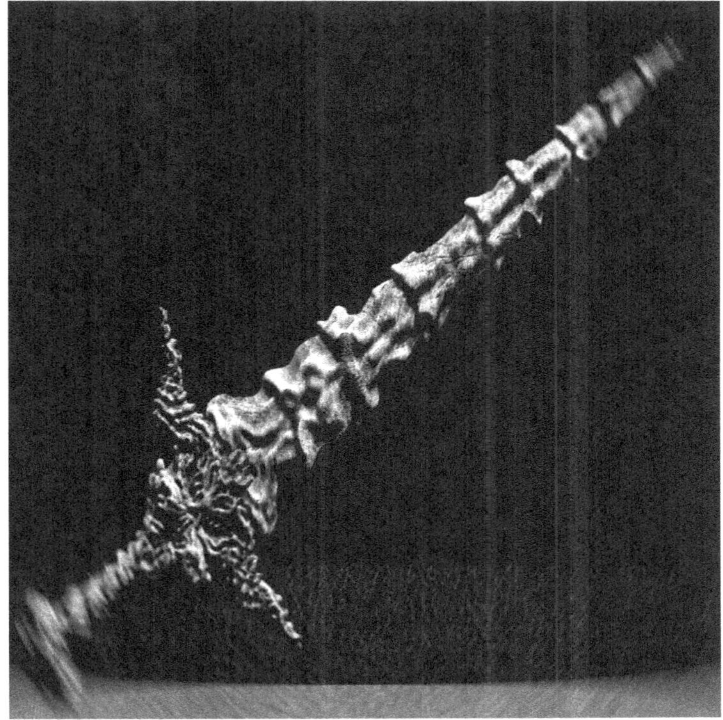

"I found it down there but that's not important right now…" Darius remembers Adam saying he has some explosives in a small back pack.

"Adam I need what's in your back pack now."

"Oh yeah; forgot I even had this… Two canisters of butane."

Darius takes one of the cans and places it inside a small fist sized hole near the bottom of the wall. "Everyone hug the one side of this wall right here; there's a way out behind this, but these stones are going to need to come out this way down the corridor. I don't want any of you getting bowled over by them." Darius says. He waits a few seconds while they all acknowledge what he's saying and lean to one side of the corridor. Darius takes his pistol out and changes a setting on it through a dial on the muzzle and then points it at the canister he just tucked inside the stone wall… "Pffhheeww" He fires the gun and hits the can causing it to explode; it sends shards of rock spraying dangerously close to them as he placed the shot perfectly into the small hole near the bottom. Then, a split second later, the entire wall begins to collapse and large chunks of rock skim by their feet on their way down the tunnel.

A blast of fresh air is sucked into the tunnel and surrounds them making them feel more at ease; that is until they hear the clattering of Giant Centipede feet coming up the tunnel behind them.

"Everyone out now!" Shouts Markov without a second glance back.

They all leap out of the newly made exit and find themselves rolling down the edge of a steep embankment along the forest floor that luckily only lasts for about twelve feet to abruptly level off. They kick up a bunch of leaves and dust as they tumble out and down the gully. Darius comes to a stop with a thud on level ground beside Adam and instantly points his plasma pistol back up the slope towards the hole they came out of. Jenkins and Markov come tumbling down to a halt beside Darius as he squeezes the trigger and fires a shot back up the slope to take off the head of an emerging Centipede. Several more behind that one poke their heads out and make a hissing sound obviously not liking the light and the blood of their kind being sprayed on them. The couple that emerged briefly, slink back down into the cave and bother them no more…

Markov picks himself up and brushes some debris off his fabri-tech suit before looking back up the slope and then to the people around him. "Well I have officially had enough of this jungle; Jenkins, Mullen, we go south and back to our pick up point. If you three wish to continue this madness and explore this jungle further, be my guest. We on the other hand are leaving now." Announces Markov.

"Nope; I'm totally fine with that…" Says Darius. "Please, lead the way."

Markov gives him a weird look because he's obviously injured and so he waves Mullen over to help him walk. Jenkins has his Smart com. on compass mode and points out the direction for them all.

"South is this way. I'll take point for now."

Outer Space – Aboard the Mir'Denack

"Captain Lucifer!" An officer among the bridge shouts. He's operating a station that scans space for threats. "The Empire's fleet will be in our weapons range in just under two minutes." He announces.

"Good! Charge the shields and activate all Knalk Cannons! All stations; prepare for battle!" Lucifer shouts at his officers. "Call up the Pey'Agus; make sure they are on rout to our location and deploy the Zeeks! Helm; continue our course to Pangaea and weapons station… Shoot down any Imperial ship that gets too close!" Lucifer commands.

An officer shouts back at him. "Sire; the Pey'Agus is on rout to our location and will be beside our flight path in less than two minutes."

"Oooh; what timing… This is going to be good… Helm! How long until we reach Pangaea?" He asks.

"At our current speed, about fifteen minutes sire."

"Oooh, too good! I'm getting chills up my neck it's so exciting!" He says and sits in his chair after pacing the floor a while. "View-screen; bring up an image of the Emperors fleet from one of our rear cameras." He orders and in seconds the image is on the screen. He can see the fleet in a backdrop of space looking like a large swarm of flies at the moment from this distance. Everyone on the bridge looks at the screen.

"That's a lot of ships." One of the officers says in the silence of the moment.

"Weapons! Open fire on that fleet!"

"Yes sir!"

Flying along in the Emperors fleet are several different kinds of space ships. The larger of the ships are the "Overlord class" called the "Craycos" and provide power to their attack crafts inside called "Stingers". These small crafts need only one pilot to operate and have a primary Voltrax coil cannon on the nose of the ship which is its primary weapon. If the coil should get damaged in battle, they have a secondary auto-tracking machine gun mounted to the underbelly. Then there's the "Battleship Class" which is mostly a design called the "Mantari". These ships get the name because they look a lot like the Manta Ray fish; having a uniquely spaded shape. In the middle of the nose is a gap where a plasma cannon is. Each outer wall in the gap is fitted with a series of magnetized energy accelerators that at full charge fires a bolt of dazzling white, red and blue lightning like energy. These plasma weapons are so devastating to other ships in space; not only does it rip a large hole into any hull, it fries out the electric circuits of the ship it hits rendering it useless. The next Battleship is called the "Leviathan" and is the Empires new experiment ship so only two have been commissioned and fly with the fleet where there are thirty five Mantari's and ten Craycos's. Every Craycos is holding close to fifty Stingers each and are also equipped with four main Voltrax coils at the front and an array of machine gun, turret pods and flack cannons along the sides and rears of the ships. The Leviathan's have a bulky, blocky look to them and are in the shape of a 3D triangle with a gap at the very front tip of the ship that houses a plasma cannon just the Mantari but also each of the two ships holds six nuclear war heads.

The two Leviathan's also have hyper-jump engines; a short high burst of power that can launch it quickly away from any threat if need be.

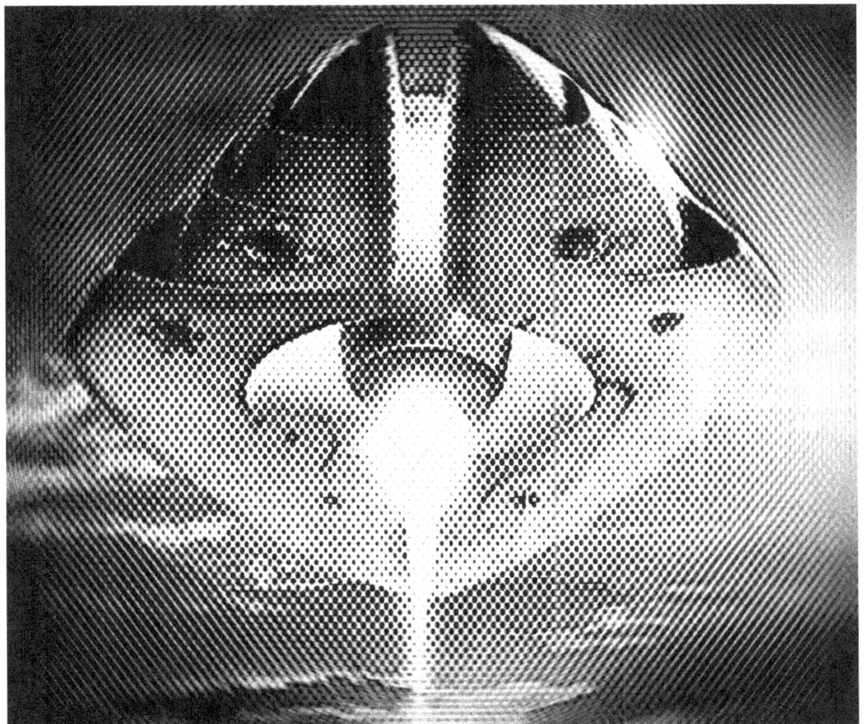

A flash of light passes with speed close to the hull of a Craycos; then another flash of light hits one of the Mantari ships and blows a gaping hole right through its whole right wing. Explosions flare out from the damage and the ship veers into a spin and out of the race.

Inside the Leviathan #2 – Command Bridge

"Sire! We seem to be in weapons range of the enemy's ship already!" Says an officer sitting in a floor mounted chair at a computer station. He's wearing the black and gold uniform of the Empire and looks a lot like Lucifer for some reason.

"How is that possible Ferradin?" Asks the Emperor.

"Not sure Milord; some kind of advanced particle weapon. Never seen anything like it." Says Micheal Ferradin.

[Separated from his family when Lucien killed them; he went on to grow up on Gorgon with foster parents and join the Empire's fleet where he quickly excelled to achieve a high rank to serve directly under the Emperor.]

"We've lost Mantari nine and Leviathan 1 is reporting that they were just hit! Massive damage to the launch bay and primary engines! Your orders Emperor!?" Shouts first officer Micheal Ferradin.

"Order the fleet to take evasive maneuvers in defence pattern Theta two! Spread us out and continue to advance." Orders Emperor Kattan. "I'll be damned if I turn and run because he has a slight reach advantage… Weapons! How long until we're in range to attack!?"

"Fifty seconds to firing range Milord!" An officer shouts back to him.

The bridge of this Leviathan ship is much like the bridge all the other big ships; computer stations and officers all about with a main view screen built into the far wall. "We just lost Mantari five and twenty one Sire! Supply ship 'Doltan' has also been hit; their com signal is totally dead!"

"Damn it Lucifer! I'm going to kill you!" Kattan shouts in frustration having never before lost so many ships, and before even attacking.

Outer space – Armies Collide

Watching the Mir'Denack; knalk canons keep firing in the direction of the Emperor's fleet while Zeek fighter crafts are suddenly pouring out of the launch-bay from underneath. The Zeek attackers don't have the unique shields currently surrounding the Mir'Denack but it matters not; they are there to fight and distract the other ships and die doing so.

The remaining Craycos ships in the Empire's fleet unleash the Stinger crafts from their launch bays; the small fighter crafts swarm about the fleet… A large ship suddenly comes out of a random point in space and stops beside the Mir'Denack; it's Lucifer's backup ship. The mining ship he long ago took over and transformed into a battleship; equipped with several of the deadly Knalk cannons that are ripping the Emperors fleet apart upon their approach.

The Pey'Agus is also a carrier ship with another hundred and twenty Zeeks which instantly are deployed as it joins in the fight alongside Lucifer in his ship.

(FFDP – "War is the Answer")

The Zeeks open fire first on the Empires Stingers with tracer volley's from their Gatling guns and blow several of them up and then the Stingers open fire on the Zeeks with bolts of white plasma. Ships on both sides blow up with an ever increasing rate as this section of outer space is now a battle zone. Stingers break through the line of Zeeks and fire at the Mir'Denack which is firing nonstop balls of super-charged death at the Emperor's fleet. The Stingers bolt of plasma streaks towards the Mir'Denack and then hits an invisible barrier just several meters above its hull all around it. The enemy's weapon causes a bright spider-web effect of electricity upon it as the shield takes the shot and absorbs some of its energy. Knalk cannons fire at the Stingers that brake through the Zeek attack wave and as they close in range are blown to bits. The Mir'Denack then continues to fire more shots at the advancing fleet. Pey'Agus doesn't have the same shields as the Mir'Denack either and begins to take some hits from several Stingers; explosions from the Stingers plasma shots break away at the hull but the vessel is so big compared to them that it barely makes a dent.

The Stingers come about for another pass but are blown away by the ships side mounted turrets and flack cannons. Seven more Mantari battleships are destroyed before the one marked "Mantari Thirteen" brakes into attack position and fires a giant and dazzling blast of electrified plasma at the Mir'Denack. Once again, the bolt of energy hits the ships shield and spider-webs out to disappear and do no damage at all. It charges up for another shot and is suddenly struck with three bullets from the Mir'Denack. Explosions flare out from the gaping holes in the ship made by the Knalk cannons; the Mantari ship suddenly explodes in a giant ball of fire and sends debris flying about. The debris hits several other nearby Stingers and Zeeks causing them to blow up too. Debris also rains upon the Mir'Denack and breaks through the shields to smash into her hull.

Aboard the Mir'Denack

Lucifer braces himself in his Captain's chair as his ship is struck with a large chunk of debris. He and his crew are rocked slightly by the impact of it; sparks fly from one of the stations because of it. "Helm! Activate evasive program Shadow Wolf one. All stations; Damage report!" Shouts Lucifer.

"Energy shields are at ninety percent and holding but hull plating in sector three is down to ten percent. We can't take hits by debris." Says one officer.

"Engines are at one hundred percent."

"Weapons systems are at seventy percent. We could miss the enemy fifty percent of the time and still have enough to finish the fight." Says Lucifer's second captain Vraad Massar.

"Captain! The Pey'Agus was just hit by a Battleship and is breaking apart." Announces another officer aboard Lucifer's bridge.

"Damn it! Keep our course and avoid debris at all cost!" Lucifer orders.

"Milord!" Shouts one of the previous officers. "We have a suicide Stinger coming up on our engines! We can't shoot it down; it's our only blind spot!"

"All hands brace for impact!" Lucifer shouts out to his crew. Within moments of the announcement he is rocked sideways in his chair; the other officers on the bridge are also jolted sideways, some fall over to the floor. Sparks fly from several computer stations as the ship is severely damaged.

"Engines; damage report!"

"Main thruster two is gone and three is badly damaged, but thrusters one and four are fully operational."

"Good! Helm put our two thrusters to use and bank the ship leeward twenty degrees!" Orders Lucifer. "I want all cannons from sections one through to five to lock on all targets as we come about and open fire! We need to kill them faster so let's get more of our guns in the fight!"

Within the span of fifteen minutes, the entire sector of space above Pangaea has become a debris field. The empire is now down to a handful of Mantari ships and the two Leviathan's remain is due to the fact that they have hung back to watch the battle unfold hoping it unnecessary to step into the fight, but now they do using their Hyper-jump engines. The two massive battleships suddenly appear at full view on Lucifer's main view screen. The Leviathan's pop up near the rear of the Mir'Denack as Lucifer has his ship making a sharp turn and they fire upon it with flack cannons and high calibre auto turrets only. The two ships target the remaining two engines and make short work of them blowing them all up and stopping the ships forward momentum but once you start a spin in space, you don't just stop because your engines are out.

LUCIFER AND HIS CREW are rocked about some more as the mighty ship of his begins to take serious damage and loses main engines all together. "Helm! Use our stabilizing thrusters to slow our spin and level out as much as we can!

And weapons! Target those two ships with all available cannons!" Lucifer commands his officers. More damages cause the ship to be rocked hard again. Lighting systems begin to fail and wall panels blow out as the ships power grid surges with back pressure of power. The back pressure is being caused by the systematic destruction of his ship as the two Leviathan ships unleash a non-stop hailstorm of flack blasts and thermite rounds from their sentry-guns.

Power from the core of the ship has nowhere to go and feeds back through the ships other systems causing overloads.

"Fire EVERYTHING!" Lucifer yells.

From space; the Mir'Denack is being picked apart from the rear, but several operational cannons near the front, lock on as the ship comes about in its spin. Bolts of death from the Knalk cannons smash into the first Leviathan blowing it apart from seven consecutive shots. Then cannon shots smash through the hull of the second Leviathan knocking out its power and severely damaging it before the Mir'Denack's main power grid goes off line. Everything comes to a halt now with the fight, as most ships are damaged or destroyed; the effort is now on rescuing those who can be saved and salvaging those ships that can be salvaged.

Back aboard the Mir'Denack a computerized male voice is announcing over the ships intercom. "Core breech critical; complete meltdown in T-minus three minutes twenty one seconds and counting. Evacuate the ship." And then the message repeats with a bit less time every time it does. Lucifer gets his ass out of his chair and makes for the door as quickly as he can. The outer sections of decks five and six on both sides of the ship are equipped with escape pods. Lucifer can make it to one in seventy five seconds if he runs fast without obstruction. He gives it all he's got. Running down the hall of his ship he turns into a stairwell and races down three flights launching himself into a run at the bottom step and pushing other officers of his ship aside. He reaches the first escape pod in seventy nine seconds, but its locked as an officer has beat him to it and is about to launch the pod. Lucifer races down the hall and catches an officer at the tenth one down trying to climb into the small hatch that's the pods only door. He grabs the officer by the belt at his waste and tosses him back into the hallway to hit his head hard on the opposite wall stunning him. It matters not; only survival matters to him right now and he didn't believe the Empire would put up such a good fight against him. He never believed he would have to use an escape pod during its construction but allowed the engineer to put them in any ways; he's glad he did now as he closes the hatch behind him and quickly gets to operating the small computer panel on the wall to his left. With the press of a few computer icons, his pod launches.

From outer space; the Mir'Denack's back side swarms with debris and is barely holding together. From the middle of the ship to near the tip, on several decks of the hull; small egg shaped pods break away. A couple at a time at first but as the countdown gets closer to zero, dozens of these small pods break away and make for Pangaea.

Gorgon – Inner mantle

THE THUMPER DRILLS have reached their target depth and stop drilling deep inside the mantle of Gorgon. Inside the device is a powerful ULF (Ultra Low Frequency) amplifier with four strong speakers to emit the disruptive sound waves. The Amps all turn on at the same time in their different spots around the planet and then the sound waves begin to pulse out from the six Thumpers. Just another fifty meters below are critical lava vents that make up the outer core. The lava in the core is the heart of a planet and flows in one continuing cycle based on the planets overall ULF. Harmony in the core means harmony on the surface and harmony of atmosphere to protect against the void of space. These Thumpers are pulsing out the same energy but at a frequency that is disrupting the flow of magma below.

On the surface of the planet, the tectonic plates begin to shift violently. Earthquakes at magnitudes of eight to nine break out all over. Those with spaceships scramble to get into them and get off the surface, but over ninety seven percent of the population isn't rich enough to own a spaceship and so are doomed to the fate of it. Volcanoes blow all over Gorgon; two of them being super volcanoes. A couple of the Thumpers get destroyed by the shifting mantle.

A pilot of an escaping space craft looks out the window to watch the entire planet self-destruct. It gets farther away from his view but he sees Gorgon die with one final explosion from the core; the planet breaks apart and chunks of it go hurling all about. Gorgon's two moons get struck with large chunks and blow up as the impacts shatter the two satellites right to their cores. "Billions of people who lived on Gorgon have been reduced to space dust and now an array of dead planet debris flies out into the solar system to seek new targets or find an orbital pattern and cause no harm… Time will soon tell." The pilot thinks to himself; his name is Lucas. Adams cousin was at the Emperors palace performing the Sebelduge; the final part of the whole ascension ceremony where you divulge all the things you experienced in the nether-realm. All your insights and revelations get recorded down into one of two books; the book of life or the book of death. Which book depends on the content of your insights.

Lucas turns to face his dash-panel and flips the switch for auto pilot before getting up and walking through the small opening that leads to the small holding bay of his small ship, confiscated by him from the half dozen that sat at the Palace's landing pads. In the holding bay he sees his girlfriend Cynthia with his new born baby boy Marcus in her arms. "We're going to have to make a run for Pangaea. Mire is still under martial law and hunting Gorgon born people… Cynthia; I don't know if we have enough life in the oxygen scrubs to get us that far."

"We'll just have to breathe slower is all… We'll make it Lucas." They share a look of deep concern. "We have the books Lucas; that means we have to make it." Cynthia says.

Pangaea – Panjacca Jungle

"We need a short break Markov." Darius says from in front of him as he marches through dense plant life on a trail through the jungle with the rest of them. Jenkins is in the lead of the single file trail with Eve and Adam right behind him; Markov has already notified the gunship pilot through his Smart com. to come pick them up. "No delays, we have a schedule to keep." He say back to Darius and keeps marching on. "The sooner we get out of this jungle the safer we'll all be. So we keep moving; it's only another five minute hike away."

"That sword you found sure does look strange Darius." Kirk Mullen says from behind him as Darius has used some jungle vines and tied the weapon to the empty sheath at his back (having lost his sword in the ruins). "What is that? Bone?"

Darius unties the sheath from his suit and holds the weapon in front of him. "Yes its bone but it looks coated with some type of clear substance that's kept it sharp and seems to stop the decay process. This has been down there in those ruins for about two hundred or more years and looks like it was just made and polished last night." He says back to Mullen as they march along. He also runs his fingers over the surface and tests the cutting edges with his thumb; still razor sharp.

"How can that be? Even Enamel would have worn thin after the first hundred years… Can I see that?" Mullen asks.

Darius pauses and hands the weapon over to him then carries on down the trail. Mullen examines it with curiosity for several paces and then hands it back to Darius. "It's one of a kind that's for sure; I'm particularly curious about that fang on the one side of the hilt there. It sticks out a bit and looks kind of like a switch, but a switch to do what? I'm not sure."

Darius looks at the fang he's referring to and wonders as well. "I'm not sure Mullen, but I'm going to call it the Reximus sword." Darius says.

Eve hears the conversation going on between Darius and Kirk which gets her to wondering about her own find. Markov gave her the belt back a few minutes ago; trading it in for a large plant leaf and some strong jungle vines tied tightly about his wounded leg. The belt she now wears is made of some tough leather and the one dagger there is set in a sheath that's attached to the belt; feels like it's made of bone too as she places her hand on the hilt. She flicks the buttoned strap that holds the weapon in and pulls it free to examine it. The blade is about six inches long and looks to be made of one very sharp and pointy piece of bone that's coated with the same substance as the sword Darius is holding on to. She places it back in the sheath and carries on through the jungle with the rest of the group.

Five minutes later Jenkins announces that he's found the beacon Markov planted at the start of their adventure, to the rest of his crew still in the trail a few feet. They all emerge from the trail into the slight clearing, not even. The area is like twelve feet in total diameter and is free enough of underbrush but is still covered by the canopy of trees up above. The all stand about looking up and then they see it; the tops of the trees shake about from the wind being put off by the Gunship's 4 thrusters and then ropes suddenly appear as the pilot did nothing to wind them up. A couple of them get tangled in the branches above for a moment; Gunship shakes her caboose a bit and frees them up. The ropes slowly come down and reach grabbing height; they wait a bit more until the ends touch the ground and then they all grab on and link the rope into their waste band buckles. One rope remains unused as Private Cutter is no longer alive to grab it.

As they begin to rise off the ground climbing with all their might, the Gunship pilot pulls up on the controls to raise the ship higher accelerating their accent out of the jungle.

As they breech the canopy of trees, Markov hears a faint humming sound that the others don't notice. Mistaking the added noise as something to do with the Gunship's engines. All of them are looking up at their goal (Gunship) as they climb and don't notice what's suddenly behind them, but Markov knows it's something else. He looks behind him and sees a black swarm of blood sucking insects they (EDF) have named Kilzmatos.[They are about the size of a 1 year old human back then but today they are small and we call them Mosquitoes]They are flying up and out of the jungle's canopy to chase after their new prey; humans.

"Everyone, climb harder!" Markov announces. "Kilzmatos swarm on our rear! They will drink your blood until there's nothing left of you but bones!" He yells to the group getting them all to look back down to the jungles tree cover and see what he sees. They all climb their ropes faster with new found motivation; the Gunship pilot helps them by continuing to fly away from the swarm but he can't go too fast without threatening to knock his passengers off their ropes. They all know the price for letting go of their rope is potentially a long fall into the jungle and their deaths if they can't re-grip the rope in time. Along with that, they have to climb fast to the drop-down door of the Gunship's loading bay. Adam and Darius have the most upper body strength so they are first to reach the edge of that door and hoist themselves up.

Adam braces himself there at the edge and waits for the next climber to reach the brink so he can help lift him (or her) up. Darius braces himself at the edge of the door and once again un-holsters his plasma pistol with his free right hand, as his left hand is gripping a fold in the door to steady him. Eve looks up and realizes that she's the farthest behind out of them all and then sees Darius fire several plasma shots that whiz past her by a foot or so; it freaks her out a bit and makes her flinch and causes her to turn on her rope so she is now facing the swarm. She sees a couple Kilzmatos explode just feet away from her as they get struck by shots from Darius's gun. She finds renewed strength and climbs harder up the rope. Adam helps Jenkins and Mullen reach the top of the door by grabbing their hand as they make it up to the edge. Markov is holding back on purpose to give the Kilzmatos another target other than Eve and hopefully confuse them a bit. She makes it up to the edge and her arm is grabbed by Adam who leans back and hoists her up with all his might.

Darius and Jenkins help Markov reach the edge and hoist him over and up. They all scramble towards the interior of the loading bay to get away from not only the danger of falling but the danger of getting blood-sucked to death by giant insects.

Markov scrambles to the wall panel about five feet into the bay against the left side and hits the close button for the loading bays one large steel door. They all watch as the door slowly closes up and over the edge of it, in flies nine Kilzmatos making it into the loading bay before the door closes and seals into the top edge of the ceiling. Adam backs away pulling Eve back with him; protecting her from potentially being attacked. Darius pulls the bone sword free from the side of the sheath that he tied it to down in the jungle; slicing through the twine with ease he tosses the sheath to the side and slashes the face clean off of a Kilzmatos. Its body falls to the decking and twitches; eight more buzz about the room along the ceiling and just out of reach of their swords. Adam and Eve are farther away from the group and look like easier targets than the other humans so three Kilzmatos break towards them; stingers poised to stab right in upon contact. Adam pushes Eve aside with his free hand gently and leaps towards the lead bug with a strong slash of his sword slicing the critter in half at the torso. He sees the next one is too close to attack and has to dive forward to avoid being stabbed by the needle sharp points of a seven to eight inch stinger nose. A nose like a straw that injects a venom once piercing the skin and before it begins to drink your blood,

so even if you kill it before it takes a second sip, you start to feel numb and tired as the toxin hits your blood stream.

This makes you weaker and easier for the rest of the swarm to consume you.

Eve takes a big step to the side as Adam shoves her aside and leaps out to attack a Kilzmatos. She instinctively grabs the hilt of the dagger she found in the ruins and pulls it free. She sees Adam dive out of the way from being jabbed by a bug which brings the Kilzmatos close to her and off its guard. She lunges out with an upward stab and drives the blade deep into the bug's underbelly. Its body convulses and wings flutter randomly in the throes of death. She rips the blade free and quickly slashes it's stinger off on its way down to the cold steel floor. Adam recovers from his dive and upward slashes at the third Kilzmatos; it flies back just out of his range and then is struck in one of its six eyes with a dagger made of bone. It's a kill shot; the Kilzmatos spins twice on its way down and hits the steel floor with a thud. Eve dashes over to its dead body and pulls the blade free.

Darius and Jenkins jump and swing their swords at the remaining five Kilzmatos but miss by about a foot each time. Markov tries a swing and misses as Darius looks at the fang on the hilt of his new sword. Some animals tooth got placed here for some reason; time to find out. Darius presses on it one way, it doesn't move. He presses on it the other way and it begins to move; sort of rusty at first but then clicks over all the way and suddenly the sword in his hand un-links at all twelve seams and droops to the floor.

The twelve separate links are all connected by an inner working of thin metal wires and small pulleys inside every link. Darius thumbs the fang on the hilt back over and presto; all twelve links whip upwards and re-connect to form a solid, one piece sword again.

"Fascinating!" Darius says as he begins to imagine the implications of such a weapon. He looks up at a Kilzmatos hovering just out of reach and lowers the sword in preparation for an upward slash; he thumbs the switch on the hilt at the same time that he whips the sword up at a bug. The links disconnect and stretch up to slash the Kilzmatos he aimed for right in half; he flicks the fang back over right after the kill and re-links the sword like a professional.

Two Kilzmatos dive down for Markov, smelling the blood leaking from his leg wound. Jenkins jumps in to defend his comrade and slashes at one clipping off its two left wings.

Markov waits for the second one to do its move; it lunges its needle nose at him. Markov leans back and sideways to avoid the stab and grabs the bug by its needle nose holding it there as it tries to fly away and escape his grip. He leans in with his other hand and grabs all four wings at its body getting a good grip on it; he could have used his sword but he is angry with these bugs and lets them know it. He rips its wings right out of the sockets and breaks its nose sideways about an inch from the base of it before dropping it hard to the steel and stepping on its head hard with his good leg. Jenkins crushes the other one under his boot leaving two to deal with.

Darius uses what he just learned about his new sword and slashes out at the two remaining Kilzmatos flying above them in the loading bay of their ride home. With three slashes of his bone sword, the last two bugs are dead. Jenkins and Mullen begin kicking their corpses off to one corner of the bay; Markov eyeballs Darius with that new sword of his. "Nice moves Darius…" He looks around at the group and limps as he takes a step towards the cockpit. "I'll be in the crapper using the medibot… Jenkins; go see the pilot and ask him to make for HQ at top speed if he isn't already. Get an ETA."

"Yes sir." Jenkins marches off down the corridor and up the stairs to the cockpit. Markov hobbles off down the hall too but turns to his left before the stairs and opens the door to the ships washroom and disappears inside. Darius stays in the loading bay with Mullen while Adam asks Eve to join him in the cargo hold section. He stops at a tarp covered crate against the wall and turns to face her, nervous like never before. He doesn't know where to begin… He wants to tell her everything but has no real idea how… maybe he'll start with this… "Eve, we just barely survived that adventure and it's made me realize something…" Adam pauses.

"What Adam? Realize what?"

"Just how important you are to me… Ever since my parents adopted you when we were kids. It was like fate bringing us together…" He steps closer to her so they are face to face; body to body, just inches away from each other. "This feels different then before; chalk it up to close brushes with death I suppose but when you reached out and killed that bug with your knife to protect me…

We protect each other; look out for each other. It just makes sense that we should… You know?"

Eve looks into his eyes and knows what he's saying; she feels it too. The connection the two of them share, it's not just a lust or a friendship. Or the love of two siblings because there is no blood relation to each other… It's a true love they have for each other that keeps them both strong and alive; glad to see each new day because the other is going to be in it.

"That we should love each other." She says to finish Adam's last statement and places her hands on his chest and inches her face ever closer to his; lips about to meet… Suddenly the air is filled with the sound of sirens as the emergency button was pressed by the pilot. They break from their near intimate moment and rush back out to the loading bay getting there just as Jenkins comes running down the stairs from the cockpit.

"Scanners have detected a ship that's coming right for us out of the north east. It's loaded with weapons and is flying at one and one third our speed; we need to get into the two manned turret pods and defend the rear! The pilot will do his best to put the enemy in our crosshairs; we got about three minutes." Jenkins announces to the group.

Markov comes bursting out of the washroom with a healed up leg. "I'm manning one of those guns!" He yells from down the short hall. Markov comes rushing into the loading bay and goes right for a hatch that looks like just a part of the loading bay wall. He pulls on a latch and opens a man sized port."Mullen, you take the other side." Markov orders before crawling into the turret pod built into the outer hull of the ship and then closes the hatch/door behind him. Mullen goes to the opposite wall and opens the turret hatch, crawls inside and closes up behind him.

"We should all get some parachutes on, just in case the unthinkable happens." Jenkins says and rushes over to a crate against the back wall. He opens the lid and reaches in; he hands one to Darius first, then Adam, and Eve. He then pulls one out for himself and two extras.

One for Markov and the other for Mullen if they should need it.

"Here, strap it over your arms like this and then buckle these buckles around your chest like this." Jenkins shows them. Darius has to wedge his new sword between the pack with the chute and his back, hoping it'll hold up in a free fall if need be. The others have the same setup, swords wedged at the back between the parachute pack.

"Now what?" Eve asks Jenkins.

"We should buckle into the chairs in the cargo hold; something tells me this is about to be a bumpy ride."

Following behind the Gunship, Liam Xavier bring the Dark Arrow (his attack craft) into attacking range and holds his gunner joypad in his right hand while holding the ship control joypad in his left. A screen beside his gun pad shows a cursor that's trying to lock on; it gets a lock and he fires. Just then Gunship's pilot steers the craft down and out of the way of the volley of thermite rounds from Dark Arrows main turret. Xavier steers hard to stay in pursuit and let's go of the gun pad to flip a couple of toggles on the ships dashboard. A display light below the toggles reads "Missiles Armed". "Tsseew, tsew, tseww." Rounds of bullets race by Dark Arrow's hull making Xavier take evasive maneuvers. He swerves his ship down then left to avoid another volley and pulls hard over on the joypad making the craft do a barrel roll and then levels out right behind his target again. Xavier thumbs town on the fire button sending streams of hot thermite bullets towards Gunship.

The volleys of gun fire pass just inches from the hull; Darius, Eve Adam and Jenkins look about the cargo hold nervously as they hear the rounds whiz by from inside.

"Shit that's close!" Jenkins shouts.

Inside the one turret pod, Markov does his best to put the enemy ship in his crosshairs but misses as he fires off some rounds.

"Attention crew!" The pilot announces over the ships intercom. "Ehdon peninsula will be below us in two minutes. Shoot that bastard down!" Markov hears the pilot and finds a new sense of determination.

Xavier veers left quickly, then back to the right and levels out to get a clean lock on Gunship with his sidewinder missiles; equipped with auto tracking systems. He looks to the dashboard screen telling him he has a lock and as he flicks the switches, firing three sidewinders at Gunship.

A volley of bullets from Markov's gun pod rips into his cockpit and tears him to shreds. Xavier dies instantly but it doesn't stop the fact that three missiles are now on their way to blow them up. He watches the attack craft veer right and plummet down out of view and looks back up to see three small flecks of metal in the distance with smoke trails behind them. "We've got incoming missiles!" He yells as he hammers down on the fire button to his mini-gun turret, trying to hit the coming missiles. They get closer and closer; he suddenly hits the one behind the lead missile and blows it up. The third missile was close enough to it to take damage; it veers to its left and down a bit before blowing up. Still, the missile in the lead seems to have luck on its side and streaks in to hit the rear right thruster and in a giant ball of fire, blows the engine to bits.

The passengers in the cargo hold get jolted in their seats, Eve screams in shock. As the ship levels out they unbuckle from their seats and stagger towards the loading bay.

The ship is sent into a spin as the three thrusters attempt to compensate for the loss of the fourth; the pilot manages to get the craft to a wobble as it slowly descends no longer able to carry the full weight of the craft. Markov climbs out of his turret pod at the same time as Mullen on the other side, they scramble to their feet as the stress on the other three thrusters overwhelms the one opposite from the destroyed thruster. Sparks fly from its casing and a small explosion flares out followed by lots of black smoke. The ship is sent into another violent spin as all the passengers have now gathered in the loading bay no longer believing the cargo hold to be a safe place to sit in.

"We need to jump!" Jenkins shouts over by Mullen, handing him a parachute while gripping the wall to keep from being knocked over by the G-forces of the spinning ship. As if the pilot hears the request; the large bay door cracks and begins to open. They are at an altitude of six thousand meters above the Ehdon peninsula in death spin; all six of them are now being tossed about in the cargo hold. Another thruster suddenly gives out sending Gunship into a head first nosedive.

The six passengers in the loading bay are suddenly lifted off their feet and sucked out of the open bay door. Adam spins and twirls as he struggles to find his balance in the fall; stretching out his arms and legs he finds that his fabri-tech suit has deployed webbing from his both his wrists to his waist and also in between his legs. Finding his balance, Adam begins to glide down slower than a free fall would have him going. Looking down he sees Gunship spin once end over end and break apart in a big explosion; he then glances around him to see everyone else in his group gliding down through the sky with him. He finds the experience exhilarating and smiles as he tries a couple of quick maneuvers. Adam slows his descent and allows the others to catch up with him, forming a gliding group.

"I think we can make the shore line of Ehdon's east coast if we keep gliding like this!" Jenkins shouts to the group and then looks over to Markov with a shocked expression. "Hey Markov! You're not..." Markov cuts him off.

"Look out below everyone!" He shouts.

Jenkins looks and sees a whole cloud of flying creatures below them and directly in their path.

"What do we do!?" Asks Mullen.

"We don't have a choice!"

"Are those more of them bugs!?" Eve asks.

"No! Those are Tyridactlin down there! Meat eating birds! We'll break right through them if we have to! We can't fall short of the shore line! Those waters are full of worse monsters!" Markov shouts to the group; now Darius takes notice.

"Markov! You have no Chute!" He shouts making the others aware of it too. "Grab on to me near the end and share my chute!" Darius yells.

"No time to plan! Here they come!" Markov shouts and points his body down and deliberately dives down a quick twenty feet to level out right on top of a Tyridaclin's back and grapple the bird from behind. It freaks out as it had no idea something would fall from the sky to land on its back and so it starts a deadly spin down towards the water.

"That man is totally insane!" Shouts Adam.

This flock of flesh eating Tyridactlin is flying right below them as they glide down and are seconds from encountering them. Darius whips out his new sword curls up like a cannon ball with the bone sword sticking out and spins making himself a deadly weapon just as he falls into the flock. He slices the closest birds head off at the neck; blood sprays out as it free falls. The other people now make their way through the spaces between the multitudes of Tyridactlin and become instant targets by at least five birds per person. One suddenly veers close enough to Adam for him to whip his sword out and slash it across the face, mortally wounding it. "Wwrraaak!" It cries as it spins out of control and plummets to its death. Another bird reaches striking distance on Adam; he impulsively reacts by darting sideways in a spin and slashes out with his sword cleaving the birds jaw in half. It's a fatal blow and the Tyridactlin goes down in a spinning death dive. Adam regains control from his spin and finds himself right beside Eve who is about to get chomped on by one of these ravenous birds. He grabs her arm with his free hand and yanks her hard from his right to send her over top and to his left in a spin. As she completes the spin there's a loud "Clomp!" sounds as the Tyridactlin chomps on air and flies over, ever closer to the falling humans looking to try for another bite. Adam still has hold of Eve's arm and looks at her now with a move in mind. "READY!?" Yells Adam.

"Ready!" Eve replies with her sword in her other hand, as she reads his mind on what he intends to do. Adam still has Eve's free hand and whips her down in a spin under himself in the free fall; Eve has her sword stretched out in her other hand and comes up with a slash that slices the Tyridactlin's belly wide open and slices the wing in half as well. Another Tyridactlin dies and free falls to a watery grave below. Several meters to Adam's left and down, Corporal Mullen and Jenkins are under attack Too. Three Tyridactlin converge on Mullen now above and behind the whole group of falling humans. One bird chomps down on Mullen's leg as the other gets his right arm; Mullen screams in pain and horror. Jenkins sees one come up to bite him from behind and uses the move he saw Darius do; Curling his legs in to flip around with his sword out. The bird's jaws snap shut just inches above his feet and then its throat is slashed wide open by the sword gripped tightly in Jenkins hands. He tries to glide in for the save on Mullen and with his sword in his right hand, torpedoes himself right for them and stabs at the closest Tyridactlin.

He plunges his blade between the eyes of the one chomping on Mullen's arm, killing it. The Tyridactlin that's clamped down on Mullen's leg twists left and dives down, away from the group. Jenkins watches helplessly now as several others join in on the kill and rip

Mullen to shreds on the way down. "Dive Hard Now!" Darius yells to the group and they all comply and dive the last fifteen hundred meters towards the sandy beach of Ehdon's south eastern coast line just up ahead. A powerful auto-turret on a hill top past the beach begins to fire off rounds at the approaching Tyridactlin causing them to scatter and abandon their pursuit of a human meal. Adam looks below and sees a splash in the calm ocean surface just several meters from the beach itself; it could have been Markov, or one of the birds we killed. He wonders if he survived the fall.

"Pull your chutes!" Darius shouts.

One after the other they pull their rip-chords; chutes deploy and safely down to the beach they float. Adam notices a man swimming to the shore below him. "Look! It's Markov! He survived the fall without a chute!" Shouts Adam while he's just about fifty feet from touching down on the sand.

Markov is swimming hard to shore and looks like he will step foot on the beech right as they will be touching down. They all land smoothly and unbuckle the back packs that hold the parachutes and lay them down on the sand; the attached chutes flutter to the beach and rest there as their job is now over. Darius, Eve, Adam and Jenkins sprint over to where Markov is laying having just crawled out of the water and is exhausted from his close brush with death. They crowd around him cautiously.

"Are you hurt?" Darius asks him.

"No." He takes a deep breath. "I'm fine; here, help me up." Markov says and stretches his arms up to them. Darius grabs on the left and Adam on the right, they lift Markov to his feet with ease. "Now that's something you don't see every day. Look up there." Markov says pointing to the sky.

They all look up and see the escape pods blazing though the atmosphere, leaving a trail of smoke behind them. They also see hundreds of chunks of burning metal that were once space ships, come raining through the atmosphere right behind the pods.

"It looks like those pods are heading our way... What do you think is going on Markov?" Darius asks him.

None of them have a clue of all that's transpired since they set off to investigate the jungle.

"I really don't know Darius but I think we're soon going to find out." Markov replies and turns to look up the beach; at the edge of the sand is gentle little hill covered with shrubs and weeds. Within seconds of him looking there; a Hovercraft comes barrelling over the edge heading right for them. "EDF reinforcements have arrived." Markov adds just as two more hovercrafts roll over the crest of the hill following the first one.

Commander Enders steps out of the first hovercraft after coming to a stop about ten feet away from everyone on the beach. "Lieutenant Commander Markov… Can you explain to me why you all got shot out of the sky? Did you find an enemy base out there?" Enders asks him.

"I can explain it all but we should be going back to base. I'll debrief you on the way." Darius tells him.

"Ok Darius, but we're not going back to base… Markov, ride with us too. Jenkins; you ride in the second one with the youngsters here… And before we go, I have to tell you all that there have been some big changes since you left this morning… Gorgon has been totally destroyed and Mire has been hit with several large chunks of the destroyed planet.

Several ships have managed to escape the doomed worlds and are above us now in orbit… There was a big space battle and both the Emperor's ship and Lucifer's ships have been destroyed. Those escape pods up there are from the enemies ship and are about to touch down on the eastern farm fields. We are all linking up with a larger force stationed at East Boundary road where we'll surround and arrest the enemy survivors… That's all I got; now you all know… So now let's all Move out… We got war criminals to catch." Adam, Eve and Darius stand there in a spell… Enders turns around to see they aren't moving.

"Destroyed? Like, all of it gone? No more home? No more

Empire? Nothing left at all?" Adam asks in a brand new state of shock. Eve walks up to him and gives him a big hug.

"Look; I never saw it coming either but there it is… We will have to adapt now to survive I'm sure… But this is what we do as humans so you all better buck up and ride out or stay here and matter to no one."

Adam can't help but think… "How perfect the role of commander is for this man Enders. The way he just passes information so dryly, with no expression on his face of any kind. He's so robotic and strategic, and that's what you have to be when people's lives are on the line and in your hands. As a leader you have to make the hard choices sometimes where feelings and emotions would destroy you every time you send a squad into battle knowing most of them will die."Everyone does what Commander Enders says and as Adam steps up into the crew compartment of the hovercraft right behind Eve, he feels glad that he's with this man and his company of soldiers while the rest of the solar system goes to hell. He also feels angry; his dad was serving the Emperor and if he wasn't killed on Gorgon when it blew up, he most likely died among the thousands of officers on one of the Emperor's many ships just moments ago. "If I see Lucifer; I'll make him pay for all he's done." He thinks to himself as he takes his seat in the craft and buckles up.

Inside the interior of the hovercrafts we have just basic fabric covered benches lining both front and back walls with the front wall having and opening big enough for one man to fit through crouching, to get to the drivers cabin. One of the soldiers offers Adam and Eve a field ration pack; they both take one and tear open the package. It looks like pepperoni pressed between two layers of crackers, good enough for the famished young couple. While they eat, there's a serious talk going on in the lead hovercraft between Darius, Markov and Enders…

"So that's how I got this here sword and we then linked up with Gunship. During our escape, the flying bugs attacked us; we fought them off and mere moments later we were being attacked by what must have been a Mirosian commandeered attack ship. After a bit of a dog fight, the craft fired homing missiles and hit a thruster engine of Gunship's while Markov peppered it with cannon fire; we both went down at the same time but they went down hard while we managed to get parachutes on. Well, all of us but Markov… You may be the bravest man I ever met…" He looks to Markov and then back to Enders. "He landed on the back of a Tyridactlin and rode it into the sea close to shore." Darius explains. "Never seen anything like that."

"Well I'll see you get a medal once this is all over Markov. Gunning down a Mirosian attack craft is quite the feat, let alone surviving the fall from the sky with no chute… very impressive…" He turns his attention back to Darius. "So this spy you slew on Gorgon was telling you lies then? About the secret base and all that… They were just after this sword you recovered then, but you found it first. That's the only reason I can contrive for why they would attack you just after leaving the jungle." Enders concludes.

"Perhaps you're right… There was another strange looking structure in there, but we couldn't really make out what it was." Darius says.

"We need to capture and question their leader and then we will know the truth of it all."

"Agreed, and we will do exactly that in less than three minutes." Enders removes a hand held hollo-com device from his side pocket and speaks into it. "Com. one, show me a feed of the escape pod's L.Z." He says to it and it obeys, lights flashing out from the surface of the device to generate the image of where over thirty escape pods have landed and people are now outside of them and getting organized.

Escape Pod's LZ

"Everyone over here!" Lucifer shouts to those who have landed in the grassy field with him. There are thirty three survivors of the Mir'Denack who come sprinting over to Lucifer. "We are close to our objective! The tree of Life lies just past this patch of forest to the east." He says and points in the direction he is speaking of. "We will take control of the fruit and use it to empower ourselves… We have to move quickly though as the defensive force of this colony is most likely on route to our location right now! So let's move out!" Lucifer commands, and the men and women with him shout "Huya!" to show their solidarity to Lucifer's command. They begin their march to the tree line as the sun in the background is just about to set over Ehdon casting a golden light over the colony. A cool breeze blows in from the nearby ocean peninsula. Only fifty yards to go to the tree line and one of the thirty three soldiers looks back and notices a large convoy of hovercrafts coming over a ridge in the farmland from west of their location; at least fifty of them at first glance. Lucifer is alerted by the one officer and as they all pause to look back and see the advancing threat, Lucifer hears Urmack's voice in his helmets comm. Device. "My lord, are you in need of assistance?" He asks through the ear piece. Lucifer looks up and sees the Saberus off in the distance. "Perfect timing Urmack! Strafe run the line of hovercrafts advancing on our position and then make to my location for landing procedures. I want my brother in this fight." Lucifer orders then addresses his company of officers. "Look up there! Back up has arrived!"

Inside an Advancing EDF Hovercraft

Having a moment at the EDFs' rendezvous location; Adam, Eve, Darius, Jenkins and Markov have all piled in to one of the hovercrafts now advancing over the farmland towards Lucifer's location. Darius gets a feeling that something is wrong and gets up to open the top gunners hatch. He releases the lock and pushes the circular hatch open then hoists himself up to have a look around. He sees the tree line to the east and the escape pods up ahead in the distance. He then turns to look back behind him and to the east where he sees a space craft up in the sky closing in on them quickly. His eyebrows flare up in surprise and he quickly drops back into the crew compartment. "We're about to be flanked by a space craft." He tells the others. He smacks open the hatch to the pilot's cockpit and yells to the pilot. "Incoming aerial attack! Take evasive actions and alert the other EDF crafts!" Darius yells through the opening. The pilot of their craft drops speed and begins to drive the craft erratically just as hovercrafts around them begin to explode. The one Knalk cannon on the Saberus opens fire from above on the hovercraft convoy. Adam and his company are jostled about in the cramped compartment of the hovercraft as a nearby hovercraft explodes from a direct hit. Adam catches Eve in mid toss as she was lifted from her seat by a hard right turn the driver pulls to get distance from the explosion. Adam looks to Darius with an odd expression, like what the hell should we do now kind of look. Darius shouts up the hatch to the pilot again.

"Break off to the east!" He yells to the pilot. "Follow the dirt road back to the shore line… We're going to do some climbing." Darius finishes saying while looking at the young couple. Adam opens the gunners hatch and looks out to see the space craft hovering above the farmland and firing away at EDF crafts below blowing them up. As he focuses on the balls of fire from exploding hovercrafts his mind begins to lose focus of those next moments.

Adam & Eve's Longhouse – Earth

THE IMAGE OF THIS SCENE fades as Adam comes back to reality; ending the story he's telling his son. "Back to reality; the reality of a world without answers." He thinks to himself as he stares into the dwindling fire in the fire place. "A world where they are alone on a planet full of mutated, lower cast, sub human species of people." He sees the wall of the hut he's built for his family and the vision of his past begins to fade away back the what's really there; sticks, stones and mud.

Cain looks as though he's asleep, leaning against Adam's forearm and resting at his side as he sits in his deer-hide, homemade couch… But apparently not so much asleep as he thinks. "Why'd you stop Father? Keep going, I wanna hear the rest of it…" Cain says to his Dad in a sleepy voice.

"In time my son, in good time…" Adam picks his sleepy son up gently and brings him to his raw-hide cot and lays him down on it; he covers him with a wolf pelt blanket and kisses his forehead. He looks across the room to where Eve has fallen asleep with Able, his body resting nestled up with Eve's in the shape of a big "G". Able's one arm resting on his pregnant mother's belly Adam looks closer and sees the scar on Eve's exposed rib cage; the place Lucifer wounded… Flashes of swords clashing cross his mind; images of Darius fighting a massive cyborg, then him and Eve fighting the cyborg. He remembers watching Eve getting slashed in the ribs and then the rage… The uncontrollable rage and darkness that took him. "How do I tell my son that I gave in to the evil within and became no better than Lucifer himself?" Adam shakes the visions cut by physically shaking and hitting his head with his hand as he gets up and leaves the cottage to sit outside on a bench in his back yard. His mind is racing… "There must be an answer… Either here or in the heavens, there has to be an answer."

CHAPTER 6

BROGG THE CHROMAG & THE LAST BATTLE

A dam wakes the next morning upon his back yard bench sore and irritated but most of all hungry. The sun has been up for a while and so has his wife and kids. The three of them are playing in living room with some toys and laughing away as though the world around them doesn't matter, but he knows better.

"Honey!" Eve shouts from inside. "It's about to happen!" She looks at him then to her big belly with a child inside. "Aaarrg. This isn't happening… It's too early in the morning."

"Adam!" she screams.

The rest of the birthing event goes by in somewhat of a blur to Adam. There's shouting and panting, then before he knows it there's a new life in his hands; a baby boy. He hands the slimy new born to Eve who grabs her non breathing baby and smacks him on the butt cheek. The baby draws breath suddenly and starts to cry, a good sign.

"Seth… Seth…" Eve says as she cradles him; Adam grabs a knife and cuts the umbilical cord and makes a knot close to the baby's belly. He knows where an extra goat skin covering is so he grabs it and lays it beside them.

"Just a second." He says and walks outside to the wash basin fed by captured rain water off the hut and picks up a wooden bowl from

202

the ground beside it and dips it in the pool of water in the rain barrel. Carefully he walks back to his wife stopping to grab a deerskin rag and then proceeds to clean the child in her arms; he then takes the newborn gently from Eve and lays him in the goat skin blanket and wraps him up snugly before handing him back to his mother.

"It's a good name." Adam says.

After spending several minutes cleaning up a bit of a mess,

he makes sure Eve has everything she needs for an hour or so and turns for the door. "I'm going to let the two of you get to know each other. Cain and I will go to the river and catch us some fish; we got ourselves another mouth to feed."

"Is that all we are to you now Adam? Extra mouths to feed?"

"Eve! You know that's not what I mean. I love you and all our children and would do anything for you… To keep you all alive… The lengths I would go to!"

Eve realizes she upset him and apologizes. "I'm sorry Adam; I know you mean the best but to go… Now?"

"Cain is becoming more a young man every day; I think it's time we had a talk." Adam replies. "Especially after this morning's event; he has questions on his mind I'm sure… Able!" Adam shouts to his other son in the play pen area; Able looks to his dad. "Be good for your mother. I'll be back soon… Cain! Come on son; let's go to the river."

Cain and Adam are at the river bank, Cain is watching his father cast his half bark thread, half human hair fishing line into the pool he made off the river bank. Two full weeks he spent moving rocks and stomping mud around to create this perfect little resting pool for fish moving upstream. Another week was spent weaving that fishing line together; after collecting the hair for two months. Adam thinks for bit of how to say this to his son… "You were young when your first brother was born, the whole thing may not have made sense to you then but you are old enough now to realize many things."

"Like how we are born into the world?" Asks Cain.

"Exactly, like that… So um, when two people love each other a lot… They umm…" Adam pauses his speech which allows them both to hear some sort of ruckus just inside the forest not even a hundred yards from where they stand in the clearing at the riverbank.

"What's that sound father?" Asks Cain.

"I'm not sure, but I think we're about to find out."

Two hairy humanoids they call "Chromags" come bursting through the underbrush at the forests edge followed closely by an animal's roar. The two Chromags are heading right for them and Adam is glad he brought his throwing spear along. He goes to grab it five feet away from him lying on the stony bank and as he turns to look again he sees a large mountain lion barrelling down on the slower of the two Chromags. With a powerful final leap, the lion lands on his prey's back and takes him down. The second one stops and turns around to see a spray of blood fly up from the waist high grass that makes up the field. He cries out in his glurrish tone that is so Chromag. "Ggrraaaal!" Which was a bad move because the mountain lions focus on the kill is now broken and another easy piece of prey stands close by.

The lions head pops up from the grass with a mouth full of Chromag flesh; the lone survivor turns and runs again for the riverbank. Adam tells his son to gather the fishing line and stay put, then sprints off in the direction of the action. The Chromag now sees Adam running towards him with a spear in hand and freaks out, tripping over his own feet he goes down in a tumbling mess of grass and limbs. Adam is now about sixty two feet away and sees the beast get ready for that leaping kill pounce he just saw moments ago. He reaches back with his throwing arm and lets his brain and perfect senses do the rest of the calculations as he throws the spear as hard as he can towards the animal.

The projectile hits the mountain lion in midair as it pounces up for the kill; the five inch blade sinks deep into the cat's chest and punctures the heart. It yelps once with utter surprise and lands hard, tumbles one time and lays still and dead right beside the Chromag.

Adam continues to sprint towards his prize and as he steps up to retrieve his spear he realizes that the Chromag hasn't moved at all but just lays there staring at the beast and wondering how he is still alive. Adam grips the shaft of the spear and yanks hard to rip the blade out from the animal's flesh. Now the Chromag moves all startled at first but then moves into a bow before Adam as though worshiping him as a god; and then gurgles out the sound "Satun Ga." He clears his throat and says it again louder.

"I think he's trying to say 'spare me' in his language." Says Cain from ten feet behind Adam. Adam turns and gives him a stern look.

"Didn't I tell you to stay by the riverbank?"

"But I saw you take out the beast so I knew it would be ok. Besides, I really wanted to see him with my own eyes; up close you know." Cain pleads his case.

"Fine, besides; I think you're right about this 'Satun Ga'." Right after Adam says that, the Chromag says it again.

Adam now steps up to the Chromag, kneels and grabs him gently by the shoulder slowly lifting him up. "I don't want to harm you… Stand up, stand up…"

A look of wonder is upon the Chromag's face as he sees the baldness of his savior's face and how straight and tall he stands. So unusual for him to see a real one. He wonders if this tall white man knows about the island of ghosts. Ghost not of his kind but of this man's kind. None the less, he is grateful to be alive and wishes to thank his savior.

"I am Adam… Adam…" Adam says pointing at his chest while speaking it slowly.

The Chromag understands and points to himself and says; "Brogg."

"Ok Brogg… Will you Help Me?" Adam asks loudly while pointing at the dead cat. Adam drops his spear and kneels at the cat's side and tries to lift it but can't. He stand there wondering for a moment when suddenly Brogg understands how he can repay his savior. By helping Adam get the dead beast somewhere.

"Chung Ga." Brogg says and kneels down to help but then Adam stops him. Adam rips at the base of some of the thicker grass clumps and instructs Brogg and Cain to do the same. Once the three of them have a good handful of four foot long grass blades, Adam grabs the lions front claws and holds the spear out so that he's crossing the paws over just above the shaft close to the blade. He then instructs Cain to do a whole mess of figure eight knots around the paws and the spear. Cain does as he is told and the Chromag catches on to what they are doing. Brogg grabs the two back paws just as Cain finishes with the front and they repeat the process, tying the animal's paws to the spear shaft for transporting. An ominous feeling sets over the three of them on their walk back to the settlement that is their home. "We walk in peace at the moment but what are these Chromags about? Would they attack us in numbers for the things I've made?" Adam wonders; at the same time Brogg wonders the same thing. "What does this white skinned, hairless person have intended for me right now?" He wonders in his simple mind.

They arrive at the camp in a few minutes. Adam opens the gate with the crude drawstring latch. Abel comes running out the front door to the hut and pauses once he see what Adam and Cain brought back; his jaw drops and as they walk into the hut Eve and Able are left speechless unable to find the words to rationalize what they see.

"What in the world happened Adam!? You said you were just going fishing; that is not a fish. And what the heck is a Chromag doing helping you? I'm so confused right now." Eve says resting on the hide covered straw bed in the middle of the longhouse with Seth in her arms.

"I knew you would be... Things happened quickly out there;

I'll tell you after I deal with this beast and string it up in the back yard... You were telling me the other day that we need a new blanket for the baby about to be born. Now the baby is here; here's the blanket." Adam says and leads Brogg to the back yard.

"Not how I expected it to happen but ok." She says to their backs as they disappear from her sight. She turns about in the bed and slowly gets to her feet then walks through the hut to the back door where she can continue watching the men at work; well, a man and one Chromag. "I'm already figuring the whole thing out." Eve says from behind Adam. "You were fishing and got interrupted by a Chromag being hunted by that mountain lion." Eve lays it out as they are working away on the cat; Adam pauses to interrupt her version.

"Actually there was two of them, and this is weird talking about them like one of them isn't standing right next to us… His friend was killed by this beast."

"I can take it from here; Eve can you take Brogg to the kitchen and pour him some apple juice?" Adam asks.

"Sure; I have the feeling his friend may have been family, he looks so sad… Cain! Come along now, you can have some juice too." Eve says and then calls his name. "Brogg, Come this way." Eve says and gestures with her head to follow her into the house. "Come Brogg." She tries again.

Adam looks back. "Go on Brogg!" Adam says loudly.

Brogg gets it and follows Eve having no idea what juice is; he trusts his savior. Eve leads them both into the kitchen and lays Seth down in his twig and fur crib then opens a hatch in the wood floor that leads to a cellar. The two of them watch her disappear down there for almost a minute then return with a clay jug; she gets two clay goblets from a shelf against the kitchen wall and pours the juice evenly into each goblet before handing them off to Brogg and Cain. Adam steps in as they are taking sips of the juice with blood all over his hands and immediately goes to the big stone wash basin he made that sits in the middle of the two large shelves that make up the kitchen. Brogg is very impressed by all that he sees; finishing his juice he hands the cup back to Eve and grunts "Urngg."

"I thinks that means thank you." Adam says.

Brogg now meanders out to the back yard curious to what all exist back there. He instantly sees the strung up mountain lion between a couple of fruit trees and cringes. Then he sees the kids play area to the far left and spots the sand box. "Zunga! Zunga mayon!" Brogg shouts back to them and dashes off over to the sand box. Adam, Eve, and Cain follow him out there right away. He looks back at them and then dives down and starts to spread the sand all evenly instead of the lumpy mess it was moments ago. With that done Brogg now uses his hairy index finger to draw a squiggly line from one end to the other.

"What's he doing?" Eve asks.

"Let's just watch for a second." Adam responds.

Brogg continues on like nothing was said. He draws out a circle where he thinks the camp is located then steps back and grunts again. "Graa." He says and stomps the ground then points down. Adam steps over and with his finger he draws lines on each side of the circle and then draws little trees on the edge of each line to represent the forest. Brogg smiles, grunts a few times and dances around in excitement over this co-op effort to map out the land. Adam too feels a certain excitement over this or perhaps he's just happy that the ape man is happy. Adam steps back and lets Brogg continue. Off the right forest is where Brogg goes to next, with his finger he traces out the path his people take through the forest to the short squiggly line that ends at the far edge of the sand box. Brogg steps past it so he's just a foot away from the dried sapling fence that borders the yard and runs his fingers up the fence a bit begins to get upset. He points to the fence and looks back at them grunting "Hooga ugga." He repeats it louder and louder and then Adam shouts out "Enough!" Brogg stops in mid pose while Adam looks closer to the squiggly line at the back of the sand box.

"That must be the ocean…" Says Adam.

"Well then why does it seem like wants to keep going?" Asks Eve.

"Because there's something just past the ocean shore he knows about." Answers Adam who steps over to him and taps his chest saying; "Do we… Come from here?" He asks now pointing at the area on the fence.

Brogg simply gives him a blank stare so Adam quickly thinks to try something different. Quickly, he turns about and kneels down to scatter the image they both drew in the sand back to a blank, smooth surfaced sand box once again. Brogg grunts at Adam to protest starting over then stays quiet and watches. At the bottom edge of the sand box Adam re-creates Brogg's sharp squiggly line and steps back to let Brogg see.

He grunts happily a couple times as he scampers over to the front of the sand box and kneels down several feet above the line Adam just drew on there. With his finger he draws a large triangle and surrounds it with a circle, stepping around so to avoid messing up the triangle as he does. He stops and looks at Adam then back to the sand and draws a human figure just inside the circle then points to Adam and grunts.

Adam looks over to Eve. "I always thought there may still be survivors." He says to her excitedly. "You know what this means right?"

"What do you think it means Adam? You think they still have law? A colony to which we can go live in? Technology? If they were there they would have found us after ten years of living out here. I've thought about it too, and I don't think it's real."

"He just drew us out on a sand map; how much more real can this be?" Adam retorts and raises his arm to gesture Brogg. That makes Brogg uncomfortable and he shy's away and goes to leave around the side of the home.

"Brogg, no! Don't go!" He stops him and points to the human image in the sand. "Is that us?" Adam asks pointing from the sand art to his own chest.

Brogg repeats what Adam just did pointing to the sand drawing and then to Adam; finishing with a grunt of confirmation. There's a long moment of silence, then Adam grabs Brogg by the shoulder and brings him inside; Eve is quick to follow. Once inside the house, Adam seats Brogg down in a pile of furs set up like a couch just beside the front door then turns to Eve.

"We're going out there to bury his companion and then I'll have him show me the start of this trail his people take. I'm going to find out for sure if he is telling the truth… Next year at the first sign of good spring weather, I'll head out."

Says Adam and looks over to Cain. "You'll be coming with me I think."

Cain's face lights up with excitement. "We're going on an adventure!? Woohoo!" He shouts.

"I don't think that's a good idea." Protests Eve.

"Come on... Adventures build character... We can talk more about it later Eve; for now, let's set our furry friend on his way with some food."

3 Months Later

"This sucks!" Cain says. Several months have gone by without further incidents and as they wait for the snow to melt outside they are all working away on making bark string hammocks. Adam came up with the design and Eve learned how to weave and knit all sorts of materials when she was young from an aunt of hers. The design will keep them safe from all sorts of predatory bugs that come out mostly at night and can be used close to the ground or high up in a tree. Yet the process of making these two hammocks is painfully boring and repetitive.

"Keep at it just a bit longer and then well stop for some dinner." Adam tells him.

Seth begins to cry from within his crib at the far end of the room close to the kitchen. Eve sets her strands of bark string down and goes to check on him while Adam goes to the fire place and sets another piece of wood inside it; the existing flames move quickly to consume the new fuel provided and Adam stares and becomes entranced in the dancing of the flames. Cain steps close to him having abandoned his weave of string. "Father, are you ok?"

"Yes son, I'm fine. Just remembering some things."

"Like what happened with you and Lucifer?" Cain asks.

"Yes; things like that."

"Can you tell me now? What happened Dad? Did you have to kill him?"

"OK son, I'll tell you. Sit here next to me." Adam says and dives back into his memories of that fateful night…

Ehdon- Before the End

DARIUS HAD INSTRUCTED the driver of the hovercraft to abandon the front assault line as it began taking fire from a random reserve spaceship of Lucifer's forces; the last in his arsenal. Commander Enders now fights his own battle and Adam has no clue what their fate was to be of the EDF hence forth. The road they wound up on took them back to the shore line at the bottom of the plateau that upon grows the sacred and holy Tree of Life. The driver stops the hovercraft as there is nowhere left to go but straight up a rocky cliff face. Darius opens the door to his left and hops down from the craft; Adam, Eve, Jenkins and the driver of the craft are quick to follow him out and ahead twenty feet over to the very base of the cliff they must climb.

"Were going up." Darius says and wastes no time to ask if anyone is with him on it or not; he just reaches over and begins to climb. Adam and Eve follow behind watching Darius carefully; where he's grabbing and placing his feet. Jenkins follows behind them.

"It's only another two hundred feet to the top!" Darius shouts without looking down. "Don't look down behind you! It will only hurt your chances to make it to the top! Just look up and keep going!" Darius finishes instructing the rest of the climbers. The driver of the hovercraft decided to stay at the bottom; oh well. They all climb up in silence but for the scraping of hands and shoes against the rocky cliff face as they concentrate to make it to the top of the plateau before nightfall.

The climb takes them just under twenty five minutes and they are exhausted when they reach the top. Adam and Eve sit back to back supporting each other while Darius sprawls out on the grassy/dirt mix surface of the plateau.

Jenkins sprawls out by Adam's feet and as they catch their breath and rest their muscles, they all simultaneously look over to the magnificent Tree of Life. Darius recalls the ancients name for it; the "Padra'Kay" they called it. There it stands before them catching the last hour of daylight behind it, causing every leaf and branch to glow in a dim orange light, with pink and light purple fluffy clouds floating close behind it in a backdrop of fading blue skies and the twinkling of the night's first stars. The sight is majestic to behold and each of them feel shivers of awe send their every hair on their bodies to stand and tingle in excitement; then suddenly the moment is shattered by the sounds of several people approaching from the main path;

the one that winds through some forested ruins all the way from the farmland about a twenty minute hike away.

The place where the EDF army has just suffered a military defeat at the hands of Lucifer. And it's Lucifer who is doing the talking among them. Seven of them approach the sacred tree Padra'Kay; Darius, Jenkins, Adam and Eve scramble to take cover behind large tufts of grass that grow scattered about the plateau and listen in on the enemy.

"Once we have enough of the fruit and leaves of this here tree, we will have the ability to withstand extended periods of time in space, and perhaps we may even discover a way to permanently reverse the effects of time and aging... Immortality for my brothers and sisters!" Lucifer says loudly as he approaches the tree with the monstrosity of a cyborg named Gabriel and five regular soldiers from within his remaining military force. "What a sight to behold here... With this power we will wait out the coming ice age on this planet. Living out in space, orbiting... And when it ends only we will remain and we will repopulate this planet with a pure race of humans. No half breeds from that cursed planet Gorgon, and we will set up a just and reliable system of law. Laws that all can agree on and prosper from obeying them; I'm so glad to see this dream of mine finally becoming real and here it stands before me as a tree... all I have to do is take it and look! Nothing stands in my way." Lucifer mocks his fallen enemies as he begins dancing the last few meters over to the trunk of the massive tree. He stops underneath its massive canopy of leaves. "Can you believe those EDF fools thought they could stop me?" Lucifer continues to rant as his five soldiers spread out; two of which decide to check out the edges of the plateau.

Lucifer's soldiers are walking right to them.

Darius knows they will be discovered soon so he hand signals to Jenkins that he's going to get the one and he should get the other in a surprise attack. Jenkins nods his head in agreement and quietly unsheathes his sword as Darius ready's his new found bone sword that he has come to call the Reximus sword. Just as the two soldiers come within a foot or two of their hiding place Darius and Jenkins strike. Darius lunges out from his grass tuft with an upward thrust into the soldier's ribs and Jenkins leaps up with a straight stab into the enemy soldier's throat stabbing right up the jaw and into the man's brain.

(Godsamck – "Straight out of Line")

The other three soldiers have guns loaded and open fire at Darius and Jenkins who both use the bodies of the men they just killed to shield them from the flurry of bullets. Adam and Eve are slinking their way over to where the other three soldiers are; standing there in a group, shooting away at Darius and Jenkins. Two bullets rip through soft tissue of the body Jenkins holds against him and rip through his fabri-tech suit to find homes in his left lung. Jenkins goes down with a shot up corpse to land on top of him. They run out of bullets and have to re-load when Adam and Eve pounce out from the low lying grass tufts. Adam slashes a soldiers neck wide open from the side and watches blood spray out at him from the man's artery. Eve leaps in with an upswing on one of the soldiers hands, the one holding the gun; she chops it clean off. The man yells in shock as holds his stump with his other hand; Eve spins about in the same motion, making one fluid move from slash to reverse thrust. She drives the sword deep into his chest impaling him upon it, then rips it free and allows his body to fall to the ground. Adam notices the last soldier click in his new clip of ammo and as the man fires at Adam, Jenkins pops up in the space between them three feet in front of the soldier; Adam is about four feet behind him. Jenkins takes five bullets to the chest as Adam pounces. He body checks Jenkins into the soldier's gun and leaps up three feet to come down with straight stab. The sword plunges into his body, piercing his heart and pops out the back side of him.

Adam rips the sword free as the soldier falls to his back. He looks over to Eve and then down to Jenkins; he's dead on the grass.

"Well well! Look at this! What a surprise to see you here Darius; looks like my assassin failed in his duties." Lucifer says to him taking him by surprise.

"How is it you know me!? And why try to kill me? Who am I to you but a humble priest of the order?" Darius asks him as he walks closer up to him and his cyborg brother. Adam dashes back to his side and follows Darius but Eve hesitates; she thinks for a second. "If Lucifer and that freak win the battle because of my inaction I would never forgive myself. Eve comes out of her spell at that moment and catches up to Adam to march at his side. Darius halts his advance a mere twenty paces away from his opponents. Adam and Eve stop at his side with swords drawn out; Eve has the bone dagger in her left hand, sword in the right. They stand there for a moment eyeing each other up.

"This is what you bring to oppose me oh great priest of the order; a young man barely out his teen years and his girlfriend. I know their names too… Adam and Eve of Mire, or should I say of Gorgon. Son of general Corso… The late General Cor…"

"Enough!" Adam shouts with a deep authoritative tone he didn't know he had in him. "You don't get to say my father's name or my mother's name! You are responsible for their deaths and will pay for it."

"Oh, so it's personal then? Well good, I wouldn't have it any other way…" Lucifer says and rips a leaf off the tree. The sun now settles a bit more and a dark shadow suddenly seems cast over the entire plateau.

"You might better recognize the name Lucien!" He says and pops the leaf into his mouth and chews on it. Adam, Eve and Darius do the same; standing under the tree at opposite sides of the trunk. They all chew on a leaf of the sacred tree and begin to feel energized. Darius is startled a bit to hear the name; the name of a long ago friend of his in the school of the Holy Order.

"That's the name of a student who died in a ship just after his ascension ceremony almost two decades ago. He was my friend and I was told that it was a malfunctioned guidance system, that his ship just didn't slow down after entering Gorgon's atmosphere and went full speed into some mountain range." Darius says and looks closer at Lucifer who helps him remember by taking off his helmet. "Lucien Ferradin! Hence the combination Lucifer… How could you!? We all believed that the seven of you had all perished and here you are! A traitor to the human race! Gorgon and Mire both destroyed by your ignorance!" Shouts Darius.

"No! It's you Darius who are ignorant! You look the other way conveniently while corruption, pollution and crime runs rampant across the solar system! My ship was a zero point powered ship; no isotope core. A magnetic core that generated power from the void of space. We all could have free power at any time; clean water, air, and food!" Lucifer shouts passionately. "We were all lied to Darius; you chose to believe those lies while I renounced them and became an even more convincing lie myself. A student of the order killed by a malfunctioned computer on a space ship. Happens all the time right!? Fools!" Lucifer paces back and forth. "You think this tree here grew from this planet? You think our kind has evolved from these planets other species? We are Aliens on this world; every one of us knows so little of our true origins… So little about the species that made us… All thanks to these shards of dark matter." Lucifer holds his sword up in front of him.

"That sword you hold… Those mountain ranges on Gorgon your

ship crashed on. They are the same ranges that were mined and those burial chambers found... That's the missing Dark matter right there." Darius says somewhat dismayed by it all.

"You're absolutely right Darius! I'm glad you are finally accepting the reality of your situation. I got off the ship by the Catacombs and then programmed the auto pilot to fly out and crash. We ventured in and found the walled off section; busted through it and found the shards of dark matter. Used their power to shield my ship from energy weapons and the other two I cast into this here sword..." Lucifer pauses to hold it out in front of him. "You see, during my Ascension Ceremony I was shown how we all came to be so long ago. When these shards were hit by their ship it caused so much damage, but how could they have detected it... The Shinue had to make us; had to have a slave race to gather minerals and ores. But once all the work was done, they couldn't agree on what to do with us... Well; here we are aren't we? God damned Empire! Ruining all my plans." Lucifer paces some more with contempt in his voice as he speaks with Darius. "I didn't think the Empire would figure out to use cannons so soon into the fight and so they gunned my ship down, but I shot them down before the final blow hit my ship..." Lucifer stops his rant and looks to his three rag-tag opponents. "Now that you know this and who I am; you must also know that none of you make it off this plateau alive!"

(FFDP – "Canto")

Lucifer finishes his statement with a speed dash towards Darius, at fifteen feet away. He leaps up with his momentum in a spinning air slash that Darius is forced to block with the bone sword yet the impact knocks him sideways and into Adam who is knocked into Eve and all three of them take a spill sideways.

"Hahaha, you fools think you stand a chance against me!?" Lucifer questions while looking down at them. The three of them quickly scramble to their feet again but this time spread out a bit and in an extra cautious stance.n"You know, I should just let my brother Gabriel have his way with you three and see how long you can all last." Lucifer says and steps back allowing his brother to advance.

"What do we do Darius? I don't think either of them are human; this one least of all... He's huge and full of metal and electronics." Adam says.

"They may not be human but they are still made of flesh and blood; flesh can be cut and blood made to bleed. They are not beyond death, just harder to kill... I never shy away from a challenge." Darius says. Adam suddenly understands what Darius is doing; you have to psyche yourself up before a fight. You have to believe in yourself or you're already beat even before the fight begins...

While the three of them ponder what to do, Gabriel goes into attack mode.

The kinetic array attached to his spine begins to extend and the air around him begins to crackle and spark from a sudden concentration of raw power. He targets Darius and thrust his gun arm towards him; time slows as a ball of sub sonic energy blasts towards him from seemingly out of nowhere leaving a ripple in space behind it like a pebble would in a pond. Darius tries blocking the shockwave with the Reximus blade and it helps him a bit but the concussion of it sends him flying back through the air about ten feet landing him on his butt and making him roll. Adam and Eve are also knocked over as though they were pushed real suddenly and couldn't keep balance. Adam is quickly back to his feet and sees Gabriel pull a metallic club with a chrome steel skull fashioned on the end of it from the back side of his black leather tunic; a hidden weapon meant for bashing bones and blunt force trauma kills. Measuring in at about two and a half feet long. Gabriel begins marching toward Darius who is stunned and helpless. Adam dashes over just in time; Gabriel comes down with the club in an overhand blow meant for Darius's skull but Adam comes in with a hard upward swing and deflects the blow. Gabriel didn't see that coming and stumbles away only slightly and quickly recollects himself. Meanwhile, Adam kneels beside Darius in his stance, his hands just vibrating from the swords impact with the club.

"Nice save Adam, but I'm afraid you just made him angry! Haha." Lucifer mocks.

Gabriel grunts and swoops in on them both lashing at Adam with a side swinging club and firing a sonic blast at Darius again. Adam throws his sword out in front of him in a block and is still knocked off his feet to roll backwards about five feet while Darius spring leaps out of the way of the sonic blast. The blast hits the ground and sends shards of rock and earth with bits of grass flying through the air in front of them. Adam tumbles onto his back from the blow while Darius is now the main target of Gabriel's club.

Darius dodges an overhand swing followed by a block on an instant backhand swing and dives out of the way of another sonic blast from Gabriel's left handed gun arm.

"Come On Gabriel! Stop toying with them and finish them!" Lucifer shouts from the background.

Gabriel hears the command of his master and steps it up a notch by dashing and swiping his club from underhand to an upward swing aimed for Darius's head. Darius leans out of the way from the back hand swing just in time and pulls his sword up to block the following downward swing from Gabriel which pushes Darius back; his feet grinding into the dirt as he slides backwards. Each swing from Gabriel is like being hit with a force ten times more than a normal man could generate. Darius has to use the iron man stance to avoid being bowled over from every block; god forbid one of those attacks connects with any part of his body, for it would be instantly broken to splinters. Gabriel instantly follows his down swinging club attack with a blast from his sonic gun built into his left arm. Darius can't react fast enough to dodge so he pulls the Reximus blade sideways in front of him to block it. The shock wave makes him smack himself with the flat of the blade right on the forehead as he is sent flying back through the air. Gabriel now realizes that Adam has gotten back up and is closing on his right flank at the same time Eve is closing in on him from the same side just at a ten degree vector difference and several seconds behind. They are seconds away from imminent attack on him; his computer brain calculates various moves they could do to him and comes up with counter measures.

Adam leaps in the air with his sword raised over his right shoulder and comes down at Gabriel who just gets his club up in time to block the attack and counters with a left hook to Adams face. He would have hit him with a sonic blast but his gun arm needs about thirty seconds to recharge and he just spent the energy on Darius. Still the punch with a steel/flesh combo fist sends Adam sideways seeing stars; he stumbles away as Eve springs into action. She strikes at Gabriel with a thrust meant for his rib cage but he quickly side steps out of the way and comes about with a full swing of his right arm trying to clothesline her. She ducks under his arm and comes up beside him with a twisting action and aims towards her targets back with a hard slash of her sword. Eve makes contact with the kinetic array on Gabriel's back and slashes through several links of it. Gabriel spins about again and catches Eve off guard with a backhand left arm swing that connects with the side of her head in a glancing blow and sends her reeling away from him and tumbling in the dirt and grass. Darius dashes back in and thrusts his sword towards Gabriel from five feet away while releasing the linkage switch; the twelve, sharp bone links disconnect from each other and fly at Gabriel who just has enough time to spin again from the momentum of his hit on Eve. Yet Gabriel is still not quick enough to avoid it completely; the first two blade links snag in the metallic kinetic array on Gabriel's back. Gabriel feels the snagging of the swords links and dashes quickly away from Darius maximizing the length of which the Reximus blade can reach. It catches Darius off guard now as he is holding tightly on the hilt of it; he suddenly finds his arms stretched out before him and his feet have involuntarily left the ground. Darius scrambles forwards struggling for balance. Gabriel stops his dash and turns about with insane speed to swing his club for Darius's head but Darius loses grip on the hilt just as he triggers the fang switch to reconnect the links. If Darius hadn't released his hand from the hilt at the last second and fallen face first to the ground, his head would have been caved in; Gabriel's blow falls just an inch shy of turning Darius's head to mush. Having been released, the swords links must now reconnect with the links caught on Gabriel's back. Gabriel tries to spin about with the momentum of his missed swing but in this race he doesn't fully win. He avoids being shredded but still gets deeply gashed on his left side; three of the links slice into his ribs before fully connecting at his back severing a few more links of his kinetic array before falling to the ground. Darius falls hard face first into the dirt layered ground of the plateau and becomes winded and blinded as he eats a mouthful of dust and it poofs up into his eyes.

Lucifer sees Darius un-armed and stunned and decides this is where he steps in, yet he is now thirty or so paces from striking distance on him. None the less, he swoops in as Darius gets up and draws his plasma pistol. Adam is back in the fight as well as Eve; they both attack Gabriel from the way he ended up facing, keeping his back turned to Darius who now takes aim at him with what may very well be the last shot in his gun as the power gauge on the side shows that levels are critically low. Gabriel swings his club at Adam who blocks while Eve thrusts at him; Gabriel spins to evade but turns in time to see the shot.

Darius fires the last shot while squinting from dirt in the eyes, yet still fires true. The glowing green ball of plasma hits Gabriel on his right pectoral muscle sending him reeling straight into Adam and Eve's simultaneous thrust with their swords; driving them both deep into Gabriel's chest. At the very same moment of Gabriel's demise is Darius' demise, for he was so focused on making the shot and blinded to a flanking attack that Lucifer reaches Darius unhindered and drives his sword sideways through his chest killing him rather instantly.

"Nooo!" Adam yells as both he and Eve pull their blades free from Gabriel's chest; Gabriel falls to his knees. Adam watches in slow motion as Lucifer pulls his sword out of Darius and his body falls lifelessly to the ground. "You will pay!" Adam shouts as he finishes Gabriel with a slash to the throat; blood sprays on his face from the wound and Gabriel falls motionless to the ground as well.

"My brother died long ago… But you did just break a very expensive machine and that pisses me off… It took a long time to put him together… You two think you can beat me!?" Lucifer says pointing his blood soaked Dark Sword at them. "I attended the holy school with this man here. He was my real threat not you two little brats; you don't stand a chance." Lucifer continues and slowly walks towards them; closing the distance on the young couple.

"My father served for Gorgon which I know you destroyed, and my mother was killed by your soldiers on Mire! You have taken everything from me!"

"No boy; not yet I haven't!" Lucifer responds and dashes towards the two of them swinging his sword sideways at them from waste height, starting from his left side and ending on the right. Both Adam and Eve lean to their left and block with their swords while leaping back to minimize the blunt force impact of the swing. Lucifer half expected to slice at least one of them in half. Not expecting a well-executed block like that; he completes the slash with a full spin to face his opponents in a defensive stance.

"Such a beautiful bride to be she would make." Lucifer says staring at Eve. "It's a shame I must kill her as you watch Adam… Or Eve… You could kill Adam right now and then you can stand beside me as my Queen of this world. How about it?"

"I would rather die a thousand deaths than side with you; monster!" Eve Answers.

"Monster!? Ha, you have no idea!" Lucifer shouts and leaps towards them both who still stand about a foot apart. Lucifer thrusts at Eve first knowing what Adam would do. Adam pulls Eve back as she parry's the thrust; Lucifer doesn't even commit to the trust. He quickly changes stance and slashes to his right at them again this time the tip of his blade grazes the fabri-tech clothing just above Eve's right breast cutting into it and into her skin. The slash continues on in slow motion to Adam's mid-section; slicing through the same special fabric given to them by the E.D.F. and cutting into his skin beneath.

Luckily the two of them had backed off enough to only receive shallow cuts.

"Oh! Did that get you!? Haha!" Lucifer Mocks as he steps back feeling confident about his coming victory.

Adam and Eve place their free hand on their wounds and at the same time pull away to look at the blood that's spilled out. Not fatal wounds, yet enough to scare them; to shake their confidence and create doubt over if they can beat their opponent… Adam shakes the feeling and grabs Eve's shoulder; she looks into his eyes.

"We can beat him Eve; same strategy, we divide and conquer. On his next move." He whispers to her.

"There may have been an outcome where you both would have got to live… If the Empire had destroyed my ship quicker, perhaps… If Darius had noticed me coming up on him and shot me with his final shot instead of my brother; perhaps then you'd have made it but that didn't happen. Not this time, and now…" Lucifer prepares for an attack. "You're time is up!" Lucifer shouts and dashes towards the young couple looking menacing in his dark armor and brandishing a dark sword.

"Now!" Adam shouts just as Lucifer comes in range with a swooping side slash on Adam, but Adam senses the move and dives to his left evading the swing while Eve somersaults to her right and both are on their feet again and in stance; Adam behind and Eve in front of him. Lucifer sees his dead brother's club laying by his body and suddenly wants that weapon in his other hand. Adam strikes first with an overhand slash, Lucifer spins to face him and blocks upward, while he quickly leans hard to his right arching his stomach to avoid being stabbed at by Eve. Eve quickly repositions her stance and swings hard upward for Lucifer's head while Adam pushes from the block to follow up with a thrust at him. Lucifer just leans back again just enough to avoid Eve's swipe, and whips his sword down just in time to block Adam's thrust; Lucifer then spring board leaps over to grab his brothers club in his left hand.

Adam and Eve are hot on his back and poised to strike him at the back of his head at the same exact moment; this is just as Lucifer completes his diving retrieval move. It's as though he has eyes on the back of his head. Just as their swords come down, Lucifer gets his sword up over his head and braces, blocking their identical attack. Immediately after the block he rears his body up and back with a swing of the sword to push them back and then follows with a fast swing of the club that he just recovered. Eve is closer to Lucifer and so it strikes her in her rib cage breaking one of her ribs. She releases her sword once struck and flies back several feet to land hard on her back; she struggles with all her will to simply draw a breath. Lucifer blocks another slash by Adam; immediately he pushes back on Adam's blade in a struggle. Adam pushes back positioning his body until he is parallel with him and then pushes his sword off hard. Both stumble backwards; muscles burning in both their arms from the face-off they just had.

"Eve! Talk to me Eve!" He yells and glances over to see her squirming on the ground.

He looks back to Lucifer, then back to Eve; Lucifer picks that second to strike at Adam with both weapons in back to back overhand swings. Adam blocks them all with upward defensive swings of the sword but is unexpectedly kicked brutally in the chest just after his last block. A dirty trick move by Lucifer but he does whatever to win; Adam is launched back and off the ground. He lands hard and tumbles right beside the fallen Reximus blade.

Unlike Eve, Adam is used to taking hits and punishment from his training at the school. Grabbing the blade with his right and recovering his short sword with his left; Adam gets up off the ground in a fuzzy world of darkening colors. Adam notices as the sun continues to set over the battle ground that it's getting harder to see but because he ate a leaf of the sacred tree, his eyes are changed and everything alive is cast in a yellow glow. The kick was a hard one and has him shaken. He looks over and sees Lucifer standing over a badly wounded Eve, poised to strike a fatal blow. He finds renewed strength.

"Nooo!" Adam screams so loudly that he freezes Lucifer for a split second. That's all the time Adam needs to close the distance on Lucifer as he reacts with lightning quick reflexes that he never thought he had. He dashes in and whips the bone sword around the Dark-sword and pulls on it just as Lucifer plunges the tip down to stab into the dirt right beside Eve. In pain and struggling to breath; Eve rolls several times quickly away from Lucifer.

Adam now leads the battle for a while; swinging both his swords furiously at Lucifer with amazing speed and yet with amazing precision also. Lucifer has to be on his best guard or the young brat could get the upper hand on him at any moment. Eve props herself up on a tuft of grass underneath the large canopy of the Tree of Life and watches the fight knowing that her rib is broken; she is useless as a fighter now. She has lost her sword somewhere but still has the bone dagger in her left hand.

Eve watches Adam swing two swords at Lucifer in a flurry of attacks where each swing would hit the target hard. If Lucifer was a lesser sword fighter he'd be dead already, but Lucifer has had a lot of training and is blocking and dodging all the attacks. Adam strikes hard on a block with the club and knocks the club out of Lucifer's hand. Adam slashes out again with the short sword; Lucifer blocks it and kicks Adams wrist. The immediate pain causes him do drop the short sword and reel back. Lucifer lunges in with a thrust that Adam blocks with the Reximus and spins about to slash him; Lucifer blocks and holds Adam there a moment. Adam leans in and slides the sword down crossways against Lucifer's. Adam loosens his wrist to let the Reximus blade and lean out as he slides against it and backwards now against Lucifer's sword. The block ends with Adam gliding his sword off and leaping back in a spin while triggering the Reximus blades to unlink themselves and then slashes out at Lucifer. The attack works and catches Lucifer off guard. Even though he gets his sword level to his body to block the move; the first two links of the sword spin into him and hit the chest plate of his armor and imbed themselves in the plate-mail.

Lucifer reels back and grabs at the thin chain between the seventh and eighth blade link of the sword. Adam lands from the leaping spin attack and releases the trigger on the hilt of Reximus as he thrusts hard away from his opponent forcing Lucifer to release the fine chain as the links pull back. The ripping momentum causes the chest plate on Lucifer to break at the links on his left shoulder plate and left rib brace. Lucifer stumbles forward too from the same momentum of the pulling force. As the links rip free from the metal of Lucifer's armor they join and make a whole sword again. As Lucifer struggles for his balance, Adam steps in and swings for Lucifer's head; Lucifer raises his shoulder as he stumbles in and the Reximus blade hits hard on the thick plated shoulder armor. Again the impact of the swing along with the special properties of the sword allow it to slice into the metal and impact enough to break the plates and links at the chest and back plates. Lucifer is bowled right over by the attack.

"That sword!? Where did you two get it?" Lucifer demands to know while stumbling away.

"We found it in a sacred place; a place full of death and fear, as well as beauty and grace… The ruins of Odaan."

"Ach! I knew it existed but could never find it. And I thought you were after the weather control device." Lucifer says and is now back to his feet in full stance and away from Adam to get a little separation. Lucifer checks over the damage to his armor.

"That's because you are stupid to think you can predict what people do… Eve, are you ok?" Asks Adam from fifteen paces away.

"Yeah, I'm ok but my rib's broken. Afraid I'm not much for fighting anymore."

Lucifer grabs his busted chest plate with his free hand and rips it off; throwing it to the ground. "Call me stupid Boy… It's the two of you that are ignorant and naive… You two have no idea… You think you are smart!? This tree you see here was planted long ago by an alien race… A race that made us to serve a purpose then die… Did you know that!? They used their own genetic code and crossed it with a sub human cast on Gorgon; Apes they were called… All to make us to fix a ship. A ship that was hit with Dark Matter after harvesting <u>their</u> fruit on this <u>here tree</u>. They have perfected genetics, and use these trees to mark the planets that they own... Once I kill the two of you I will lead the human race in the same path; a path to perfection and kill the Shinue should they try to intervene... How much of that do you know about if you think you're so smart? You also think you are strong? You can't kill me! I'm already dead...

I died long ago and all that remains is Lucifer..."

"Prepare to meet true darkness. True evil!" Lucifer shouts and then grabs and tears off the rest of his armor until he stands before them wearing only his black slacks. Adam just watches and regains energy as the flurry of attacks he's made on his foe has left him rather spent. Adam also notices his short sword off to his right and goes to pick it up. Lucifer doesn't attack, instead he begins to do a series of moves waving his sword above and around him fluidly and then spins twice to raise his sword up high. He raises his left leg and comes down planting his foot hard in the dirt. The last of the daylight disappears at that moment, thankfully two large bright object loom in the sky and are reflecting the suns light. Adam thinks "moons" but then remembers that Pangaea has no moons.

He looks up and sees the giant chunks of a destroyed planet up in space, mere hours from hitting the planet. "This is my power!" Lucifer says in a non-human voice; sounding more like a voice of a demon instead, all low and growl like. "No one escapes my wrath!" He shouts and glides towards Adam with insane speed and as he does he begins to shimmer in the darkness; as though he is in seven or eight places at once but each image of him is right beside another. Adam is unsure of what to do and suddenly he is forced to block a slash from the left, then the right, left and down to up slash. Lucifer is suddenly all over Adam with attacks from seemingly out of nowhere and if Adam didn't have two swords he would have been killed several times as Lucifer steps up the pace. In a flurry of swings against Adam, Lucifer's swing is met with a block from the short sword and he follows it so quickly with a forearm smack with his free hand right on Adams wrist causing him to release his grip on the hilt of his short sword again. He thrusts at Lucifer with the Reximus sword but misses. Now they are both down to one weapon once again…

The two of them back apart and pause for a moment. Lucifer looks around for the club but can't see it; at the same time Adam quickly looks about for his short sword but can't see it either.

"You're a skilled fighter Adam… It's not too late to pledge your loyalty to me and rule by my side in a new world… Once those chunks of rock up there hit this world, things will change and you'll want to be on my side boy. I'll even allow you to save your wife from dying." Lucifer tells Adam with 100 % certainty.

"If that's true it's only because you did that to her! You monster… You asshole! You're the one who doomed us to die! Doomed her to die! Aaahh!" Adam screams at Lucifer and with renewed energy he leaps in and attacks Lucifer with just the Reximus blade in his hands. Swords clash as Lucifer defends himself against a vicious series of attacks; Adam down slashes and Lucifer blocks holding him there for a moment.

"I told you I can help you save her!"

"I don't care what you tell me; it's all lies." Adam shouts back and continues to attack with a strong push off Lucifer's sword; a well of anger, hatred, despair and rage all flow through him at the same time giving him the power to attack his enemy with furiously strong hits. Lucifer blocks several strong side slashes and one strong overhand. After blocking the attack and holding again for a moment, both push back away from each other. Adam follows the push off quickly with a thrust, slash, and thrust combo. Lucifer dykes out of the way of the trust, blocks the slash and spins away from the last thrust to come around with a slash of his own. Adam is forced to back away as he blocks the slash and dodges a thrust then leans out of the way of another slash. Closer and closer to the tree of life they get with each maneuver. Lucifer finishes his twelve swing combo with a twisting slash that Adam struggles to block and then "Boom." Lucifer delivers a swift spin kick to Adams gut the moment he blocks the sword attack. Adam is launched back to land hard on the ground at the base of the tree of life; still gripping the Reximus sword.

Lucifer lunges in to stab Adam as he is on the ground but Adam reacts instinctively now rolling his hurting body over just as the blow would have impaled him. He hears Lucifer's sword strike into the dirt beside him and as he completes his roll he gets to his knees and thumbs the trigger on his sword to release the links and whips his sword at Lucifer who just pulls free from the dirt and backs up just in time to avoid having his arms chopped off yet the Reximus blade has now wrapped itself twice around Lucifer's sword. Adam reverses the trigger while getting up to his feet also swinging the hilt away from Lucifer; the links force themselves to retreat back to normal form and rip the Dark sword out of Lucifer's hands. Lucifer tries to hold on the best he can and reels towards Adam having lost grip on his weapon in the midst of the move and reacts instinctively with a strong side kick to the back side of Adam's right rib cage. Adam doesn't know its coming until it connects and winds him badly. He releases the Reximus sword in mid back swing, hurling both weapons away as he reels sideways to his left to stumble right up against the trunk of the sacred tree.

Lucifer has been hiding a special dark matter replica dagger in the waist band of his black slacks right at the crack of his butt, and decides that now is the time to pull the dagger out and finish his stunned opponent. He grips the hilt of it and pulls it free then lunges at Adam who does the only thing he can at the moment and reaches up with both his hands to grab at Lucifer's wrists as he tries to plunge the dagger into his chest; his back is against the trunk of the tree. The situation is tense to say the least with Lucifer trying to stab Adam and Adam trying to hold the dagger back and live.

"You should just give in." Lucifer growls as he pushes down, the blade tip inches closer to Adam's chest. "You don't have to worry about your woman; I'll make it nice and quick for her too!" Adam presses back with all his might and looks over to where Eve was last laying fifteen feet or so away and to his left. She isn't there anymore...

Eve sees that her man is in trouble and sucks in as deep a breath as she can and crawls over forcing herself to get to her feet. She staggers over just as Lucifer has Adam pinned against the tree of life with a dagger aimed for his heart. Right behind him now; Lucifer is oblivious to her as he's so focused on killing Adam. She jumps on Lucifer's back and wraps her right arm around his neck in a tight choke hold; pulling him away from his attack on Adam and then she drives the bone knife into his ribs. Lucifer releases his knife attack on Adam as he's pulled back up to his feet but kicks him in the gut as a last measure of attack on him. Lucifer now has to deal with her so he pulls back and switches the position of the blade in his hand and trusts backward just beside his left ribcage (the one that Eve just stabbed) and slices into the same rib of Eve's that he bashed and broke minutes ago with a club. Eve screams and releases her choke hold to fall hard on her knees, holding her wounded rib with both hands; she falls on to her good side writhing in pain. Lucifer turns his head to look back to Adam while he looms over her, pulling her dagger free from his side and dropping it. He towers over her with his dagger poised in his right hand to come down on her with a killing blow.

Adam is winded but can see what is about to happen and digs deep to find the strength to leap up and grab Eve's dagger with both hands from behind him and plunge it deep into Lucifer's mid-section from behind; Adam follows up instantly with a tackle push, knocking Lucifer down to land hard on his face and cough out a bunch of blood as he hits the dirt. Lucifer is still holding the dark blade in his hand and spins over to look at Adam the expression of complete surprise on his face.

(BLS – "Angel of Mercy")

Adam scrambles over to Eve's side and looks her over noticing all the blood coming from her left ribcage. "Hey Eve; you're doing great... I'm gonna fix you up and we're gonna get outa here." He tells her brushing her hair away from her face.

She puts her bloody hand to his face to caress his cheek. "Nearest hospital is in the colony; we'll never get there in time." She replies.

Adam doesn't like how she is resting against a grass tuft. "Here; I'm gonna pick you up and move you over to the trunk of the tree there." He says and places his right arm through her left at the armpit and around her back. He cradles her legs with his left arm at her knees and lifts her up then carries her to the tree trunk and gently lets her down to slide her back up against the trunk, wincing in pain.

"What can I do Eve? There must be a way I can stitch you up or cauterize that gash somehow." Adam says.

"It's not just cut but my rib is broken up inside… Aaahh!" Eve shouts and cringes in agony. "I need surgery soon or I'll die Adam."

"No, this can't be happening. I can't let you die Eve; you mean too much to me…" He says crouching beside her. A tear falls from his eye.

"I never did get the chance to tell you… I love you Eve. I love you so much I can't bear it any longer." Adam says and leans in.

Their lips meet in a gentle and passionate kiss. They break away from the lip lock after a few.

"At least we got to do that before the end." She says and brushes his thick long bangs aside to better see his face. "I love you too Adam, ever since I met you…" She coughs and stirs in pain. "I fantasized as a child that we were boyfriend and girlfriend and as I became more aware of the taboo things in society, I buried my feeling for you… But there's no reason to hide from them anymore is there?" Adam looks into her eyes and shakes his head, then leans in and kisses her again.

Lucifer looks over to them and sees the concern on Adam's face; something stirs in his dying heart. Lucifer, in his final moments feels more human than he has in decades; he feels sympathy for the two of them as crazy as that may be and he barely believes it himself but he feels compelled to tell them. The demonic spirit within him has let go, and so he feels compassion once more as he lays there dying. "There's a way you can both survive this… Look above you.

Where can you go to escape that?" Lucifer asks.

Adam looks up at the oncoming meteors. "You're delirious…

You say we can survive and then show us our demise; it doesn't make any sense!" Counters Adam.

"It does when you realize what's right above your head." Lucifer tells him.

Adam looks directly up and sees the tree of life glowing in the dark of night. "The fruit of life and death." Adam says under his breath.

"Yes… You're both in love and that will take you to Hovani.

That's the ancients name for heaven; a realm where the physical becomes meta-physical." Lucifer tells them and coughs up more blood. "Many things are possible in that realm… I'm bound for Hades; it's the realm where my counterpart comes from and so I shall return to be with him there. I made an unbreakable deal you see, but you two have a choice. Eat the fruit and live; don't eat it and die here, now." And with that said Lucifer draws his last breath and dies.

Adam watches for a moment to be sure Lucifer is truly gone then looks back to Eve and asks. "What should I do my love?"

"Get one of those fruits." She says. "I don't want to die Adam, not yet."

Adam's Longhouse – Earth

…ADAM STOPS THE STORY at that with a long stretch of silence.

Cain looks at his father hoping he will pick up on it real soon but he doesn't. "Father? What happened? Did you two eat the fruit?" Asks Cain.

Adam continues to stare into the fire as he thinks over his next words. "Yes son; we ate the fruit and everything changed…" He imagines the moment when the world began to melt away in front of him.

"We as humans, Physical beings, are made up of many different molecules and atoms… We kissed right after eating the fruit and

231

then we kind of dissolved into the universe; it's the only way I can really describe it. The entire world melted away and the universe was suddenly opened up to us... We both seemed to melt into each other in a state of pure bliss and became like a comet flying though the galaxy, and to us it seemed like it could last forever. Just floating through the galaxy in a state of pure ecstasy... Passing through other galaxies and colliding with stars; experiencing the universe first hand... But nothing lasts forever. We both felt this urge to return to the physical world but we couldn't, not like before. It was because Eve was badly wounded before we left. I knew I could fix her somehow, and it was like... As soon as I thought to fix her, a part of my body's energy moved to her body's energy and fixed the broken energy. You see my son, it all makes so much more sense when you think of things as energy... Atoms forming molecules that vibrate at certain frequencies; and it worked Cain. We re-materialized into this world over by the riverbank both whole and healthy. Neither of us knew how much time had passed from the day of the battle with Lucifer..."

"Although; as we emerged into this world we remembered the battle we had, and the meteors that were about to fall. We looked up to the heavens in a panic and then we knew... We knew that very night when we returned simply by looking in the night sky... Only the one smaller chunk of Gorgon hit this planet some time long past, and the second one got trapped in the gravitational pull of the planet to become the moon we see at night now... That pale moon that shows a quite gloomy face to us when at its fullest... As if reminding us that we've had a horrid past; full of evil deeds and heroic attempts that were met with a form of failure... We found ourselves alive in a new world; that's all we knew at that moment and so we set out to make the best of it."

"So did the meteor make people turn into Chromags then? Cain asks.

"No Cain, I don't think it works that way..."

"So this is why we're going on the adventure? To find out how it happened?"

"That's right son, but you already knew that… You're nervous about it aren't you?"

"Yeah, I guess so… I can't help but wonder if the answer will be worth the trouble and effort we're gonna have to put into it." Cain says.

Adam looks at him in the fire lit room and sees the truth in his eyes. "You're just bored with twisting bark strands; I know you want to find out as bad as I do. It's not in our nature to leave big questions unanswered. The human way is to dig up every last clue and exhaust every avenue before giving up on answering questions of great importance." Adam tells his son and thinks about the weapons he made in the last few weeks using the lion's teeth and claws. His son's birth date is close to this time of year and thinks to give his son the club.

"Stay here son, I'm going to get you something." Adam gets up and Cain goes to the wood pile and adds a couple small pieces to the dying fire while waiting for his dad to return. Adam comes in from the back yard with the club in his left hand and kneels to be eye level with his son. With his free hand he holds his son's shoulder. "I want you to have this weapon in the event that you have to defend yourself or anyone of your family members here. Never use it for senseless killings and blatant murder of anything from rodents to Chromags. Do you understand?"

"Yes Dad, I understand; it's only to defend ourselves." Cain answers.

He looks at the weapon being handed over to him. It looks like the bark was peeled back perfectly in halves and the inner cambium dried and carved with small holes to accommodate twenty two of the beasts sharpest teeth placed about the top of the club in random fashion. Then the bark skin was worked to fit back over and secure each tooth in place; finished with a couple strong strands of the beasts own dried and stretched stomach lining held in the wood by carved in notches. The strands are woven tightly around the areas with the teeth spikes making it one deadly looking club.

"Your first task if you wish to continue to own it is to find a safe place in the hut to stash it; a place where your brothers won't find it. Secondly, you will make a soft leather casing to cover it and a modification to your clothing so you can carry it along on the journey without it being in one of your hands."

"Yes father… Can I name it?"

"Sure you can name it. What name are you thinking of?"

"Liondal…"

"Good choice son; well named."

Winter comes and blankets the valley in snow for a while causing some grief for the young family as a section of the roof caved in one night from all the weight of piled snow on it. Yet it also causes some joy as Cain and Able enjoy a sunny day in the yard making snow forts together and having a snowball fight; playing and laughing as kids should do making Adam and Eve pause for a while to watch and laugh along with the kids as they pelt each other harmlessly with soft snowballs. Winter doesn't take long to fade away and give in to the spring and the valley is transformed again from a white world to a lush healthy green one. Adam and Cain help Eve with preparing the garden quickly after the last nightly frost of the year. On one particularly nice day, Adam and Cain set about collecting all the gear they will need to comfortably make their journey. Both of them have backpacks with their hammocks stuffed inside taking half the space; the leather sleeping bag and small pillow take up the rest. Adam has a spear, short bow with arrows in a quiver, and three smaller knives in leather cases with tie strings to attach tightly to his waste and one on his upper thigh. There's also the fishing line, climbing rope and a large satchel of dried foods and small vials of oils, spices and healing potions they have collected over the last few years of comfortable living.

It took them a long time to build the home and yard they have today so that they could have things like pottery, and the means to make medicines. Adam looks around and feels hard pressed to leave it behind for even a short while. Cain has his Liondal bane club and small spear that he made himself by studying the one his father has. He also has a large leather water skin to carry, holding a total of seven liters of water; that he will carry at his back with the help of his spear. He thinks of the amount of work that's going to be needed to finish this journey through and suddenly doesn't want to go.

Adam and Cain stay one more night having collected all the gear they need. Eve cozies up next to her man as they settle into bed for the night; the burning embers in the fireplace provide a warm little glow from across the room.

"I wish you two would stay and forget all about Brogg and this quest. I for one think you'll find nothing but ruins and death. The people that once lived have all gone and are no more and all that remains are these Chromags. Is that not a good enough answer?" Eve asks.

"I can't believe that… Brogg showed us a place where he had seen us before. Why would Brogg lie about that? …Besides that, we need to think on the future of our kids… If they are to raise families of their own they will need to find partners that are not of our blood… Remember those cults of in breeders back on Gorgon? How they turned out deformed and crazy? We can't allow that to happen with our children." Adam replies.

"Hmm; I see… You're right my love. It amazes me how deeply you think about these things… I won't argue about you leaving anymore. Instead I'll leave you with the memory of this." She leans over him and kisses him passionately. They shift their bodies on the bed to meet face to face, belly to belly and make out some more. Both Adam and Eve are fully aroused by their mingling of tongues and saliva; Eve reaches down to find his manhood eagerly waiting for her.

They quietly make love to each other in the comfort of their animal hide bed, then fall asleep in each other's arms.

The morning falls upon the valley quickly and intensely as there is no cloud in the sky; the air is crisp but warms fast as the sun blazes down on the valley unhindered. Bodies are stirring inside Adam's home. Everyone is awake; Eve is making up a quick breakfast of boiled oats from last year with the first of the years strawberries. Adam is working to consolidate his gear to easily pick it up and go and so is Cain. Abel is entertaining Seth in the play pen with some of the wooden toys Adam has carved over the years. The two travelers quickly eat their breakfast and get to strapping up their gear on their bodies and shortly after this day's Earth dawn, they are ready to go on their journey. Cain gives his mother a big hug and is first to go out the sliding front door; he goes to the fence gate and starts to open it but pauses to look back for his dad. Adam pauses at the door way of his house to give Eve one last kiss before the journey; he breaks away from her warm embrace painfully and walks over to meet his son at the gate. Both disappear from Eve's sight…

Excerpt from "Earth Dawn Two – Tribes of Atlan'Taka"

Looking from space, a small shuttle craft shaped like a bullet departs from the docking bay located on the rear end of the ship. Thrusters on the craft's hull fire up and steer it on a path through the planet's atmosphere.

Inside the craft we see the occupants strapped into seats that are mounted to the inner walls. Orron is in one of those chairs; he is big and muscular unlike most men and barely fits in his chair. "Think you guys would have a seat more my size?" He asks jokingly as they are hitting the atmosphere. The ship begins to shake violently as they all begin to chuckle at Orron's joke of the situation. This is a group of hardened veterans.

Moments later the ship is landing in a field next to a fairly wooded plateau that overlooks the ocean; the field is littered with dead bodies and the burning hulls of hovercrafts. Lucas, Brayden, Orron and a half a dozen other soldiers exit the landing craft down a short ramp on the rear of the ship and observe the aftermath of battle.

"Through the path to the tree! We have to get what we can as quickly as we can!" Shouts Lucas.

They all march off quickly into the wooded area. They march past the old gates and ruined doorways that once marked a glorious path to a sacred place. Now it looks like an eerie path to a place of doom as all the stone structures are over gown with vines and moss. Moments later they all stumble upon the plateau, which looks like a recent battle ground…

"Everyone stay where you are for a minute…" Lucas says and slowly weaves his way through the tufts of grass piecing together from the evidence at hand that there was a major fight here… Foot prints there, a bit of blood spatter there and then he sees the hulking corpse of Gabriel ahead of him by ten feet. He tip toes over and follows the trend of scuffed ground and hacked up pieces of grass over to the tree of live where he discovers the corpse of Lucifer. He looks over to his right and sees the body of Darius; he walks over to him slowly and kneels beside his body.

With a heavy sigh he says to him."Find the fountain and be at peace my old friend." Lucas pauses a moment here and then gets up seeing the signs of other combatants.

Lucas follows the path around the battle ground and finds the corpses of five more men dressed in Mire's black uniforms. He makes his way back to Lucifer's body and to the trunk of the tree of life. He runs his hand down the bark of the trunk and asks himself. "What in the heaven's happened here?" His hand still on the tree and as though a dream in his mind is occurring he sees the final moments of the battle between the three… Adam and Eve were here… He breaks away from the tree and looks around for other bodies. He sees nothing. "Where did you two go?" Lucas asks to no one looking about.

"Commander; are you ok?" Asks Brayden as he grabs Lucas by the shoulder unexpectedly.

Lucas looks distant but answers. "Yes Brayden; I'm fine. Collect as much of the fruit as you can… we march out in five minutes." Lucas commands his group.

They all get to work at picking the fruit while Lucas walks away and kneels at Lucifer's body. Laying close by and covered in blood, Lucas recovers both the dark sword and then the Reximus blade. He stands up holding both weapons as Brayden stands close by looking back at Lucas with a strange sword in each hand; a hint of worry in Brayden's eyes. Like Brayden knows the carnage those two weapons can cause in the wrong hands. Lucas looks back at him and meets his gaze with the same look of worry.

They are running now down the path of the tree of life, but they aren't running towards it, they are running away from it back to the open field where their shuttle craft waits for them. Nine men in total, with Lucas leading the way; every couple of seconds he looks up to see the meteor streaking thorough the atmosphere. And then it happens; he looks up in mid stride and doesn't see it anymore… Seconds later the ground under his feet quakes with a violent vibration; ahead of him by thirty feet he sees the exit of the path and his shuttle close by that. A few of them stumble as the ground quivers but quickly recover… Lucas clears the edge of the path first and sees the carnage in the distance; he doubles his efforts like the other eight men behind him. They make it to the shuttle and quickly climb aboard. "Go, Go, Go!" Lucas shouts to the pilot of the craft as he quickly takes his seat and buckles in. The outer door automatically closes and the pilot kicks the thrusters into high gear. A massive wave of water hits the entire colony and washes over it just as Lucas and his crew aboard the shuttle speed away just, barely avoiding being swept away with it. Orron looks over to Lucas. "Well, that was fun." He says as the shuttle breaks out of the atmosphere and makes for the loading dock on the Mantari ship from where it came. Looking out the window beside him Orron sees a multitude of other ships that have escaped the death of the three planets in the solar system. Gorgon, Mire, and Pangaea. "So Lucas; what are we going to do now? There's several tribes out here that will be in need of some leadership… Think you're up to the challenge?" Asks Orron. Lucas looks out the same window and answers him. "I don't know Orron; I hope so."

www.ingramcontent.com/pod-product-compliance
Lightning Source LLC
Chambersburg PA
CBHW070625170726
48291CB00003B/878